BIKER'S BABY GIRL

JORDAN SILVER

Creed is an ex sharpshooter turned bike crew President, with a rough upbringing and the scars to prove it. Nine years ago an old drunk offered him his twelve-year-old daughter for his next pint.

Knowing that as fucked up as he was he was still the kid's best bet, he took the deal. He left her with an aunt he thought he could trust because Uncle Sam owned his ass for the next little while, and he had no choice.

Then his babygirl turned eighteen and shit went south, literally. He knew he had to stay the fuck away from her or she'd be under him before she could blink, but he made a deal with himself.

When his babygirl hit twenty-one he was taking her no matter what. Her birthday was three days away and though he'd kept his distance for the last two and a half years he's been keeping tabs on her. It was time to collect.

This book contains cameo appearances from Colton Lyon, The Lyon series- Travis Mallory, Rough Riders, -Blade Master, Man of Steel, -Lawton Daniels, Anarchist, -Jake Summers, Bad Boy, - and members of the SEAL Team Seven series.

Discover other titles by Jordan Silver

SEAL Team Series

Connor

Logan

Zak

Tyler

The Lyon Series

Lyon's Crew

Lyon's Angel

Lyon's Way

Lyon's Heart

PASSION

PASSION

Rebound
The Pregnancy Series
His One Sweet Thing
The Sweetest Revenge
Sweet Redemption
The Spitfire Series
Mouth
Lady Boss
Beautiful Assassin

THE PROTECTORS

THE GUARDIAN

The Hit Man

Anarchist

Season One

Eden High

Season One

What A Girl Wants

Taken

Bred

Sex And Marriage

My Best Friend's Daughter

Loving My Best Friend's Daughter

THE BAD BOY SERIES

THE THUG

Bastard
The Killer
The Villain
The Mancini Way
Catch Me if You Can
The Bad Girls Series
The Temptress

Forbidden

Deception

Texas Hellion

Illicit

Queen of My Heart

The Wives

JORDAN SILVER WRITING AS
JASMINE STARR

THE PURRFECT PET SERIES

Pet
Training His Pet
His Submissive Pet
Breeding His Pet

http://jordansilver.net

This book is dedicated to all the butterflies that have followed me from the beginning, and those we have met along the way. Thank you for your continued support for not only me, but for all the Indie authors out there who you give a chance just at a mere mention. Thank you sincerely for being you. May we enjoy many more smutastic days together....

CREED

Three days and counting! I looked at the little calendar I kept on my phone for this one purpose with a smirk. Almost there thank fuck. The last six months had been the hardest, though it seemed like I'd been staring at this thing for the whole two and a half years or so since I started the countdown.

I'm kinda surprised I made it; half the time shit had been touch and go. There were nights when my need was so strong I almost lost my fucking mind.

In the beginning I'd tried losing myself in other things, but that shit only went so far to leashing the beast. He knew who he wanted and there were no substitutes.

I opened my wallet and studied the little dog eared image I kept there. My heart did its usual pitter-patter bullshit, and I was pleased to note that it no longer freaked me the fuck out. I was getting used to being owned by her.

Damn, if my crew knew about this shit they'd laugh their asses off. There's always been speculation about my indifference to the women who threw themselves at me, especially here of late.

No one knew that the badass biker king had given up his Cut so to speak, to a little half pint female no less. And the funniest part is that she has no idea. All that's about to change in the next few days though, and my dick can't wait to feel all that tightness.

She'd better be fucking tight. Of course she is, she's my good girl, my babygirl. I laid my head back against the chair as I pictured her beneath me. There was no sense in trying to curb my thoughts; they always came back here.

I could almost imagine the feel of her skin, the taste of her pink lips. Did she still have that cherry flavored smell? In my mind I saw her much tinier form dwarfed by mine as I took her in my king-sized bed.

I could feel the tightness of her virgin pussy as it

wrapped around my cock, sucking me in, milking me. "Shit."

I pressed down on my cock when it started to grow behind my zipper. No fucking way, I was saving this all for her. I tried talking myself down, pulling myself back from the brink.

Fuck. I had to stand so the blood could flow to where it was needed in my dick. This always happens when I think of that first fuck, that first taste.

As much as she has me twisted, she'd better be cherry, there had better be blood at the end of my dick when I breech her for the first time, or her little ass will pay the price.

My phone rang in the middle of my mini meltdown and I answered it absently. "Soon babygirl." I kissed the plastic like the sap I'd become before putting it away again. "Yo."

"MAX, I have to be out, got a little situation just came up." I hung up before my second in command could answer. He didn't have any choice in the matter but to hold shit down until I got back anyway.

I threw some gear in my saddlebag and headed

out of my place with a determined stride. I had my open carry on my hip and a concealed around my ankle. My Bowie was in my back and I had backup in my cache, so I was good to go.

If I get pulled over anywhere between here and my destination, the cops could go fuck themselves. Wasn't a one of them I couldn't outrun anyway. It might be legal to carry, but some shit just wasn't made for the streets, or so they say.

I was in a killing mood after that phone-call, but no one would be the wiser. That's part of my M.O. never let a motherfucker see you coming.

Though I wasn't breaking a sweat about what I was heading into; I never do, I can hold my own. But I was a little out of sorts because of her, the female I was going to rescue.

I didn't want our first meeting in more than two years to be like this. I had plans all laid out, had been working that shit out in my head for the better part of the last few months, and now this.

I switched gears in my head and looked ahead to when this shit was behind us, to after I'd handled what I needed to.

I was purposely keeping my mind from drifting too far off into what I was gonna find at the end of this ride. For one, there was nothing I could do before I get there, and for another, I was too fucking pissed to think.

I hopped on my ride and rode out alone. Not something I usually do, not since I formed the crew a few years ago. But I didn't want to waste the time it would take for the crew to mount up. The sooner I get to her and assess the situation, the better for all involved.

Plus I didn't like men around her, not even those I trust. Not yet anyway, not until I'd staked my claim and put my brand on her. Shit would be easier that way, might save a lot of unnecessary ass whippings.

Life was going to be a basket of fucking laughs from now on, because my place was always crawling with testosterone. I hadn't worked out how I was going to deal with that shit, didn't have to really.

I'd been planning to bring her home in another three days. That was about the time I was planning to tell them I had an old lady. Fuck they need prior warning for?

When I start explaining myself to anyone that's the time I need to hang shit up. I'd done enough of that shit in the army, never a fucking gain.

Like I said, I'd had shit all worked out in my head

for a few days down the road. But now some asshole had stepped out of fucking line in a big fucking way and I had to move shit up a couple days.

I was studiously avoiding thinking of the report I'd just received each time it teased the edges of my mind. That shit was only gonna cause me to wipe out on the highway, or end an asshole in a road rage situation.

And the only blood I wanted on my hands this night was the motherfucker's who'd thought to touch what's mine. Yeah, I felt my fingers beginning to get twitchy. Pull back Creed; take a deep breath.

I hit the road for the three-hour ride that was a straight shoot on I80. She had no idea I was coming, no idea that I had even been planning to come get her before this. I'd kept her in the dark too, because my mind was already made up and that was all that was needed.

I didn't need anyone's permission, not even hers. She was mine plain and simple, had always been. If anyone needed time to play catch up with that shit that was on them. I pretty much didn't give a left nut about that shit.

She'd better be of sound mind and body when I get there though, or that little town was gonna go up in flames. I sped up a notch and let the wind propel me through the night, taking me to her, my destiny, my babygirl.

JESSIE

I didn't have to see him to know who was out there. Just the sudden wild beating of my heart and the tingle down my spine were enough. "Creed."

His name was a whisper on my lips as I ran down the stairs just as the engine went dead outside. I was all but vibrating, hopping from foot to foot in my excitement.

Until I remembered that I was no longer a little girl and it was no longer appropriate for me to run and jump into his arms the way I did when I was little and cute.

That only dimmed my excitement for a half a sec. Somehow this time I couldn't bring myself to care, he was here and that's all that mattered. It had been so long...

He came through the door like he owned the place just as I reached the bottom stair. "Creed." I couldn't hold back the sigh of his name as my knees went weak. Still the same!

It's as if he knew, the way he came in and just stood there watching me without saying a word. I don't know how, but I felt it. And under that look, that stare that seemed to see right through me, my newfound confidence faltered.

I wanted so badly for the last three years to disappear, to be that same young girl who was still cute and adorable in the way she adored her 'uncle Creed'. But I was afraid those days were long gone, and what made it worst, was that he knew it too.

I'd been careful to keep from giving myself away, but lately, the more I thought about it the more I was convinced that something had let my secret out of the bag.

How else could I explain the long absence? Or the fact that he'd just disappeared from my life with just phone calls between us instead of the visits I had so looked forward to in the past.

I wasn't about to whine and moan to him though; he'd done so much for me already. I knew it was the greatest folly to expect more. But how I wish…

"Come." That one word spoken in his sweet baritone, which still had the power to make me weak, was all that was needed to have the barriers come tumbling down and send me running towards him, as his arms opened to accept me.

I let myself enjoy, just suck in the enormity of the moment. It had been so long since he'd held me, since I'd inhaled his scent. Home, he felt like home and my poor young heart seized for what could never be.

"You're here." I whispered the words into his neck as I felt the floodgates about to open up and suck me under. I had promised myself that I wouldn't do this. Each time I thought of seeing him again I had sworn to myself that I wouldn't break down like this.

I'd told myself that the next time I saw him I would be all grown up. But just the sight of him had everything flooding my mind at once and I couldn't hold back. He held me closer, tighter, his arms offering comfort as I struggled with my emotions.

Just as his arms closed around me I heard movement behind me, and not long after her voice and I stiffened. Why must she spoil it? I felt the loss I knew was about to come and he hadn't even put me down yet. I got in one last squeeze and inhaled his scent before the inevitable could happen.

"Stop that Jessie, you're too grown to be acting

like that." I started to pull away at the censor and disapproval in that tone, but the arms around me tightened. "Stay where you are." I looked up at his face and my heart hurt. He's so beautiful that it was torture just to look at him.

I wanted so badly to run my fingers over the ink that covered his arms and part of his neck. Not to mention the markings on his chest that I'd gotten a glimpse of just once, so long ago.

It hurt because he could never be mine, not in the way my poor stupid girl heart had wanted for so long. And because I knew he'd never take me in his arms and love me the way I've always dreamed. Dreams that had become harder and harder to avoid here lately…

I felt the old familiar bitterness in my gut start climbing up my throat to strangle me. It wasn't right to feel this way I knew, but why was my life always so unfair? I've never caught a break as far as I can remember; except for that fateful night he came into my life and saved me. That, I must admit, was the best day of my entire existence and probably always will be. Only he could top it, and…

I did my little internal monologue thing, where I told myself to be grateful. Things could've turned out so differently back then. There could've been someone else in that parking lot that night, someone less honorable. He'd done so much already, I shouldn't want more, but I did.

I tuned out of the past and back into the here and now when I realized that no one was saying or doing anything. Not since he'd told me to stay put, which was a first, but one that gave me pure joy. He held my head against his chest with one hand at my nape, while the other covered the back of my head protectively.

"Screw you, she stays right where she is." There was such venom in his voice.

"Creed?" I tried to pull my head back to look into his face. There was so much anger, I could feel it radiating in his body now. "Shh, you're fine."

He was staring back at her but not in the way he once did, like everything she said was truth. I felt the first stirring of hope in a long time when he kissed my forehead, gave me a tight squeeze, and pushed me behind him protectively.

"Where is he?" I wasn't sure what to think about his question but I started to get nervous. She didn't answer him right away but instead glared at me, which is her usual. I fought back the fear as I clung onto the back of his shirt. He seemed to sense my discomfort because his hand reached back and covered mine before he turned back to her.

"What's going on? Why are you here without letting us know you were coming?" She started doing that nervous cleaning thing she always does, as I watched him watch her. One part of me was hoping that he knew the truth finally, and another was too embarrassed to even contemplate it.

"I said where is he?"

"If you're talking about Sal he's not here." She made herself busy as my pulse raced in fear and hope. I was beginning to think that someone somewhere had told him, because I sure hadn't; but who, how?

"Baby I want you to go upstairs and get your stuff together. Just what you need for now, like your important papers and stuff like that." His words were whisper soft in my ear as he turned just his head to me.

That second kiss, this time closer to the corner of my mouth made my heart do cartwheels in my chest, and my body tingled in that old familiar way I was getting used to whenever I thought of him.

I didn't stop to question, not even when she asked him what he thought he was doing. "What're you doing? You can't just come in here and change things up without any notice. What's she doing up there?" I didn't hear anymore after that but I sure did move fast getting what little I needed together.

I had hoped and prayed for this day for so long that it was hard to believe that it was actually here; but why now? And why was he acting like he knew more than he should? I wasn't about to question anything though, this is what I wanted, what I'd always wanted since my feelings for him had changed.

It wasn't even a gradual build up either that change, it just hit me one day out of the blue, like a ton of bricks falling from the sky, and I haven't been the same since.

And now he was here and he was taking me away with him. I didn't care where just as long as he was there I knew all would be well. I wouldn't let my heart really enjoy until I was well away from this place though. Please don't let her sway him like she usually does.

I hastily threw the only things that meant anything to me into my little cloth sack at the thought. There wasn't much, mostly mementos and keepsakes from our times together over the years. Whatever she hadn't found and discarded every chance she got that is.

I didn't want to take too long, just in case it was a dream and he was gone when I got back down there. Or worse yet she was able to convince him with her lies. I couldn't stand that, not after he'd held me like that, not after the promise of being taken away from here. I'd just die.

CREED

I looked at the woman in front of me wordlessly. I hadn't come here for this, not yet, not in front of my babygirl. I'd made a conscious choice a long time ago that none of the darkness of life would ever touch her again. That I would stand between her and whatever came. That's why although I was prepared for war, I'd come here knowing that I wouldn't shed blood in front of her.

*I*n fact I'd come for one thing and one thing only, to take what was mine and get the fuck out. I'd done nothing but think on my way here and I could kick my own ass for leaving things this long. I should've come for her as soon as she was of legal age and fuck society's mores. If I had none of this would've happened.

"Did you know?" I barely kept myself from crossing the room to her, because even as I asked- I already knew. I watched her now as she fidgeted; nothing but nerves. She was about to become the first female I fucking offed. Hold it, babygirl's upstairs, remember? No bloodshed asshole.

"Know what, what's gotten into you? First you show up out of nowhere and then you ask all these strange questions." I could break this bitch's neck. Not only because she was a fuck up, but because she'd fooled me into thinking that she could be trusted, and by so doing had put my babygirl in danger.

My babygirl fuck! There was a time when that meant something a whole lot different than it does now. Back then it meant pigtails and cotton candy on a bright summer day. Now, now it meant hot nights and sweat.

Yeah, that's what I think about now when I picture her. Under me, with me buried so deep inside her there was no end and no beginning, and the heat of our bodies making us sweat. I shook it off when it was getting to be too much. Now was not the time, but soon.

I moved forward towards my prey, willing myself not to strangle her ass before I got my answers. "Did you fucking know what he was doing to her?" It was the flinch that gave her away. If she'd looked confused in the least I would've given her a break, but her reaction convinced me that she either knew or suspected, either way she was aware.

"Tell me where the fuck he is or you can get some of what he has coming to him."

"How do you know it's even true? You know she's always making things up to make us look bad."

Hearing her say that in that familiar way, reminded me of every time she'd convinced me of just that shit in the past. Every time my babygirl would write or call me with a complaint, she'd give me the same half ass excuse. And me being a fucking hump would always fall for the okey-doke.

Now as I stood there I recalled plenty of things that were warning signs, if only I'd paid attention instead of running. There had been so much that I missed because I was too fucking lax.

I'd bought this one's bullshit over the years hook line and sinker. What had that done to the young girl up those stairs? What else had she been subjected to, what had she endured because of me?

I felt shame and rage fight each other for dominance within me, as I dealt with my part in this farce. How many times had she cried out to me before I put a wedge between us? A wedge that I thought was needed to protect her from me.

How was I to know that someone else would try to take what's mine, what's always been meant for me? When I thought I was protecting her I was leaving her in harm's way all along. Somebody was gonna pay for that shit.

"She didn't tell me shit, it's fuck this shit o'clock, and I just rode a long way. Now start talking before I break every bone in your body starting with your fucking back." I was this fucking close. That haze of rage was threatening to overshadow everything else, even my need to protect my girl from bullshit.

I could see the lies forming in her eyes before she even opened her mouth, and felt sick to my stomach. How many times had I seen that look, how often have I fallen for it? What a fucking cluster fuck. Later, you can kick your own ass later; right now you have a couple enemies to annihilate.

"Jessie's been acting up a lot lately, you know she's started college these two years past and she thinks she's an adult. Sal and I do everything we can for that girl you know that, but she's a tad head-strong and ungrateful..."

It was the same fucking spiel I'd heard a thousand times before, only this time I wasn't buying that shit.

How had she felt all those years when she'd been trying to tell me the shit that was happening to her and I believed this bitch's word over hers? Granted that shit was nothing compared to this but still?

Would I have ignored her this time as well, had she tried to tell me? Since it had been a while since she'd even tried. Would I have been able to see the truth? I hope to fuck that I would've.

Or maybe it was because someone I trusted, someone I had served with and who had no reason to make this shit up, had passed on the news to me this time.

I admit now that in the past I was afraid, afraid to have her too close and that's why I allowed myself to accept this bitch's trumped up excuses. Jessie had never given me reason when we were together, to think of her as a liar. Still when she was young I'd always accept this one's excuses.

She hadn't complained to me in a long fucking time. It hit me in the gut then. I'd stupidly believed that things had smoothed themselves out. That she'd outgrown her growing pains, which was this bitch's excuse for the young girl's behavior.

Now I see that it was just her way of giving up on

me since I was never there for her those times she reached out to me. Fuck me! I felt that shit to my soul before I pulled myself back, reined it in. I'll get to the bottom of my own shit later, but for now it was time to clean house.

" Do you know it just occurred to me that it's been a while, a very long fucking time since she's tried to complain to me about anything. I wonder what the fuck else I missed." I slammed my fist down on the table as she scurried away to get out of the line of fire.

Was it because I'd always taken this evil bitch's word over hers? Is that why she'd stopped believing in me? The thought left me cold. What the fuck had I done?

How was I to know that she was lying? I believed her when she said that kids lied to get their way, hadn't I done the same as a youngster?

But it was only now, now that I wasn't blinded by my own bullshit that I could clearly see how I'd wronged her. How I'd made it impossible for her to come to me.

What else had I missed? What other horrors had she endured while I buried my head in the fucking sand because it served my purpose, kept me out of the loop when I was too chicken shit to face up to what was?

I'd thought it was the only way to protect her, to keep her safe from my lust. In the end it looks like I'd done more harm than good. I'll spend the rest of my life making it up to her, some way somehow.

"When we leave here, I'm taking her to Doc Stevens. If he finds that she's been messed with in anyway I will light this fuck to the ground with you in it." Like fuck I was taking her to some other fuck to put hands on her, but this lying bitch didn't need to know that.

"He didn't touch her-it didn't get that far...." Her voice trailed off when she realized what she'd given away with her hurried words, but she'd already told me all I needed to know.

The story I'd heard pretty much correlated with what she was saying, but I'd needed to know just how much she knew and how accurate my Intel was. Now I know.

"So you knew, you unconscionable bitch." I was about to snatch the bitch bald when I heard the tires on the gravel outside. My head whipped around in that direction as I scented my prey.

"Run Sa..." She opened her mouth to scream out a warning but my hand around her throat lifting her off the ground cut that shit off. No I didn't give a fuck that it was female, what the fuck?

"You make another fucking sound and you're done." I added enough pressure to let her know how easy it would be to carry out that threat, before pushing her ass back against the wall next to the door with my hand still holding her pinned in place.

I heard babygirl moving around upstairs and hoped she stayed put until I was finished doing what I had to do.

"Dee whose hog...?" The fucker didn't get another word out because I dropped one prey for another. I flung her aside like the garbage she was and grabbed him with my other arm before slamming my fist into his gut.

Her screams were annoying the fuck outta me only because I knew my girl would hear them and come running, she hated for me to be in danger. I used what time I had left to pulverize his kidneys before letting him fall like a rotted sack of potatoes.

"You're lucky she's upstairs or I would end you. Not to worry though, I'll be back you sick fuck, and next time I'll finish what I started." I moved away from him just as she came down the stairs.

"You ready? Lets go."

"Are you...?" Her eyes were wide with fright as she searched me for damage.

"No babygirl I'm fine we have to go." I tried blocking her view of the two people who were still trying to make it up off the floor, as I took her little backpack and threw it over my shoulder.

"Let's go baby we're done here." I led her outside and to my ride before turning to the other that was now sitting there. I used my boots and the Spurs on my heels to destroy the shit.

Only real men should ride, assholes like this piece a shit who owned this, gave the rest of us a bad name. I did as much damage as I could before drawing my bowie and slicing the tires to ribbons.

She didn't say a word but she was watching my every move, wringing her hands and looking worried. "Stop that baby I'm here now, no more fear." I could only hope that it's that fucking easy.

I fitted her helmet on her head and made sure it was straight before zipping up the lightweight jacket she had on. I could feel her body trembling slightly as I helped her on the back of my ride, so I reminded her again.

"You're safe now, stop worrying." I didn't have time to reassure her more than that; that will come later. I walked away a few feet and pulled my phone.

There was one last thing I had to do before this fuck took matters into his own hands on my behalf.

"Law, I've got my girl, thanks for the heads up brother."

"You end that fuck?"

"Couldn't, not in front of babygirl. By the way, you never told me how you came to know about this shit." Not that I was surprised, Law knew pretty much everything that was going on in his town these days.

"Brand's woman dropped the word in his ear. Seems your girl almost let it slip a time or two in the last couple of months. After she got settled in here she figured we were into helping damsels in distress or some fuck."

"She's not too far off on that one brother, I owe you one."

"You want me to take care of it for you since your hands are tied? My prey went into hiding and I'm bored as fuck."

"Nah brother, this one's mine, I'll catch you later."

It was a given I'd be back this way soon. Law had kept me and pretty much everyone else out of his troubles because it was his blood to shed, but after doing me a solid like this there was no way he wasn't getting my help.

I hung up and got on my ride because I wanted her away from this fucked up place as soon as possible. "Hold on tight babygirl."

We rode out with her little arms wrapped securely around me and I felt at ease for the first time in a very long while. At last I had what was mine, it felt like the best fucking thing to happen to me in my whole damn life, having her wrapped around me as we headed for home.

CREED

*T*here was a lot of teeth gritting going on-on the ride back I'll tell you that. Especially when I thought of the fact that we were gonna have to stop somewhere for the night. I hadn't factored in that little dilemma when I'd headed out earlier.

There was no thought of getting separate rooms though. My baby had never spent the night alone in her life and I knew with everything that had been going on she had to be scared. No way was I leaving her alone in a strange hotel room.

I bypassed a few low-end travel lodges and motels until I came upon a halfway decent mid size hotel. "We'll stay here for tonight and head home in the morning." I hopped off and helped her short ass down to stand in front of me. How could I have forgotten how tiny she is?

My dick started his shit and for the first time I didn't try to quiet him down. He knew the time was fast approaching when I wouldn't be harnessing him, wouldn't try to stop him from breaking out of the gate to get to her.

"Home?" Her voice sounded hopeful as fuck. I looked down at her in the moonlight and prayed for patience. "My place, Wyoming."

I'd forgotten that she'd never been there, never seen me in my natural habitat. The look of uncertainty on her face made my gut hurt. Has she lost faith in me? It hurt to even think that shit, even though it was just what I deserved.

I was about to broach the subject but she beat me to it. Good thing too because I wasn't sure that I would be able to give her the time to get that shit back. In three days give or take a few hours she was on my dick.

"Creed, am I staying with you now or...?" I knew what she was going to ask before she said it. "You don't ever have to go back there not ever." Her whole body relaxed and made me doubly glad that I had taken her out of there.

I wasn't going to ask her about the report I'd

received tonight, but tomorrow I was going to get to the bottom of it. it was enough that she was out of it now, that she was safe with me.

The fact that she relaxed against me told me that I hadn't lost her, and she didn't look too torn up at the prospect of living with me. In fact she looked downright joyful. Granted she didn't know that she was going to be in my bed before the week was out, she'd find out soon enough.

I checked us in and took her up to the room, where there were two queen- size beds. I dropped my gear on the one closest to the door and waited for her to move away from the doorway. I wasn't gonna be able to deal with her being afraid of me, fuck that. She needed to know that with me, she was the safest she'd ever be.

Life with me wasn't going to be a bed of roses that's for sure. I'm a hard fuck in more ways than one, but she never had anything to fear from me.

Unless she lost her fucking mind and laid with someone else. But it was up to me to see that that shit didn't happen either so she was safe.

"I don't like you being skittish around me so let's clear this shit up right now. I was wrong not to listen to you all those times you tried to tell me how things were. I let you down I know I did, but I can't go back and change that shit. I can only move forward and promise you, that nothing and no one will ever fu...I mean mess with you again in this lifetime."

Okay so I'm not the most tactful motherfucker in the world, but she got my meaning. If she was going to be fucking with me from now on and I'm pretty sure that's just what the fuck she would be doing, then she was gonna have to get used to this side of me.

Until now I'd only shown her my softer side, whatever the fuck that was. And that fucker didn't show up too often. She's gonna have to get used to the real me; the one that fucked shit up when it was needed.

She gave me her patented innocent little girl look and I wondered how in the hell she'd been able to hang onto that shit after the life she'd had living with those two fuckups. That innocence had a way of digging under my skin though and right about now that could be dangerous for her.

She still looked unsure as she looked around the room anywhere and at anything but me. I sighed and relaxed my stance a little. Can't expect her to come around in one night Creed.

"Come 'ere." She's the only thing breathing that I have any patience with; it's always been that way since I've had her. Before that in my day to day, I was known to be hard with not much give, if any.

The men of my crew know not to fuck with me, not even once, because I don't forgive worth fuck and I hate the fucking word sorry. I'd as soon gut punch an asshole as listen to his pansy ass excuses for fucking up.

So my rep is that of a straight up motherfucker. I give a fuck. Like I said, she's the only thing I've ever given a damn about in my whole fucked up life and it looks like I'd done a piss poor job of protecting her; that all ends here tonight.

When she was standing in front of me I took both her hands in mine and looked into her amazing eyes. Her hands were almost childlike as was the rest of her, except for her rack.

There was nothing childlike about the Double Ds on her chest, which were about the only things that differentiated her from a teenager. Thank fuck she didn't have them the last time I'd seen her at eighteen, or little Jessie would've been well and truly fucked. Even then she'd come pretty fucking close. Down boy! My rod was working on memory overload.

"You know you have nothing to fear from me right?" She nodded her head but I wasn't convinced.

I was pretty sure that I was gonna have to regain her trust.

I studied her for a long time, weighing the pros and cons of questioning her now, of getting to the bottom of whatever hell she'd been through. I had a need to know every single one of her hurts so I could put them to rights.

No, better wait until there was more road between me and Sal the fuck, or I might go back and kill his ass while she was in the same air space. I wasn't about to introduce any more fuckery into her life, but that fuck's day was coming. "Get to bed we've got a long day tomorrow." I squeezed her hand and released her.

She went into the bathroom and I jumped off the bed and hit the door. I couldn't even risk being that close with her in the next room naked. It's not like I don't think about her every second of every fucking day, but at least I get to keep my distance. Me having to be here, be in the same room with her, is going to fuck with my program.

How the fuck was I gonna make it the next three days until her birthday? My cock was unruly at best and this one he really wanted. He's been waiting three years to humble her; three long fucking years of beating off and second grade fucks, which were never anything more than a quick release.

I'm not sure if I'm in love with her, though I suspect that I'd been falling in love with her a little bit here and there over time, but I do know I've never felt for anyone the way I feel for her.

Love isn't something I was familiar with, not until her at any rate. But even there the shit was confusing, because what I'd grown to feel for the little girl, was nothing compared to what I now bore the near woman. And fuck me sideways with a crowbar if this shit wasn't scary as being in the warzone.

I didn't really have a basis for what she does to me, nothing to compare it to I mean. As a man of action I like to know what I'm dealing with. I like shit spelt out for me like I'm a two year old so when I have to fuck somebody up for their shit, at least we were both on the same page before they fucked up.

The shit she makes me feel has no rhyme or reason. There's no pattern to the fucking madness or the way she consumes my every thought even when I don't want her to. Shit's not fair, it's like I didn't have a choice. And that right there is why I think I might be in love. Fuck!

It wasn't like the shit changed gradually either,

no. One day she was the sweet little sprite I'd rescued, someone I had resigned myself to having in my life in one way or the other for all time, but of course in a conventional way. Then one day out of the blue, she changed and all that shit went out the window.

I wasn't equipped to deal with the rapid changes back then, and I probably handled shit all wrong. All I know is that when I started dreaming about her, staring at her body like a sexual thing, it was time to go before I did some fucked up shit that would make her first years seem nice in comparison.

I only ever wanted what was best for my baby-girl, and nowhere in my mind was that me. I'd lived a rough and sordid life, a life on the streets and then buried in war. I wanted better for her, she deserved the white picket fence and all the other bullshit that went along with it. Shit that I was never gonna be able to give her.

So I'd stayed the fuck away in the beginning, tried to keep my thoughts clean where she was concerned, that shit didn't last too long though. But still I'd had the strength to stay away though it almost killed me. I'd told myself I was giving her time. Because once my mind was made up, there was no changing that shit. Still, I maybe should've handled that shit better.

It had been way too long since we'd seen each other; that too was my fault, my own cowardice I guess you can call it. But I'd wanted her to at least finish school before I tied her down to me for good. Because I know for a fact that I wasn't letting her out of my sight once I'd taken her.

But now that I'd seen the new grown up Jessie, it would be a minor miracle if she made it to her birthday with her pussy in tact. She was even more beautiful than I remember if that were possible. There was barely a hint of the girl in her anymore she was all woman.

Those curves, fuck me, who would've thought she would become this from the scruffy little urchin who'd wrapped herself around my heart all those years ago?

'Maybe you don't have to wait, she's legal.'

'No you fuck I said twenty one...'

'But she doesn't know that, you're the only one who...'

'Shut...the fuck...up.' My conscience needs a

fucking conscience, that fuck thinks with his dick twenty four seven when it comes to her.

I paced outside in the hallway like a fiend needing a hit while she took her shower. I couldn't go too far, not with her in there naked, and with who knows who staying in this fucking dump. But I daren't risk going back in there either. Not with visions of her wet and naked, and fuck me she was going to give me blue balls again.

This is why I stay the fuck away from her. If I didn't, I would lose my cool; that control I was always hailed for would go out the fucking window in a heartbeat and she'd end up under me.

As it stands, I know that when I finally get inside her it would take at least three days before I'd had my fill. Is it sick that I've already been to the pharmacy to pick up some ointments and shit to see to her pain after I tear her?

Just the thought of her sitting on my thirteen and a half inch cock with her little virgin pussy makes me wanna howl at the fucking moon. My mouth was already salivating at the thought of getting near those tits, and I'm not even gonna get started on that ass of hers. A fucking work of art!

Shit Creed, think of something else before you do something fuck stupid. Like go in there and just pin her. It had been a while since I'd fucked, not a long while but long enough for someone like me who liked pussy on the regular.

Because I knew I was going after her soon I'd cut down out of respect for her. But now that I think about it I may not have done her any favors. My dick was already harder than he'd ever been just from sniffing around her.

I actually checked my Tag to see just how long I had to wait, down to the days, hours, minutes and seconds. Seems like the closer we got to her birthday, the harder it was becoming to control my urge. A cold shower wasn't going to cut it this time.

I was afraid even as I paced that hallway that I was fooling myself. There was no way I was going to make it three days without taking her.

Before this shit had jumped off I was able to put thoughts of taking her aside for long periods of time. I'd needed to just to get through the day, or I would go get her from her bed in the middle of the night and just slake my lust inside her. Something I had promised myself I would never do.

When I finally do take her, it's going to be the special shit that she deserves; the first couple of times at least. Because if my dreams and daydreams were anything to go by, I had a world of hard fucking planned for her future.

It was the only way I knew to fuck and as little as her ass is I'm sure it was going to take some doing to get her accustomed to my size. I'd already taken all that shit into consideration, hence the pharmacy run weeks ago.

It may appear that I'm plotting the demise of her virginity; I like to think of it as my finally staking my claim. Mind you I'm going on the assumption that she wants this shit too, but I'm honest enough to admit that it won't make a difference, I'm taking her one way or the other. If I have to talk her around so be it. But, that pussy is mine no if ands or buts.

For fuck sake Creed, don't think about this shit with her so close, it's only a couple more days. Yeah but I've been wanting her so fucking bad for so long now that just the thought of how close I was to finally having her was almost more than I could take.

CREED

*W*hen I thought enough time had passed I ran my hand over my cock with a stern admonishment to stand the fuck down and went back in. I'm just gonna go to bed turn out the lights and get some sleep. She's just one little girl Creed stop being a bitch it's not a good look.

"Fuck me!" I stopped short in the doorway.

"Ahhh." She screamed at my sudden entrance. I'm not sure which of us was more surprised her, or me. That was before she dropped the fucking inadequate towel and I nearly swallowed my fucking tongue.

We both stood staring at each other and I was amazed that I was able to drag my eyes away from her amazing body long enough to look into her eyes.

"If he'd touched you, I would kill him in the most horrific way possible."

She didn't need to know that I meant to end the fuck anyway, and I'd just told her in not so many words that I knew what had been going on. Not how I wanted this conversation to start, but she'd given me such a shock I'd just sworn in front of her for the first time in her life.

"Creed?" She looked white as a sheet.

"Don't be scared baby, it's gonna be okay." Damn, I was reminded once again just how jumpy she is around me, how aware we've always been of each other. Well not always.

I wanted to hold her and offer comfort, but I couldn't risk that shit. I know one thing for sure; two days and twenty-two hours couldn't come soon enough.

I swallowed hard and fought for control. I might not fuck her, but there wasn't a chance in hell that I was going to be able to keep my mouth off her tits. I was also fascinated with the bush between her thighs. Fuck my dick was hard.

"You're beautiful." The smile that broke across her face went to the heart of me and helped ease that knot in my gut. I hadn't lost her after all thank fuck.

My little Jessie, my babygirl, was all grown up.

My mind went from the vision I'd just seen before she snatched the towel up and covered herself; to the first time we'd met.

JESSIE and I share a long and sordid history. One that I try not to revisit too often because I don't like hurting her, and any reminder of the way we met was bound to hurt her in some way. Looking back at it, it was a stroke of luck that I'd been the one to be there that night. I like to think that there was a bit of fate involved there too.

I can't imagine life without her in it, couldn't fathom the last nine years being any different. Even when I wasn't there with her, just knowing she was in my life, that she was mine and only mine, was enough to get me through.

She was my own little good luck charm. The one thing that had gotten me through some of the toughest hellholes in Baghdad, and that was before I knew I was going to make her my woman some day.

I was a young twenty-four year old soldier on leave after coming back from my second stint in the desert, and looking at my third in a few days. That's where I'd met Lawton. We were both serving in the same platoon, two young upstarts full of piss and vinegar, who'd hit it off right away.

I didn't have any family to speak of since I'd aged out of the foster care system one month before I joined up years before, so he'd dragged me home with him.

It was in his neck of the woods that my whole life had changed in one hour. We'd only been back one day when something came up and he'd had to make a run somewhere else, leaving me with his family. My own foray to the local liquor store had landed me in the middle of an alternate universe.

There was an old man who was obviously drunk or high, with a young scruffy looking kid tagging along behind him. It was hard to tell whether it was a boy or girl at first. All I saw was an unkempt kid that reminded me of my time on the street.

The kid looked to be about six or seven, but I later found out she was a twelve year old under nourished kid with extremely long lashes, and the most amazing blue-green eyes I'd ever seen on a human being.

Something about her eyes tugged at me even then, and things only got worse for me when the fucker offered to sell her to me for his next pint. I didn't know if to knock him the fuck out, call the cops, or laugh in his face.

But something in the helpless way she looked at me told me that I was this kid's only hope in life. I don't know where I got that conviction, but it was strong and it was real.

The fact that the fucker had all her important paperwork handy in a dingy Ziploc bag, along with a paper bag with a few dirty tops and shorts inside, told me that he was dead serious. He even had a legal enough looking document, that I could sign if I was so inclined. Only this didn't say he was selling her, but giving her up for adoption.

I knew if it wasn't me it would be someone else, and that someone else might not be as nice as I am. I shuddered to think what could happen to the young girl at the hands of a predator. I knew they were plenty fucked up individuals in the world. I'd run into my fair share when I was a helpless kid with no one to stand between me, and them.

I gave him the money for a couple pints, hoping one of them would kill his ass, and because I thought she was worth more than the one. I couldn't see calling the cops and having her put in the system, I'd done that shit and it was a hell I wouldn't wish on…

nah that's a fucking lie, I would wish that shit on my enemies, fuck them.

So there I was a twenty-four year old who was shipping out in a few days and had just landed myself with a new dependent. I didn't know where the fuck to start. It wasn't like I could take her with me.

I questioned the poor frightened girl the best I could and got the information that the mother had a sister in town, but the mom herself was long gone, and there was no one else.

She didn't act weird when she mentioned the aunt so I figured she wasn't afraid of her and she was maybe a little better than the father. And since I was in a crunch, I searched her out and things went from there.

I did check around the best I could with what little I had which in retrospect hadn't been enough. But at the time, I thought I was giving her the best I had to offer. Someone she knew, a relative no less, and one that hadn't asked too many questions or seemed too surprised that the young girl had ended up in her plight.

To make a long story short, I told her I adopted the kid, told the kid never to mention to anyone that her old man had sold her, and to pretty much wipe that shit clean from her mind.

I wasn't old enough to be her dad, so I was just her guardian until she came of age. I did all the necessary shit the army makes you do when you have a co-dependent just in the off chance shit went FUBAR on my ass, then she'd get what was mine. But in the meantime, I was leaving her with the aunt who I paid a healthy stipend each month to see about her.

We worked shit out in the best interest of Jessie, or so I thought, and I went off to my next deployment with her heavy on my mind. I was in essence the new father of a pre-teen girl who I knew nothing about, but those eyes; they haunted me.

Over the years I'd go see her. In the early days I'd even taken her on trips and shit when I was home in between deployments. She was a shy little thing back in those days, but as time went on she started coming out of her shell.

She was never too talkative, but she wasn't shying away from me as much, and she felt safe enough to ask me a few questions here and there. Once she opened up she was a regular little chatter-box, but funnily enough, she never mentioned the old man and never talked about her life before me.

It never crossed my mind to bring her to live with me on post when I was stateside. Plus the fact I was moving around a lot back then with the army and their bullshit, and she needed a stable home.

I didn't know much about kids, especially the female kind, so I wouldn't have known what to look for if anything was out of whack, but I knew the times I saw her she seemed happy enough, and I grew to love those times.

I'd especially grown to like the way she'd run and jump into my arms whenever she saw me coming, until she remembered her shyness and would back away again. But in that split second of recognition her barriers would come down and I'd see what she really thought of me.

I always kept her close at those times, because I knew she needed it. We'd come to mean the world to each other even though we spent so much time apart.

I saw so much of me in her back then. The unwanted orphan that had everything stacked against us. It's why I'd gone overboard with everything when it came to her.

I never wanted her to know hunger and want the way I had. Never wanted her to feel that shame like the rest of the world was looking down on you.

I'd bought her every device known to man so we could keep in touch when I was gone, and had kept up with her schooling and the things that I could handle as a man. The rest of that female shit I left to the aunt.

When I was told about her having her period I walked into the neighborhood with my gun on full display on my next leave to let the young fucks around there know that she was off limits. I'd wanted to bundle her the fuck up and put her somewhere safe.

Back then she was still my sweet little babygirl, even though her body was changing and she was outgrowing her babyish ways. It was plain to see that she would always be a little bitty thing though, which I used to think was cute, but now found sexy as fuck.

It's when she hit eighteen that shit went south on my ass. The little scrawny kid had blossomed into a fucking knockout on me practically overnight.

The only thing that saved my sanity was the fact that she was still that sweet shy little girl that I'd acquired in that parking lot, or I would've fitted her ass with a chastity belt.

She didn't seem to have any idea about her new appeal, and I'd had a talk with Dee about teaching her certain things without divulging too much. Although I wanted her to embrace her new woman-hood, I never wanted her to lose that innocence that was so fucking beguiling.

I didn't want her dumb enough to fall for some lame fucker's bullshit lies either, and that's why I'd asked Dee to have the talk with her, fuck I know about teenage girls and hormones and shit?

I read some books but that shit didn't make any damn sense. At least they didn't seem to be describing any of the females I'd been acquainted with. I'd been fucking since the age of thirteen and it wasn't just thirty year olds I was fucking.

I didn't want that shit for my little Jessie. I wanted her life to be ten times better than the fuckery I'd endured, and so I'd gone above and beyond to make sure she had every opportunity. Boys were out though. I let her know that shit in as many ways as I possibly could. Maybe that's why she was still so skittish around males. I'd maybe shel-tered her too much.

In my mind she was still the same little urchin I'd met that night. I never had a wayward thought about her. I'm no fucking pervert, and would've maimed any motherfucker who'd looked at her cross-eyed.

But then shit had changed up on me when I was least expecting it.

I'd come to see her on my last deployment before I timed out and got the shock of my life. I'd been expecting my sweet little girl who'd grown some over time, but no big surprises. What I found was a fucking cover model with a body to rival any porn stars'.

I'm ashamed to say that I'd been angry back then-angry at the thought that someone else was one day going to enjoy all that. Then I was pissed at myself for looking at her that way, for even thinking of her in the same way I'd thought of other women I'd bedded, that meant nothing more than the hour or so I usually spent on a fuck.

It's when I realized that what I was feeling was actually a little bit more than that that the fun really begun. I was in a fucking quandary and that's a fact.

There was no doubt that I wanted her, but how could I do that shit? I'd spent all our time together trying to get her not to feel obligated to me in any way. How could I now take her?

Would she give herself to me out of some misguided sense of loyalty? I didn't want that shit. But I couldn't keep my eyes off of her that whole fucking weekend.

I found myself wanting to fight every male that came within ten feet of her, and was actively glaring fuckers away. She on the other hand, didn't seem to notice the men flocking to her like moths to a flame. She was still the same shy, sweet Jessie, only now she had the body of a fucking siren.

When we talked, I wondered if she realized that I wouldn't even look at her? I daren't risk it. No joke, everything about her made me hard that weekend and even as I sat having dinner with her in the only diner the piece a shit town had, I was mourning the loss of her innocence, and whatever ease we once had, because I was sure we were never going back there again.

It got so I had to physically restrain myself from touching her. When she spoke I found myself following the movement of her lips with my eyes with my breath held. It was pathetic.

I'd come way too fucking close that weekend to crossing the line. After the childhood I'd had, I'd taught myself not to deny myself anything.

I fought hard and fucked harder and made no bones about it. I'd stopped believing the world owed me something, but that weekend I was starting to look at her as my prize. My gift for doing something good for once in my fucked up life, and that was no good.

My dick stayed hard and my thoughts never stopped wandering to the nearest bed. It was a minor miracle that she made it intact that weekend. I spent the time taking her in, studying her, listening to her. I was preparing myself for not seeing her again. It was the only way.

After that I stayed away more and more even when I got out. I was too chicken shit to even Skype anymore and I knew I hurt her with that shit, but it's what was best for her, or so I told myself at the time.

I just sent money for whatever she needed, got a progress report once or twice a month and stayed the fuck gone. It almost killed me to leave her, and in the beginning when she'd beg me to come it would tear a hole in my gut.

I COULDN'T TELL her why I was staying away after all, but I think somewhere along the way she started blaming herself for my absence. That's when she stopped asking.

But then the inevitable happened and I ended up seeing her again not long after that; that was the last time before I really cut and ran.

That was more than two years ago. That's also when I'd seen that look in her eye that had scared the living fuck outta me.

It was one thing for me to find myself wanting her, but something else entirely to see lust looking back at me from her beautiful eyes. I'd run that day and kept running until this.

CREED

*N*ow she stood staring back at me from across the room with the piece of crap towel clutched against her chest. "Go get dressed babygirl." Yeah, and do that shit quick before I lose my shit and fuck you way too fucking hard and a couple days too soon.

The shot I got of her ass as she turned to walk away didn't help matters any. How the fuck did she fit all that goodness on that five foot fucking frame? I had to shake my head to dispel the vision that came into it.

I'm six five, when I put her under me she's going to be covered from head to toe, and the thought of that shit made my dick stand like an iron pike in my jeans, making that fuck an uncomfortable fit.

I kept my fucking head straight and my eyes crossed when she came back out the bathroom wearing some shorts and tank combo that was designed expressly to get her little ass nailed. And you've got fucking on the brain Creed you fuck. What makes you any better than the hump you're supposed to be saving her from?

I headed for a long cold shower after securing the door with my own shit. I don't trust fuck after the shit I'd seen out there in the world so I always go above and beyond, especially when it comes to her.

I doused my head first to calm the fuck down and let my mind wander. I knew in a few days both our lives were gonna change forever, there's no way I was letting another motherfucker taste that, fuck no. Even if I'd suffered an attack of conscience on occasion in the past, the split second sight I'd witnessed put paid to that shit.

I soaped up my dick and gave it a few cursory strokes with a tight fist, but my heart wasn't into that shit. The next time I offload it is going to be deep inside her, way inside her. Where it would do the most good. My dick and heart thumped in sync with each other at that last incendiary thought.

"Fuck." I knew just where my mind was headed. For a long time now my mind has been obsessed with breeding little Jessie. Don't ask me where the fuck it came from. Just one day out of the blue it was all I could think about and now it hits me at least once a day, the vision of her suckling my son.

It could be the size of her rack or some fuck that triggered me, but I knew it was a done fucking deal. First chance I get I'm planting one in her.

Fuck Creed this is not the kind of shit you want to be thinking about in a situation like this. She's in there sitting on that bed with those next to nothing pieces of cloth on and your dick is already heading out the gate. Think of some fuck else because now is not the time my man.

That little pep talk helped to calm my breathing a little but that was it. My dick stayed hard and my mind stayed on the pussy.

I doused my head again and gritted my teeth against the rising need in my balls. No way was I going to disrespect her by rubbing one out in her honor while she was in the next room all innocent and shit. 'Yeah? But if you don't do something soon you're liable to fuck a hole in the poor girl in a few days.' Would you shut the fuck up?

'Just saying.'

It wasn't easy but eventually I got myself under control enough to stop thinking about what was between her legs. The fact that she was more to me than a quick lay may have had something to do with that. Whatever it was, I was able to pull myself back, rein myself in and think of something else.

WHEN I'D TIMED out of the army a couple years ago I already knew what it was that I wanted to do with my life. I'd used Uncle Sam to farther my education of course, and the only expenditures I'd had while serving was her upkeep. Everything else I'd socked away for the day I got out.

I had a nice nest egg at the end of my journey with the army, which I took and invested in my own bike shop. With all the discounts and other incentives given to veterans I came out on top and hadn't had to dip too heavily into my savings.

I didn't even have to touch the little fund I'd started for her way back when. Her college fund was gonna go to something else, I don't know what yet, since she'd received a full scholarship. My baby is a smart fuck.

My thing was always to have something to leave for her if something should happen to me. I hadn't given much thought to her future other than school and a career. The idea of a husband and kids never really entered my mind. I just had it down on paper and in my head that she was always gonna be mine, and therefore I was always going to be responsible for her.

Two and a half years ago when I saw that look of longing in her eighteen year old eyes I'd ran back to my hometown. Days later when I couldn't get it out of my mind, I'd given it some thought and decided that I wasn't going to do anything to influence her, but I was going to watch from afar.

I'd been harboring a serious hard on for her since then, but I have more control than to take advantage of the young girl who'd been dependent on me her whole life.

Instead I made a deal with myself. If she was still single at twenty-one I was gonna take her no matter the fuck what. Now I know that that's a lie. I would've moved anyone out of the way to get to her. Thank fuck it hadn't come to that.

In all these years she'd never even hinted at a boy, and she'd never really outgrown that sweet shy thing she had going on that made me want to wrap her up in cotton balls and keep her safe.

I'd kept my ears to the ground and selfishly hoped that she never fell for any of the little fuckers who were always sniffing around her. It had taken everything in me not to beat the fuck outta the kid who'd asked her to prom, but she'd turned him down, she wanted to go with me.

I maybe should've talked her out of it, but what the fuck, I've never been one for guile. In the end I'd taken her to prom, which made her the envy of all her little girlfriends if I do say so myself.

And when the same kid had given her shit later about it and someone had given me a heads-up, I'd dropped in on him for a nice little chat. That little fuck never had much to say to her after that.

After the prom I'd gone back to keeping my distance, even though I must've studied the million and one pictures I'd insisted we take that night, a hundred times or more.

By then I was a selfish bastard who wanted all her firsts to be mine. As much as I stayed away, I lived for the days she'd call me, so that just the sound of her voice could soothe the beast.

We still had a standing appointment to talk on the phone every Sunday night no matter where I was, and I travelled a lot, and was always up to some fuckery. It kept me from going crazy for want of her.

But no matter what was going on in my life, I always made time for her, she always knew that she came first; at least I hope she did. It was because of her that I'd taken up the cause I had, freeing young girls from fucked up situations.

My boys and I basically travelled the country wherever there was a need and put douches in their fucking place.

We like to put a beat down on any asshole who thinks it's cool to abuse or in any way fuck with the female of the species. In two years we'd built such a rep for ourselves that we now had a backlog.

I'd found someone trust worthy to run the shop, which was the crew's main source of income, along with the few apartment buildings I'd bought for cheap and cleaned up.

I had more money now than I'd ever dreamed of, but realized early on that the shit was only good for but so much. It couldn't erase the ugly that was some people, and it couldn't remove the pain. It did have its purposes though, and I was waiting not too patiently to shower her with all the shit it could buy.

Everything I did was with her in mind. I never wanted her to be that helpless little girl again, and me being me back then there was no guarantee that I'd always be around to protect her. Lately though I've been thinking really hard about a long life. A life with her and my kids!

It was the first fucking dream I'd ever allowed myself, the only one I haven't tried to kill at its inception. As the day of her twenty-first birthday drew near it was all I could do to stay the fucking course. I'd been lining shit up in my head almost everyday, when I wasn't killing myself to stay busy until the time came.

It figures that as soon as the time drew near my patience was at an end. But I made myself hold on for her, and because of the secret promise I'd made myself. I told myself she was worth waiting for, and that if I could hang in there until D-day, well then I would've proven just that to myself, and in the bargain, proven that she meant more to me than the rest.

Then word had come through late last night from my boy Law that the aunt's piece a shit racist fuck boyfriend had been going into her room at night. Word was that he hadn't struck as yet, but I wasn't gonna give the fucker the chance. I'd been on the road not long after I'd heard that fuckery, not even taking time to safeguard my own shit; she comes first always.

I don't even want to remember the way I felt when I heard that shit. If the asshole had been standing in front of me then he would've been dust.

The idea that he'd even looked at her beauty was his death sentence. No one else was supposed to lay eyes on that but me, the fuck.

I couldn't just go around offing motherfuckers though, I had too much to live for and a hell of a lot to look forward to. But there were still plenty of ways to deal with his ilk, and I knew them all. I just needed to get her to safety, though it was hard as fuck not retaliating right here and now.

I'd been so focused on what laid ahead for her and I that my head had even cooled a little where he was concerned. I didn't expect that shit to last too long though, just thinking about what the fuck he had in mind when he was standing over her was enough to make me say fuck it and just do the fuck.

I flicked off the water and hoped like fuck that she was asleep by the time I made it back out there. My cock was tenting the towel and I hadn't had the presence of mind to bring shorts with me, since I usually slept in the raw, so there was no way to hide it.

She was gonna have to get used to me like this soon anyway, so I just tightened the shit around my hips just in case she was still up. Hopefully he doesn't pull one of his moves and slip through the cracks. My boy's a pussy hound and he's been hounding this particular gash for way too fucking long.

Of course she was wide-awake with the TV on, sitting in the middle of the bed Indian fashion with her hair in pigtails. Her innocence almost made me weep as I just stood there looking down at her, while the glow from the screen highlighted her cheekbones; willing myself not to look any lower.

My dick was already leaking like a fucking faucet, not that he had been acting any different since I'd entered the house earlier and got my first look at her in almost three years. I was giving some serious thought to sleeping under the stars tonight to preserve her virginity. I had about an ounce of self-control left and that's being generous.

She felt my stare and turned those slanted orbs my way, and not for the first time I wondered what kind of beauty her mother had to be, because the old man hadn't been much to look at.

In fact, after I'd had her for three or four years I'd done an extensive search to make sure that she really was his, and it turns out she was. But I still didn't know anything about the mom, and all the aunt would say was that she was a bitch.

Law had helped me out there too by finding out that the dad had been part of a crew a few towns over. From there I'd learned that her mom had been one of the sheep, one of those women who follow crews around and are shared among the men who were interested. He'd knocked her up at an early age, before she had run off and left the kid behind.

I never told her anything about her mom and had forbid Dee to tell her anything negative about the missing woman, but I was sure now that she'd probably been doing just that behind my back, the hag.

It was late but neither of us seemed ready to sleep, and since fucking wasn't on the menu tonight I decided to go with the next best thing.

"You hungry babygirl?" She smiled and nodded and I picked up the menu on the little side table that said twenty- four-hour room service. "What do you want?" She shrugged her shoulders and picked at the sheet under her.

I never made much of her shy behavior before, but something about it bothered me now. After all the horror stories I'd heard in the last couple years I was always suspicious of shit, what if this wasn't the first time someone had fucked with her? What if... my gut dropped at the mere thought but what if?

Maybe what I'd always taken as shy reserve had been something else. If anyone had hurt her, they were in for a world of fuckery. Before the week was out I was gonna get to the bottom of all the shit she'd endured while I'd been off saving the world, and heads were gonna roll. But fuck it; if someone had out hands on her I was sure to end up in the pen.

Looking at her now I questioned everything I'd been led to believe over the years. All those reports I'd had from the aunt that had kept me from worrying, and made me believe she was growing the way a young girl should. Even her school reports had been encouraging, and the aunt had nothing to do with those.

But I was beginning to think there was something else going on here other than an innate shyness on her part. Not my Jessie, not my babygirl. I would've endured any kind of hell to see that she never suffered any of the shit I'd seen.

I hope to fuck that it's just her sweet shyness and nothing more, but whether it was or not, I didn't want her to be one of those timid types who were afraid of their own shadow. Whatever had happened before today I will deal with, but she was no one's victim, I wouldn't let her be.

I'd done everything I could over the years to foster her independence. I paid for extra shit that the aunt said she was interested in to try to break her out of that shell, but I couldn't see where it had helped much. That got me to thinking now that I wasn't such a blind ass.

"How's your karate class coming?" She looked at me like I was speaking a foreign language and I could feel the blood starting to burn under my skin.

"What karate lessons?" She had a befuddled look on her face and I cleared my throat and tried for peace. If there's one thing I hate it's being made to look like a fool, and right now I was feeling like the world's biggest ass.

If it wasn't for her and my need to get her as far away from Sal the fuck as possible, I would go back there and finish what I started. "Did you take ballet or piano or anything like that outside of your regular classes?"

Those are all the things I'd been told in the almost three years since I saw her that she was suddenly interested in. Of course I never thought to ask her until now.

Though I'd looked forward to those calls I'd always kept them short and Dee was usually hovering somewhere in the background.

I knew she was going to say no before she started shaking her head at me and was already in motion. That was the last fucking straw, this bitch was either crazy or fuck stupid. Either way she was beyond fucked.

I held up my finger for silence, before dragging on my pants and heading towards the door. I didn't want to do this in front of her and I wasn't in the mood to wait. I hit speed dial and was answered almost immediately.

"Jason, I need a solid. I need you to look up Dee Reynolds and Sal Jones in Dorset. I want all their financial information down to the penny. Call me back as soon as you've got something."

My next call was to her old home. That call was answered in pretty much the same haste but for different reasons I'm sure. Jason would know that a call from me on his secure line at this time was serious business. These two I'm sure were waiting up in case I came back for their ass.

"By my reckoning you owe me quite a few grand for the past few years of bullshit classes that she never took. I'm going to give you exactly one day to have my fucking money or I'm gonna break your fucking neck."

"What money? We've had the care of her for almost nine years and..."

"And I paid you for her upkeep and then some.

67

What the fuck did you do with my money?" I was getting more heated by the minute.

Not only because she'd ripped me off, but because all this time I'd been thinking my girl was getting a wide and varied education, while all the while this bitch was doing who the fuck knows with my money.

My phone beeped while I was on with her. "You would be wise to have my shit when I get there, and if you even think about running this shit will be ten times worse you lying bitch."

I switched over to Jason because other than strangling her ass, which was impossible at this very minute, I had fuck else to say to her.

"What you got for me?"

"They have a shitload of crap bro, but no real cash to speak of. I found about twelve grand in cash, which I can move you just say the word. "

"I want it all, down to the house they live in now, all that should be left is the clothes on their backs and nothing else, not even a bus ticket." I hung up the phone and went back inside with a heavy heart.

I'd fucked up; there was no other way to look at it. I could pass the blame but I don't believe in lying to myself. How the fuck had they got the drop on me though? That shit hurt. Not that they'd hoodwinked me, but that they'd hurt her in the process. My baby-girl: fuck.

All this time I thought I was giving her a better life and these fuckers were taking advantage of both of us. How the fuck had I made it so easy for them? How long was this going on? Was it only after I pulled the runner two and a half years ago, or was it always like this? I was more inclined to believe the latter.

There was no point in rehashing the shit in my head now, best to move forward and make up for my screw up. But this shit's looking more and more like somebody's gonna end up dead. I hate to be fucked with.

I headed back to the room and her, once again with that feeling that I'd let her down eating away at me. What must she think of me? Was I any better than the old drunk that had sold her to me?

At least with him she knew there was no hope. But me, I came along and sold her dreams and happily fucking ever after and look at this bullshit. Cluster-fuck me up the ass with a sledgehammer.

As I hit the door I realized I'd forgotten all about room service. Damn, looks like I was still fucking up. I didn't like the way any of this shit was making me feel.

I had been looking forward to us, her and me. To spoiling the fuck out her for the rest of our lives. For a long time now I've had this picture of her in my head. She was always laughing and happy. The shit I was providing for her was making sure that she never knew a day's want or neglect.

I hated the fact that I'd been such an ass. All these years I'd been no better than the fucker that had sold his own blood to me. That shit left a fucked up taste in my mouth.

I felt a burning in my gut as I thought of the hell those two must've put her through while I was playing possum. How fucking blind had I been? And all because I was afraid of my dick, I was beyond disgusted with myself.

She was waiting up for me when I got back inside. I wasn't about to burden her with anymore bullshit for tonight. I wanted her to get past this shit and move the fuck on herself, though I knew that was gonna take some time.

But there was one thing I needed to know. One thing that just couldn't wait. I couldn't have been wrong about all this shit, could I? If she erased that image I have of her as a happy kid I think I'd fucking lose my shit.

"Did you ever have any interest in any of those

things I asked you about?" she was back to picking at the sheets again as she gave it some thought. Then she looked up at me with those innocent eyes and I felt the pull in my gut.

"I did use to, but aunt Dee always said it wasn't needed, that it was selfish of me to want those things after everything else you'd done." I think I'm gonna fucking cry.

"Tell me sweetheart, was there ever anything you were interested in doing outside of school that you got to do?" I held my breath hoping against hope. It had meant something to me, knowing all these years that I was doing something good, something decent.

Knowing that I was saving a little girl from the same fate as me. That shit had got me through some tough shit. Knowing that there was someone halfway around the world who needed me had kept me warm on many a cold night.

Hearing that it was all a lie was like being back in the midst of hell again. I could tell she didn't want to answer me, maybe because my face was starting to look like I'd slaughter half a damn village with my bare hands. "Answer me sweetheart."

"You mean other than our trips together when I was little?"

"Yeah baby, that's what I mean." She shook her

head and broke my fucking heart. I covered my mouth with my hand to hold back the tidal wave that was coming.

Now that I'd unerringly opened the floodgates I wanted to know it all, down to the last fucking detail. But instead of diving head first into the conversation, I decided to change shit up. There was only so much control I could exert over myself and I think I'd reached my limit.

I already knew what had to be done, but I was dead serious about her not ever having to face this bullshit again. So it was best if I left this shit alone for another day. Maybe after I'd shown her how life with me was going to be, then we could take this shit out and shrug at it.

Right now though I was feeling pretty raw and I knew she had to be too, so once again I moved away from the fuckery for both our sakes.

"We forgot to order, what do you want? You can have anything you'd like." I kept my tone light as I moved over towards her and sat on the bed. She bit her lip as we looked over the menu together. So fucking innocent. Mine.

She was hesitant to do even this and I had to bite back the anger. Good thing I knew what she liked and since it was already late I went ahead and chose for her.

"I'll get you the buffalo wings and that salad that you like." They were about all she ever ate when we were together so I knew they were her favorites. "Do you want dessert baby?" Her blush didn't make sense until she told me that the bitch had been denying her dessert for the last couple of years because they would make her fat and ugly.

It seems that my staying away had given her carte blanche to fuck with what's mine. Too bad for her, she'd chosen the wrong motherfucker to fuck with.

I didn't let on to anything that was going on inside me, just placed the order and added a slice of double chocolate cake for her. Her eyes lit up at mention of the treat and I added a few more thumps to Dee and Sal's asses when I got ahold of them.

By the time room service showed up she was a little more relaxed. I'd stopped asking her the hard questions and had kept things light, just asking her about some show she was into on TV. I'm surprised the bitch let her enjoy that much, because it seemed like she'd been bent on destroying my babygirl's every pleasure.

I wasn't surprised that Dee and Sal had taken me for a chump. There was no way they could've known my true nature, since I'd never shown it to them. Not that many knew it to be honest, except for those who'd ran the streets with me, and the men and women I'd served with.

The fact that I'd been an absentee guardian, had no doubt given them the impression that I didn't really care. And so they'd taken that as a green light to continue shitting all over her the way her father had for the first half of her life. Little did they know, he might've gotten off easy, but they were in for a world of fucking hurt.

I made sure she ate, and by the way she picked at her food I was inclined to believe the bitch had monitored even that. I had a lot to make up for it seems. What must she think of me? It couldn't be any worse than what I thought of myself.

"Get some sleep sweetheart, you don't need to clean that up." I took the dirty dishes from her and placed them back on the tray on the table. She'd eaten all her food and seemed surprised that no one was going to stop her halfway. Just what the fuck had those two monsters done to her anyway?

Don't think about that shit Creed, not now, it's late. Take your hotheaded ass to bed and get some rest. Come at it fresh in the morning. Sometimes I wish my conscience would take a flying fucking leap off a bridge.

With food out of the way, my mind went back to its earlier pastime, which was making love to her in every way imaginable. Poor kid, by looking at her it was hard to tell if she'd ever be able to handle me, all of me, and not just in the sack. I'm not exactly the easiest person to get along with. I have some fucked up ways and ideas that I'd picked up along the way.

I'd made up my own rules and by-laws since I'd been old enough to understand how shit worked. It was fucked that she'd lived the life she had, and was now in my clutches. I won't abuse her, far from it. But I'm going to be a restrictive fuck where she was concerned.

Because of the shit I'd seen along with my natural instinct to dominate, she was in for it. I know me, and I know what I want from her, and for her.

I know that when I fuck her for the first time, it will be more of a branding than anything else. I'd already made up in my mind that she was going to belong to me in every way possible. The kid I was planning to plant in her was just the beginning.

I've already started moving shit around in my head to accommodate this change. No one knew I was bringing her home. Those who knew of her existence were few and far between, and none of them had any idea of what I really felt for her. The only one who knew that I was all the way gone over her was Lawton, and that was because I'd gotten toasted one night and spilled my guts.

He'd since lost his family so he probably didn't remember that long ago night and what had been said. If he did he never once brought it up. Not that I was worried about being judged, Law now had his own young bride and from what little he'd told me, he wasn't in any better shape than me.

I had one glaring problem that I could see, and that was the men around me. My life was one of hard living and the men and women I surrounded myself with were of that ilk.

I've never denied anyone anything, by that I mean I've casted off many a female before who'd moved on to someone else in the crew. It's just the way of these things. Some innocent soul might lose his life over this one though. I'm pretty sure if any one of those fucks looked at her cross-eyed they might lose that eye.

I've never had occasion before now to worry overmuch about my life choices, but now with her, things were going to be different. I couldn't subject her to the same bullshit I'd let the other skirts endure. I know for damn sure there wouldn't be any moving on from me for her. She'd be lucky if I ever let her out my damn sight, at least for the first couple years.

That right there is why I'm pretty sure that if anyone else looked at her there was a good chance I'd try to end the fuck. How the fuck was I supposed to keep that shit from happening when I'd never implemented any kind of restrictions in the past? More importantly, how was she going to adjust to my way of living?

I wasn't really too worried about the guys. One five-minute conversation with them should clear shit up; it was the women I was more concerned about. I'm not that fucking stupid that I don't know what it would mean taking an innocent like her in the midst of those hardcore women.

Especially since I'd bedded a few of them at some point or the other and had left it there, no strings. I was also aware that more than one of them was still holding out hope of getting that brass ring, and might see her as competition, when there really was none. She was it, she's always been the one, the only.

I've been in charge of shit long enough to know that women don't heed too well, especially when there was a younger and prettier model as part of the equation. I'd never given any woman false promises about anything that we'd shared, but I know that that didn't stop some of them from hoping.

What the fuck are you thinking about, are you pussy? The crew is yours, the place is yours, whoever don't like the way shit is can get fucked. With that shit finally settled in my mind, I put it away for later and tuned back into her.

She was fluffing the pillows and tugging on the sheets before settling down. Every move, every twitch was caught by my eyes as I laid on the other bed trying to control my cock with my mind. This fuck was gonna stay hard for the next few days until he got what he wanted and there isn't shit I can do about it.

Instead I amused myself with ways to destroy her aunt and the fucker she was shacked up with. If I'd been any kind of guardian, I would've imposed some stipulations. One of them being she couldn't have a man around my girl. Silly me, I believed her bullshit about wanting what's best for her niece.

When she finally settled down and stopped her tossing and turning I was able to rest easy thank fuck. I closed my eyes and settled my mind with my ears pricked for any sound that didn't belong.

I really wanted to ride through the dark, back the way we'd come, and finish the two who'd used me to hurt her, but I wasn't going to leave her in a hotel room unprotected. From now on, I'm gonna make sure she's shielded at every turn.

With my mind settled and no more movement coming from the other side, I let myself relax and drifted off. With all the bullshit out of the way the reality that she was here with me kicked in and I smiled in the dark.

Who would've thought this day would come? That the little girl I'd rescued that night so long ago would come to mean so much to me? How was such a thing even possible? If I were into that sappy shit I would think it was fate.

But I had to admit if only to myself, that it was almost like we'd been destined for each other. We both came from fucked up beginnings and had seen the shittier side of life at a very young age. Then we'd found each other in a most unconventional way, but still, she was mine. Had been in one-way or another since the day we met.

Now in a few more days if I make it, she was going to be mine in every sense of the word and nothing and no one was ever going to fuck with her again. I'll make it up to her if it's the last thing I do, make up for all the heartache I'd inadvertently caused by being a fucking dupe.

On that note I turned on my side and prepared to sleep until morning. Tomorrow was the start of our life together. I might have to wait a few days to put her under me, but starting tomorrow I was going to start staking my claim.

I hope like fuck she was able to deal with this shit because there was no alternative. I'd already made up her mind for her.

JESSIE

I'm too excited to sleep. What does it all mean? Why had he come? Why now? And the way he looked at me, the way he reacted when he saw my naked body. It had given me butterflies, nothing at all like when...

I cut myself off before the thought could take ahold of me, not here, not now. I wanted to think only of Creed. He was back. It had been so long. Sometimes I thought I would never see him again, I cried myself to sleep many a night over that.

But now he was here, just a few short feet from me, but what did it all mean? Am I gonna go live with him now, or will he find somewhere else to pack me off to?

That sounded really disloyal and I don't mean to, but sometimes I get so mad that no one lets me have any say. If they did I would've told them a long time ago that I wanted to go live with him.

I guess that some would say that I was old enough to leave. I was smart enough to get myself a little job and maybe a place of my own. But he would never let me. I knew from other conversations that he would never let me go out on my own, even if he had stayed away himself.

There were times I thought of it though. Times when I got so mad at him, at her, at everyone that had any kind of say in my life. But then I would become ashamed of myself.

I owed him my life, and though she'd not been nice to me, at least she had kept a roof over my head, food on the table.

I'm pretty sure Creed had a lot to do with that, that he was the one looking out for my welfare from afar.

Each time he came in the past it was always like Xmas and my birthday rolled into one and when he'd leave I'd die a little. Especially when he was going off to war.

He'd always tell me where he was going, when he

could that is. It was the times when he couldn't that scared me the most. But the times it wasn't some top-secret mission, he'd show me on the globe he'd got me for my room where he was going to be.

Every night I'd focus on that exact place and imagine him there and pray for him to be safe. I never understood never questioned really, how we just meshed from the very beginning.

I never feared him the way I did some of my dad's friends that use to come around all the time. He's the only person I've ever felt safe with, the only one I trusted. It was as if we'd known each other all our lives, from the first second he had taken my little hand in his.

I think in the beginning we both were scared, I know I was. I had no idea what was going to become of me that day. The old man had been threatening to do it for a while, but somehow I'd always talked him out of it.

Looking back now I wonder why I even bothered, since he was never much of a dad. But that day he'd gone into one of his rants about what a burden I was and how he had to get the monkey off his back.

That was the first time I couldn't talk him down. I remember being so afraid; I just knew he was going to sell me to one of his friends. At twelve I wasn't as very well aware of what their leering looks and hungry eyes meant.

I remember the raw fear, the panic and the taste of defeat, as I stood in that parking lot in the dark, defenseless, nowhere to run, no one to help. And then he came along. I thought he had to be a movie star or somebody famous the way he moved and his beautiful face.

He'd made my young heart jump. I watched him under my lashes as he walked across the lot from his car, his stride confident, sure. Nothing like the men I was accustomed to being around that's for sure.

I remember a moment's pang of regret as he walked by. And then it happened. To this day I don't know if the old man had noticed my reaction and was doing something good for me, if he was it would've been a first.

But he'd called out to him and I'd known a new fear. You see; if he turned him down, then the first dream I'd had in forever would die a quick death. But if he kept going then I could always imagine for a long-long time.

He'd come over and stood there towering over us, I know now that he'd six-five or thereabout and his arm was covered with tattoos. The thing that had once driven fear in me because up to that point the only men I'd known with ink, were all pretty much losers like my dad, had seemed so beautiful on this stranger.

When he opened his mouth to speak I know I fell a little bit in love, but when he looked into my eyes, that's when I knew that I would never have to fear him. I think he felt it too, though I could never be sure, but I think there was something.

Not sexual of course, I would've known if it was. It was I who years later had started mooning over him, me who chased him away most likely. But back then, that night when my life hung in the balance, I knew he would protect me.

When he'd looked like he wanted to beat the tar out the old man she knew he was the right one. And when all was said and done and he'd taken my hand and led me away I'd felt real hope for the first time in my young life.

Even days later when he took me to my aunt's it didn't matter, he'd already promised to take care of me and somehow I knew I could trust him. I didn't know my aunt well, but from what little I did know, she and the old man never got along.

That had been enough for me back then. And the way she'd gone on while Creed was there, fussing over her only sister's little girl, I'd thought for sure my life had really taken a turn for the better. Little did I know what was hiding behind that sticky sweet smile of hers.

None of that had mattered though, because I had him and I knew for the rest of my life I would, he'd promised. I had been able to swallow a lot because of that fact.

He'd kept his word, always coming to me whenever he was home. Sometimes he'd come to me before he did anything else, just show up no matter what time of the day or night.

Those times he'd grab me up and hug me so hard, I always cried, and though I could see the emotion in his own eyes, he always kept them contained.

Over the years we'd grown close, almost like best pals. When he was home he'd spend as much time with me as he could, taking me places, showing me new things, and each year I fell more and more in love with him.

Then, when I turned eighteen, everything changed, and not just my body. That thing inside me for him had grown out of all proportion and I didn't know what to do with myself.

I knew then that I was in love with him, and it scared me as much as it excited me. I knew it would never happen, that he'd never cross that line, but my young heart had yearned and wanted so badly that I think I'd somehow let it slip a little.

And then he'd disappeared. When I'd asked him to prom it had taken every ounce of courage I had. I'd been so afraid of his rejection that I'd thrown up for two days before I finally fond what it took to ask.

That night had been the best of my life. All the girls had been green with envy, but that's not what made it so special. He'd treated me like an adult that night, almost like a date.

He'd catered to my every wish, making the other boys there seem so inconsequential. And when one of the other girls, one that I absolutely hated had asked him to dance, he'd politely turned her down.

Now that had made my whole time at school worth all the pain and the heartache. Kids can be cruel and in my case they took every opportunity. My aunt had had no problem sending me to school in the cast offs of someone else and since the town was so small everyone pretty much knew.

In the beginning when I'd been younger, I'd tried to tell Creed that she wasn't what she pretended to be, but somehow she was always able to convince him that I was lying. I'd eventually just stopped trying.

But that night, when I was wearing the best dress because he'd insisted and I'd got my hair and nails done because again he'd said his babygirl deserved the best memory of that night. His babygirl, I use to love the way he called me that. Still do, but for different reasons.

But that night had been magic, and then it was over and he was gone, until now. Of course we'd talked on the phone, but even those conversations had become stilted and hollow.

It had almost broken my heart when I realized that I was losing him too, not Creed, he was supposed to be mine for always. But the last almost three years had been almost unbearable without him.

There were so many times when I felt like just telling him the truth about how I felt, or running away and hiding. Those were the two choices I'd given myself, but in the end I could never leave my Creed.

Now he's back and he's taking me away with him and I'm afraid, afraid of what was going to happen if he left me behind again. I'm not a little kid anymore and by all rights he doesn't owe me anything.

My heart hurt at the thought of me losing him. What if he gets married and has a family of his own? What if he meets someone that doesn't understand or accept my place in his life? Why can't he choose me?

I know he thinks I'm just a silly little girl who won't fit into his life. He probably thinks I'm too stupid to even know anything about that, but I've always known everything about him.

Like how he'd saved a bunch of people when he was away at war, or how he'd burned out a whole village to save his fellow soldiers when they'd been captured and were about to be beheaded.

That one had scared me a lot. It was the first time I'd realized that being in a war was nothing like the romantic movies they showed us on TV.

The only reason I'd learned about any of his exploits is because I'd signed up for every army social media in our area. I'd had to pretend to be the daughter of a deployed soldier, which I kinda was, except…no better not let my mind wander there too much this time. Not with him just a few feet away.

This was the first time in years that we'd been alone together and I was determined not to do anything to mess it up. I didn't want him to go away for a long time again, and since I was never too sure what had made him leave last time, I wasn't about to take any chances.

My aunt Dee had said it was something I'd done, probably my complaining to him about stuff. But that couldn't be true because I never complained about anything, not anymore. Not since the beginning when she would convince him that everything I said was a lie.

I'd resented him for that as well, and though it wasn't in my nature to yell and scream, I've wanted to with him a couple times. But always I'd remember his smile and his kindness. That he was the only one in my life who'd ever treated me with true kindness, and my heart would melt.

Besides, I wasn't that dumb that I didn't see what was going on. She had him fooled just like she had everyone else. She'd only stopped hitting me because of the one time Creed had noticed a mark and as is his way had asked about it.

She'd slithered her way out of that one too, and though I'd tried to tell him with my eyes that she was lying he'd fallen for her made up story once again. Two days later I'd learned why he'd been so preoccupied. He'd been given orders to go in and bring out his comrades.

The papers had been very vague about the rescue,

and of course he wasn't the only one involved, but they'd hailed him personally. I'd never been so proud in my life, and I'd forgiven him for disappointing me once again where she was concerned.

I'd just always told myself that one day I'll make him listen to me and then he'd be sorry that he hadn't all along. But that was when I was young, before the changes.

As time went on I learned to keep my mouth shut and stay out of the way, she'd convinced me that he only listened to her anyway, and that nothing I said bore any weight. It was only as I got older and started hanging around other people that I started to doubt her. But by then there was a sort of rift between him and I. One that I had no idea how to fix.

I knew he couldn't be the uncaring oaf I'd sometimes come to think of him as. I mean his new thing since leaving the army was saving kids from distressful situations. The local papers from the surrounding towns were full of the stuff he'd been up to since coming home.

Even the online Topix forums were mostly about him some days. That's where I got my fill of stories about him. It's also where I learned about his reputation with women.

That one had hurt for days, a physical pain like I'd never known…

"What's the matter?" Oh shit, I'd groaned out loud and now he was sitting up in bed looking at me. I felt my face heat up as I opened my eyes the rest of the way even though the room was shrouded in darkness. "Nothing, uh, I was just thinking about something."

He looked at me like he wasn't sure whether or not to believe me. I can imagine. I'd heard that sound I make before and it usually sounded like I was in horrible pain. No way I was going to tell him the true source of my distress though. He'd probably find a way to put even more distance between us.

I was never sure if he hadn't caught me mooning over him the last time we'd been together. He'd stayed away for almost three years after that. If he knew how torrid my thoughts were these days concerning him, he'd probably lock me in a convent and throw away the key.

I could still feel his eyes on me like he was gauging the situation to see what if anything he needed to do. That's the thing about my Creed I always knew he'd protect me no matter what, though I wasn't sure he'd be in time this last time. I still hadn't found a way to tell him and he'd shown up anyway. Like magic.

What would he do if he knew? That's one of the things that bothered me most. On the one hand I reveled in my aunt getting what she deserved if I told him the truth about her treatment of me over the years, and on the other I dreaded his reaction and what it could mean.

I'd read more than just the news reports on him and his motorcycle crew, and some of them had claimed that he was all but tempting the law to lock him away and throw away the key. I didn't want that at all. And as much as he'd taken her word over the years, I never doubted for a second that if he ever knew the truth he'd go after her.

His eyes were staring back at me in the dark and I held my breath in waiting. Will he roll over and go to sleep? Or will he dig? I didn't have long to wonder when he sat up and turned on the light. I wasn't sure I was ready for this. All I wanted was to be away from my home for good, never to return if I could help it. If he gave me that I would forgive him for every time he'd not listened to me.

I sighed as if tired and closed my eyes, feigning sleep. I remembered to slow my breathing like I did when asleep. My heart was about to give me away though because it was beating so fast and so hard I was pretty sure he could hear it from the other bed. I was tempted to open my eyes to see, but I could almost feel his stare.

He hit the light and I breathed that much easier again and felt my muscles relax and my heart calm a little. Better be more careful in the future don't want to give him any reason at all to have any doubts about taking me home with him.

The thought made my tummy cramp and I was back to feeling lost and alone. I wanted so much to enjoy this time with him, this new experience. But the fear of what came next was almost too much.

What if I mess up really bad this time and he leaves for good this time? What if I do something that makes him think I wasn't worth the trouble? That's one of the things aunt Dee had always drilled into my head. How I should be careful, and not whine to him about every little thing.

At the time I believed her judgment that he'd wash his hands of me if I were to do that. He didn't really owe me anything after all, and she was my blood. He could easily just forget the promise he'd made to a stupid nobody little kid like myself who he didn't even know.

Could she be right? it was hard to tell because

he'd always treated me like I mattered. But he'd been gone for so long this last time I wasn't sure that there wasn't some truth to what she'd said. So maybe yeah, maybe I have to be more careful. I was back to being scared again, the sweet feelings that the memories evoked gone again.

CREED

What the fuck noise was that she'd made in her sleep? Sounded like she was severely hurt. She said she was fine but I still kept my eyes on her. That's how I knew that she'd conned me the first time, she'd never been asleep.

Now I'm a pro at this shit, I did it for a fucking living. It's one of the ways you survive in the thick of shit. So why would a young girl without a care in the world need to learn how to regulate her breathing to fool anyone that she was out?

The answer had me jackknifing in the bed and hitting the light next to my bed. "Sit up, I know you're not sleeping." I hated that fucking wary look she gave me like she was expecting me to hit her or some other foul shit. I studied her bent head for the longest while as I tried to put my thoughts in order.

This wasn't the easiest fucking thing to discuss for me so I know it was shit for her. But if the fuckery was gonna be fucking with her all night so she can't sleep, it was best I get the shit over with now. "I want to know about Sal, everything." My gut twisted and I clenched my fists in preparation for what came next.

Oh yeah he's fucked. The look that just came into my babygirl's eyes, said it all. She started to tear up and look distressed, but there was no turning back. "Tell me." For the first time in her life she shook her head no at me. I didn't like it, didn't know I'd have such a strong reaction to it either.

"What?" I tried keeping the sting out of the one word but I did a piss poor job of it. She almost jumped out of her skin but I wasn't about to apologize. It was best she know now that that shit was a big fucking no-no. "I asked you a question, I expect an answer, don't ever tell me no again." Are you trying to help her or scare the fuck out of her asshole?

Funny, I've helped my fair share of young girls and some not so young in the years since I'd been stateside. Heard the word no in different variations more than once. I don't recall ever having this kind of reaction to it. I literally wanted to force the issue, wanted to make her tell me what I wanted to know.

If she could draw that shit out of me for something as little as this, who knows what life was going to be like. I'd probably tan her ass for looking at me sideways. And why the fuck did that shit make my dick hard?

"But you'll blame me and you'll leave..." Her voice brought me back from the brink.

"What the fuck?" Is that what she thinks of me? That if she tells me what happened to her that I'd somehow blame her leave her?

Aren't you the one who left her with them for the past two and a half years, what the fuck do you expect her to think? Fuck, now I'd sworn in front of her, something I never do.

That was a hard fucking blow though, but no more than I deserved. She refused to look at me after that and it was all I could do not to go to her. I wouldn't risk that shit, not with her being so vulnerable, shit might get out of hand. Instead I asked her to look at me again.

"I'm sorry I gave you the impression that you mean so little to me. I know in the past I listened to others, but that's only because I didn't know, I thought…it doesn't matter what I thought, all that matters is right now.

I need to know what happened from the time I took you there when you were twelve until last night when I took you out of there. Don't leave anything out, even if you think I might become upset."

"But you know all of it, aunt Dee said. She always said she told you stuff and you always agreed with her." I'm gonna fuck that female up no fucking joke. I had to struggle really hard not to show her any of what was in me because she wouldn't be scared anymore; she'd be fucking terrified.

"I don't expect you to believe me, no scratch that, I do expect you to believe me. I've never lied to you, I might've been a blind fool, but I never have and never will be anything but honest with you." I was trying hard as fuck not to cuss in front of her. For some reason I've never been able to, she's too fucking pure for that shit, but it was touch and go dealing with this fuckery.

She finally got down to telling me all that had been going on in her life since the first day I took her to her aunt, with the one little overnight bag I'd found her back then, with the new clothes I'd bought her after throwing away the rags she'd owned.

It was because of those rags that I'd given her

aunt a very large clothing allowance for her every year, especially for school clothes. Because I remembered how it was being the poor kid in school and the shit the other kids put me through, I didn't want any of that for her.

Hearing her tell how her aunt would go to the Salvation Army and get her the leftovers made my eyes burn. Hearing about how the games and shit I'd bought her had been sold to buy shit for Sal made me commit murder in my mind a thousand times.

Instead of the privileged childhood I'd paid out the ass for, she'd had quite the opposite. While I'd been patting myself on the back thinking of the great job I was doing providing for her, she was being neglected and abused.

I let her words wash over me, tasting the bitter regret in my lungs as I called myself ten kinds of fool.

I could blame the aunt but in the end it was all on me. It hurt like fuck to know that I'd had a hand in that shit, all I could do was promise myself that from here on out, her life was going to be as close to perfect as I can get it. She seemed to sense my turmoil and her voice trailed off. "Finish it."

She shared some more of her aunt's fucked up maternal skills which were nonexistent, and then she came to this latest fuckery. As I sat there and listened to how he started coming into her room and standing over her in the dark, before it graduated to him touching her ankles up to her thighs, which caused her to live in terror, it was all I could do not to jump from the bed and go do him now.

I was afraid I was going to break one more silent promise to her before the dawn. I listened with a growing rage just being held in check as she described his fucking perversion the sick twisted walking dead fuck.

She was such an innocent still, that she had no idea what she was describing when she told me about the strange breathing and the wetness on her tummy after he'd lifted her sleep top and she'd laid there in stark fear pretending sleep.

That had been two nights ago, the fucker had been escalating. I'd gotten there in the knick of time. I broke out in a cold sweat when I thought of what could've happened had I not gotten that call when I did.

When she started shaking hard enough that I could hear it from where I sat, I knew that I had to go to her. There was no more danger of me fucking her tonight. Her little story of near rape had squelched that shit for the time being.

I had a hard-on for something else now. It had been a long time since I'd capped an asshole. Whether on foreign or domestic soil, I have no problem pulling the trigger. This one was gonna take some careful planning though.

I laid on the bed next to her and pulled her down into my arms, holding her close until she got over the shakes. When I felt her relax a little I was able to breathe easy again.

"You're okay babygirl, you're going to always be okay from now on. I'm sorry that happened to you, sorry I wasn't there to protect you, that's on me not you. Look at me." I lifted her chin with my finger so that I could look into her face.

"None of this was your fault do you hear me? Nod your head so I know you hear me." I waited for her to acquiesce before going on. "Tell me you believe me." Her little voice assured me that she did. "I believe you." I pulled her into my chest and tried to show her with that one touch just how fucking special she was.

It was almost surreal to be here with her like this finally. I inhaled her scent thinking she was safe enough, what with the conversation being what it is.

Big fucking mistake. My dick perked right the fuck back up at the first whiff. She was cuddle soft and sweet, a very dangerous combination right now. I was like a fucking deer in headlights.

I couldn't very well jump out the bed and run, but I couldn't let her feel my need either, not after the story she'd just told. She'd probably think I was the worse kind of asshole.

I tried breathing exercises, counting fucking sheep, everything I could think of to take down the swelling in my too tight jeans, but nothing worked.

I wanted her and I wanted her now. It was only years of discipline that kept me from turning her to her back and sliding in between her thighs. She had no idea the whole time of the war that was going on within me as she rested against my chest.

I let my mind drift, anywhere but here and now. I mulled over what I had to do next to make up for the complete fucking mess I'd made of things.

The one good thing was that she still seemed pretty well rounded and sweet as fuck even after all that she'd endured. I was going to do everything in my power to erase the ugliness from her memory, but there was no way I was ever gonna forget.

I didn't let my mind dwell on what she'd told me, I couldn't lose my shit in front of her. I never wanted her to fear me and I know me in a rage was sure to do that.

I kept my lower body well away from her even as I held her in my arms, because contrary to what I'd thought when I came over here, her nearness alone was enough to leave me hard as fuck.

I didn't ask her anything more, just held her until she calmed down and dropped off. I didn't want to move, she felt so right there in my arms, just like I knew she would. I kissed her hair, I figured I could give myself at least that much, and she sighed and snuggled closer.

CREED

I listened to the rhythm of her breathing until it evened out in sleep. A quick look at my watch told me that it was already close to three in the morning. She had to be tired so that should give me a solid five to do what I had to do.

It had taken me longer to get here because she was on the back of my ride, but if I make the trip solo it would take me half the time. Back and forth, in and out, this shit could not wait.

I made doubly sure that she was out, left a message just in case she woke up before I got back, secured the door and headed out. No one was getting past that door I made sure of that shit.

I hadn't planned on doing this now, had thought I'd put some more distance between us, get the whole story shit like that. But what she'd shared with me tonight was more than enough.

My crew will pitch a fit when they find out I'd done something on my own, they've become over protective old women lately. Like they think success had broken my teeth and turned me into a fat cat with no more spine.

Then again that can't be true, they know I still fuck shit up, but they like to think they're protecting me. My fucking entourage!

I should probably call Law as backup, but somehow that wouldn't be the same. I needed to do this on my own, needed the satisfaction of seeing their fear, and being the one to exact vengeance for what they'd done to me and mine.

I could hear her little voice and see her body tremble as she relived the horror of that disgusting fuck standing over her pulling his fucking plug. I'ma give that fat fuck something to pull on. A fucking stub!

I ATE up the distance between us, making it in half the time. The streets tend to be empty at fuck this shit o'clock in the morning; people got shit to do when the sun comes up.

It was just me the open road and my thoughts. I had to talk myself out of killing them both once I got there, but I couldn't see doing that shit while she was in a hotel room all vulnerable and shit. I couldn't take the chance of backlash; nothing was going to come between me, and her.

When I do them there won't be a fucking whiff of my scent anywhere near. With that shit finally set firmly in my head I was able to think clearly again. I might not be able to end the disgusting fuck, but I was gonna make him sorry he'd ever even had the fucking thought to touch her, the fuck.

I killed the lights and the engine a little ways down from the house and walked in. The lights were out but he hadn't gone anywhere, the pieces of his ride had been picked up and laid up against the garage.

I made sure to keep to the shadows just in case some enterprising night owl was lurking about as I headed for the backdoor.

I made quick work of picking the lock and eased my way in, heading straight for their room. It registered that I'd never really paid much attention to the place before, but at least I knew the layout.

It was easy enough to see his lump under the

covers in the moonlight. I made my way to his side of the bed and just stood over him, letting the hate fester. The pig was snoring loud enough to wake the neighbors so I was pretty sure if he stopped she'd notice.

Fine! I moved over to her and wrapped my hand around her neck and one over her mouth. She startled awake but I was prepared. "You got off easy." I put her to sleep and went back around to him.

"Wake up asshole." I punched him in the face to get his attention. He jumped up screaming about his face and I pulled him around by his ponytail.

"You jacked off on her you sick fuck?" I reached down between his legs and found his dick through his pajamas. You ever heard a hog squeal when it's being stuck with a knife? That's the sound he made when I twisted his shit until it was left hanging. He blacked out from the pain but I wasn't done yet.

I went to work on his ass, not enough to kill, but enough that he'd remember me everyday for the rest of his life. I stopped short of cutting his dick off and stuffing it in her fucking mouth, which was my first choice. It was enough to know that he wouldn't be getting any use out of the shit ever again in this lifetime.

When I was done with him I went over to her

next. It wasn't my style to lay hands on a female, but I stood over her prone form for the longest three minutes of my life thinking of ways to make her pay.

I recalled every word Jessie had said to me in that dark room earlier. All the times this bitch had put her down or belittled her. She may not have put it together yet; she was too innocent by far so her mind didn't work that way. Me on the other hand, I knew exactly what was going on with this bitch.

I headed downstairs to the kitchen and straight to the butcher block before retracing my steps. Up in their room I picked her head up off the pillow and jacked into her hair with the knife in my hand. When I was done she barely had enough fuzz on her head to escape being bald.

Next I went through the house looking for anything that could be of use to babygirl, like mementos of her mom or some shit. There was nothing of her anywhere downstairs. How had I missed that shit before? Always too focused on her back then I guess.

Upstairs her room was a stark four walls. Looked like something you'd find in a convent. Nothing of the things I'd worked hard to provide her with was here. It made me pissed the fuck all over and it was only because she needed me that I didn't give free reign to the anger that coursed through my veins.

I was tempted to light the shit after I packed up what little she'd left behind. I left all the second hand shit the bitch had bought and headed out. They may or may not call the cops but I wasn't too worried. If he did, then he'd have to explain why I'd rung his dick off at the root.

I was sure I would be seeing him again, the crew he ran with was known for their retaliations, not that I give a fuck; I relish the chance to end his ass, but on my terms and not with her caught in the middle.

I gave the place one last look, bemoaning the fact that I couldn't end it all right here and now, but their day will come. I'll see to it.

I MADE good time getting back to her and found her still asleep all curled up like an innocent. I'd never seen her like this before, and I took the time to really study her without interruption.

Her face was soft in sleep, her dark tendrils framing her beauty in the stark waning moonlight that came through the window. "So gorgeous babygirl." I whispered the words in the dark as I sucked her in.

My heart literally moved in my chest at her incomparable beauty. Could this really be all mine? Could I really have lucked out after a lifetime of nothing?

When I look back on my fucked up beginnings I don't see this, how could I? Born in less than stellar surroundings, to a woman that could barely take care of herself because of the ounce a day habit that she had to sell her body to afford. And most likely to one of the men she'd sold herself to, I never stood a chance.

I was shifted from foster home to foster home where I had to learn survival skills even before I could walk. By the age of five I knew how to fight off predators, how to hide at night when the sun went down.

As soon as I could I hit the streets, but even then I always wanted better. Couldn't see it, but wanted it nonetheless. When I was sixteen it was an old bum who lived under the same bridge I had chosen to call my home for the summer who had taken an interest in my wellbeing.

He was an old army vet who still had connections, or so he said. I didn't believe shit the old man said. Why would anyone with so-called connections be living under a bridge?

No I just thought he was a lonely old man full of tales. Since he was no threat to me because at that age I was already well on my way to my six-four height, I listened to his tales, thinking nothing of them.

Until one day he brought someone to see me. An old buddy of his who promised to get me into some program or the other if I would enlist when the time came. All I had to do was stay in school and keep out of trouble.

Since the only trouble I ever found was when someone fucked with me that was easy. Even though I was skeptical as fuck at first, I'd gone for it and never looked back.

I did go back once looking for the old man, but neither the recruiter nor I had ever been able to find him again. I'd gone through basic training like I was born for it, surpassing everyone's expectations. Then again that wasn't so hard to do, there weren't that met for the kid who came from the streets.

I'd taken all the pent up rage and shit that I had believed myself long over and honed it into a particular skill. One that may not have gained me much in the way of a career stateside, but there were still plenty who would be willing to pay me top dollar to do what I do. I'd just have to sell my soul first.

Until she came along, I had no real direction. I had enough sense to know I never wanted to be on the streets again so I learned everything I could while I was on their dime and looked ahead. I socked away my pay like a miser, getting by on the bare essentials.

I was never going to be Gates, but I won't starve. After her, things changed. In the beginning it was because of the little kid I now found myself responsible for. Then later it became something else.

Now she's the woman I'm going to marry. The one I want my forever after with. Everything was about her now. My sweet little babygirl!

I reached out my hand and touched her hair, trailing my fingers down her cheek as soft as a butterfly's wings so as not to wake her.

Beyond the hardening of my cock was the irregular beating of my heart; that more than anything told me that I was well and truly gone. It was as if the last two, almost three years hadn't been, as if time stood still and we were back there under the stars with her gazing up at me with lust reflected in her eyes.

I'd been scared then, but now, now I wanted that

and more. I wanted, no needed, to be the man she turned to for everything. I wanted to erase all the hell she'd been through and fill her only with the good.

I wanted her every thought to be of me, to know that no matter what had come before, that she could depend on me. It might take some time, but if it's the last thing I do, I'd make her want me as much as I now wanted her.

She made a soft sound in her sleep and I eased my fingers away from her skin, not wanting to disturb her rest. Would she wake in terror thinking she was back there at his hands again? The thought had me folding my fists and wishing I'd done more. She looked so fucking perfect lying there, like the most perfect thing ever created.

What the fuck was I doing? Could I really give her everything I'd always wanted for her? Or was I being a selfish prick? That's one of those questions I keep asking myself. Especially when it's late at night and I have nothing to keep my mind occupied. Always it reverts back to her, and always, after I've convinced myself that I was the only one for her, the questions would start.

I hate my fucking conscience sometimes; shit's always trying to fuck with my program. But this was my Jessie, my babygirl. When I look at her I know that not even I am good enough for her, she's so fucking perfect.

Yeah and if you don't take her someone else will. Like fuck! As usual it only took that reminder to get me back on track. With one last look of longing and a lingering kiss to her brow I turned and walked to the other side of the room.

I stripped down and climbed into bed feeling ten pounds lighter now that she was safe with me. Tomorrow I'll figure out what to do about my lifestyle and all the other bullshit I was gonna have to change to accommodate her.

No hardship, there wasn't much I wouldn't do for her. I fell off into sleep feeling better than I had in years if ever. Just a few more days and I'll never sleep without her next to me again.

I felt a weight hit my bed some time after I fell out and didn't have to open my eyes to know it was her. I didn't ask her any questions, didn't dwell on what demons had driven her to my bed. I was just immensely grateful that she trusted me enough to come to me.

I turned and wrapped my arms around her as she snuggled in close. I didn't sense any fear in her and sent up a silent thank you that I hadn't fucked up too badly.

"You okay babygirl?" I held her as close as I could, like I was trying to blend our two bodies together. "I am now." There was a lot of meaning in those three words, and I smiled in the dark before falling asleep with her held tight in my arms. Right where she belonged.

CREED

$\mathcal{W}$e were both a little tired the next morning so breakfast was a rushed affair before we got on the road. I wanted to leave early because I wasn't sure what, if any play Sal was gonna make, and I didn't want her caught in the middle.

If I'd been thinking straight I would've waited until she was out of harm's way like I'd planned to, but what's done is done. After her little trip down memory lane, I couldn't, not go fuck his shit up. He's lucky his ass is still breathing the sick fuck.

"If you're gonna fall asleep back there let me know so I can secure you." She'd still been a little sleepy in the restaurant because I'd woken her early, and she looked like she could hardly keep her eyes open.

I fixed her helmet and made sure she was seated properly while she assured me that she would stay up for the whole trip. There was a sense of excitement in her voice that I hoped to fuck I didn't kill somehow.

She'd already dealt with so much bullshit, I shudder to think how she was gonna put up with mine and I had a lot. My restrictions might be a lot different from her aunt's, but they are restrictions nonetheless.

For her this might seem like a new adventure, and after the way that fucking hag had denied her everything that was good in life I'm sure it very well might be. For me it was the beginning of our life together. A life that I was sure she was going to take time getting used to.

I'd already mapped out certain things in my head, things that were needed to keep her safe and not from the outside world but from me. I already know my triggers and since I never want to hurt her, not even with words, I think it best to get that shit out of the way at our earliest convenience.

Like the fact that if she ever even thought of

cheating on me she'd be dead, that one was nonnegotiable. There were others, but none as serious as that one I think. I wasn't planning to micromanage our relationship, but I was going to be on top of her every step of the fucking way for at least the first coupla years.

I've seen the shit people in love can do to each other I'm not down with that fuckery. There will be no do-overs in my little kingdom, fuck that. So to avoid any bullshit I'm going to introduce her to my rules as soon as fucking possible as well as getting to know her likes and dislikes. Because along with my shit that she's gonna have to put up with, I'm gonna be making damn sure that she's as happy as it's possible for one little lady to be.

If I was even half way decent I'd probably give her a few more weeks or even a couple days at least to get used to the idea. Nope, not gonna fucking happen. Blue was not a good look for my balls and swear to fuck my dick might revolt if I even contemplated such a fuck stupid move.

No way, two and a half years was more than enough I want in there like yesterday. And after seeing her again that need was ten times worse. Imagining her under me was one thing when there were miles separating us, now with her in my vision, her scent in my nose, she'd be lucky to make it the next two days.

I'd spent the most restful night of my life last night and was racking my brain to figure out how to make that shit a repeat performance tonight when we reached home. She didn't say what it was that had sent her running to my arms and I didn't push.

I'd just studied her over breakfast and since she looked like my bright eyed little girl I let it slide. I was hoping to leave all that darkness behind, a fresh start with none of the ugliness of her past or mine.

"You ready babygirl?" She didn't seem to mind her new nickname, in fact each time I called her by my secret name for her she blushed prettily and smiled. She nodded her head and I got on the bike.

Once again her arms went around me and she held on innocently as we rode out, headed for my home, her home now. Maybe one day I'll tell her that I built it with her in mind. Thinking of that reminded me of all that I'd done with her in mind. Everything was 'would she like this?' or 'would this be good for her?"

It was easy to look back on my life now and see how much she'd influenced every decision I'd ever made. Some of them probably saved my life come to think of it. Before her I wouldn't have thought twice about running headfirst into trouble, I never met a bar fight I didn't like. I spent my life scrapping, fighting for everything that meant anything to me.

The bitch that had birthed me had dumped me on her way to somewhere better a few short hours after I came into the world. I never stood a chance. Found in the worse part of town, high as a fucking kite even though I didn't know a pipe from a tit, they didn't give me much hope of surviving. Did I forget to mention it was thirty below when the bitch wrapped me in newspaper and left me for dead?

After I beat the odds life wasn't through with my ass. I was then passed around from every degenerate family within the city limits. Thank fuck I escaped the horrors of sexual molestation, but everything else was on the table. My life was a smorgasbord of hellacious bullshit.

I was used as a mule to run drugs to and from school, was taught to steal with the best of them by the time I was six or seven, and by the time I was fourteen before I lit the fuck out, I was servicing my fifth foster mom and her pals. I didn't see that shit as abuse because those bitches taught me all I needed to know and then some.

The one thing I learned throughout was that there was only one way out of the hood. I was a smart little fuck but I had to use my head. A scholarship might be nice but contrary to the feel good bullshit they show on T.V. no one was giving someone like me a full ride, not unless there was some fuck in it for them.

So when I met old man Steve at sixteen and his pal set me up with the boy's home I finally started feeling human. At eighteen is when they had some kind of job fair at the high school and they sent recruiters from the army. I listened to every fuck they had to say that day and found my calling.

Now the reason I knew so much about my beginnings was on account of this old dude from the neighborhood. Even though I'd ran away I never went too far, just to show you how hard they look for kids like me.

Anyway this guy I remembered from when I was much younger. He was always hanging around outside in his yard and whenever he'd see me he would stop to chat.

He had no idea who my real incubator was, but he knew everything else. Old Silas was an old army dog; he was the closest thing to a human being I knew back then before Steve, and I figured if the army produced them I could maybe stand a chance.

Everyone was of the general opinion that the incubator had been passing through and there was no way to find her. By the third foster home when I was nursing broken ribs compliments of the last asshole who was just using me for a paycheck from the government, I no longer gave a fuck.

Those beginnings had given me a thick skin and a don't give a fuck attitude. Until her I didn't fear death, wasn't too worried about someone sticking it to me, I could always hold my own. But then she came along and shit changed.

Even in the thick of battle, I kept thoughts of her in the forefront, reminding myself everyday that I had to get back to her. That's when she was still my sweet little innocent Jessie. It killed me to imagine her out there on her own at the mercy of the same fuckery I'd had to deal with.

Then in the last few years after the change, I'd kept her there for other reasons. She was my reason for breathing plain and simple, and I was gonna spend the rest of my life letting her know that shit. It was my greatest wish to erase everything that her dad had done to her from her memory, and to fill it with only good things, the things I meant to give to her.

Now because of my ignorance and her fuck of an aunt I might have to start all over. All the work I'd believed I was doing to distance her from that parking lot had been a lie. I'd just been paying someone else to mistreat what's mine. I bit that thought off before I fishtailed and headed back to finish what I'd started.

Instead I concentrated on the days ahead, on the things I'd only imagined thus far that were now closer to reality. My dick thumped against my zipper. Maybe that wasn't such a good idea either, but it was hard not to celebrate the fact that she was finally mine, that I was going to have her just where I wanted her after all this time.

There was no question of whether or not she would be accepting of me; I wasn't about to give her a choice. She was mine plain and simple. Had been for a long time. She didn't need any fucking choices where that shit was concerned. Now the only thing I had to worry about, the only hurdle I could see up ahead, was getting my cock into what I was sure was going to be the tightest pussy I'd ever tackled.

I didn't suffer even a moment's guilt at the thoughts running through my head. I knew better than anyone what was in me for her, that's why I knew that no one would ever, could ever feel for her what I did.

I pulled myself back to the here and now as we raced through the morning, trying to beat the rising sun and the heat it was about to unleash on us. Her slight weight against my back warned me that she had indeed fallen asleep so I slowed down a little, but didn't stop since we were already so close to home.

I spent the rest of the ride reliving the feeling of waking up with her in my arms for the first time. My morning wood had been poking her in her middle and my first inclination had been to pull away before she woke up and felt that shit.

After what had been done to her I didn't want her having any bad moments. But she felt good as fuck against me first thing in the morning, the way a day was supposed to begin. I allowed myself a few extra moments to smell her hair and relish the feelings of absolute joy that ran through me. Just one more minute and then I'd let my little innocent go. That's what I kept telling myself.

In the end I'd decided against that shit, this was me she was never to fear me, never to lump me in with anyone else. And though my heart raced in my chest at the thought of putting any kind of fear in her eyes, I held onto her.

I needn't have worried. The smile she gave me when she opened her eyes went a long way to convincing me that she was going to be fine. It had taken everything in me not to kiss her smiling lips. I'd settled for a quick peck even though I'd wanted to suck on her tongue for the next week or so.

CREED

We hit my place just after eight in the morning. I didn't call ahead because it was way too early when we left, and so when we pulled into my place she got an eyeful. Mattie, one of the more popular hangers on, was just coming out of the clubhouse, still putting herself together.

The look on babygirl's face was priceless, but I checked my first inclination to shield her. She's gonna have to learn. She was gonna see a fuck of a lot worse before long I was sure like I said, I'm not in the habit of censoring or curtailing my men's activities as long as they don't do any shit to harm women or kids.

With that much leeway some of these fucks run the gamut. I pretty much expect anything and try my best not to react to some of the fuckery they can get up to.

I waved at the other woman when she hailed me but kept it moving. I didn't want Jessie's introduction to my world to be one of the sheep, and especially not one I'd fucked in the past.

Shit, was she going to be able to deal with the fact that some of the women here had once shared my bed? Or would she understand that none of those encounters had meant anything more than a quick release?

It wasn't something I'd given a hell of a lot of thought to, I mean she was just a kid for fuck sake and I'm a grown fucking man. It wasn't like I could wait around for her to grow up; I'd have gone out my fucking head. 'Yeah but if she'd have done the same you would've flipped your shit.' Who the fuck asked you?

"Come on let's get you settled and maybe you can get some more rest." I took her hand and led her in the opposite direction across the way, to my private residence, while she looked back at the colorful woman who wasn't too quiet as she left.

Was Mattie always that damn loud in the mornings? I hadn't noticed. I'm pretty sure she was putting it on for Jessie's benefit. Then again...I saw two of the guys come out behind her scratching their nuts and grinning.

I just shook my head and hustled my little charge inside before she caught wind of that shit. Fuck me she'd be corrupted in five seconds flat.

I saw her to the guestroom across the hall from the master suite, made sure she was all set and bounced. I had left some shit up in the air when I went after her, might as well get back to it because there was no way I was gonna get any more sleep with her here.

"Creed?"

"Yeah baby?" She called out to me in that half sleep voice that sounded like a cross between lustful sin and innocence. I went back and stood in the doorway not trusting myself to go any farther.

"Where are you going?"

"Just across the way to my office, you're safe here no one's gonna bother you. If you need me just call okay." She nodded and put her head down to sleep.

Even though I knew she was safe and that no one would even think of entering my place without my say-so, I still went around the house securing the place. I wasn't about to take any more chances with her, and the last few hours had taught me not to take shit for granted.

I knew I could trust most of the men in my crew, but as with all crews there were some unknowns who'd skated by by the skin of their teeth.

Friends of friends or somebody's fucking cousin. I was going to keep an eye on the unknowns, though I didn't think any one of them were dumb enough to fuck with me, still to be on the safe side.

When I was sure everything was set I looked in on my baby one last time before heading out the door. Sound asleep already. "My little innocent babygirl."

The place was just the way I'd left it, like I'd been in the middle of shit and had to bounce in a hurry. I'd probably fucked the deal I was in the middle of but I couldn't find it in me to give a fuck. I'd do it all again if it meant going after her.

For the first time since getting Law's call I was able to truly breathe. She was here she was safe I didn't have to worry anymore. It was a few days early and definitely under the circumstances I'd envisioned, but here nonetheless.

Now I had to figure out what to do about this new pebble in my fucking shoe. Because it involved her, I was going to have to put everything else aside and take care of this shit once and for all.

From what little I knew and what Law had told

me, Sal was in bed with a very bad group of assholes. The kind who believed that they were above the law and made it their life's mission to be fucking annoying to the rest of the general population and that's putting it mildly.

CREED

*T*he first thing I did was call a meeting. I needed all my boys to know who she was and how she was to be treated, not just here but in the county period.

I also needed to give them a heads up in case Sal's people tried anything. He knew where I lived I was sure, because of his association with Dee, and I wasn't taking any chances in case he and the other fuck-wipes he hung with decided to pay me a visit.

From what Law had told me these people were heavy into hate and low on sense, a bad fucking combination if you ask me. I never even knew she was around that kind of shit, just one more thing that I'd failed her in.

Dee was gonna get her turn, but I knew her shit was money. I'm just waiting on Jason to take everything she owned so she'd get the picture that it was never too wise to fuck with me and mine.

That little buzz cut was child's play compared to what the fuck I'd do to them both if they fucked around. She didn't seem too badly scarred by their shit, but then again it had only been one day, who knows what the fuck she was holding in?

The men came straggling in one by one, which told me what kind of night they'd had while I was gone. At least the fucking place was still standing and the asshole cops weren't at my door; progress.

I waited until they were all there and looking as attentive as they could be at that time of the morning after a long night. I wanted their full attention because the first one to step outta line was getting FUBARRED and I didn't want any fucking excuses.

"Listen up, my wife is here." That woke them the fuck up. Between the eye popping and the what the fuck looks thrown around the room I think all remnants of sleep had disappeared.

"It goes without saying that she is to be respected as my wife any slip-ups on that one you're out I don't care if you shared womb time with me and none of you here have. Anyone even look at her with anything but brotherly love will lose a nut."

I let that shit settle in and watched as they shifted from leg to leg with pained looks on their faces. Good, they were a little more awake, not all the way here yet, but enough.

"I'm gonna need you lot to be on guard for the next little while because of some shit that's gone down. She's asleep right now, but I'll introduce you as soon as she's up and about." I threw out the pictures of Sal and Dee that I'd blown up in my office five minutes earlier and made copies of.

"If you see these two anywhere in the vicinity, detain them, but leave them for me to deal with. All you need to know for now is that they are a danger. Any questions?" I'm pretty sure I knew what it was going to be and I wasn't disappointed. Like I said, not many people knew about her or my attachment.

No doubt they thought it was one of the many women I'd paraded in and out of here over the years. Though why the fuck they'd think that when I hardly ever gave anyone a repeat performance was beyond me. "Yeah boss, when did we get married?"

"A long fucking time ago Jimmy." Let them make

of that what they will. I wasn't in the habit of explaining myself when it came to personal shit, I'm sure they'll piece it together eventually.

The others pretty much kept their opinions to themselves for now, but I had a feeling that had more to do with the booze they'd downed the night before than out of any respect for my privacy. I'm pretty sure I'd be bogged down with questions before long.

"One more thing, I'm gonna need y'all to keep the sheep on a leash for the time being. My girl is kind of on the innocent side, I don't want her seeing certain things." The fucks looked like they expected me to start censoring, and curtailing their natural proclivities, which I wasn't about to do. When there was nothing more forthcoming they relaxed again.

"She's an unknown then?"

"Yes Max, it's Jessie." I saw realization dawn in his eyes and the slow smile that started to spread across his lips, nosy fuck. Of course he knew who she was he was my right hand and the closest thing I had to a friend outside of Law.

I dismissed them since they didn't have anything else to say and took Max aside to fill him in some more. Like I said, he was my right hand man, the only person other than Law and babygirl that I would consider trusting, and as such knew a little more than most.

"I don't expect to be away from her for any length of time, not now anyway, but I want you to promise me that if anything happens to me, or if I'm not around for whatever reason, you'll make sure she's okay."

"What the fuck Creed? You expecting trouble?" His hackles were already raised and his stance changed automatically to protective mode. That's one of the reasons he's allowed so close. You save a man's life once and he thinks he has to have your back forever and a day.

"Calm down brother, the barbarians aren't at the gate, not yet anyway. You know I've always done what needed to be done, never thought twice.

The kind of life we live, the shit we do, there's always going to be some asshole gunning for us. No, let's leave that for now. Let's focus on this shit. I just need to know that if anything goes down that everything is hers. I already have it in writing, but I'm telling you, and I'm asking you to watch out for her."

I hated like fuck to have this conversation, but it was something that needed to be done. I didn't fool myself that everything was fucking roses. No I wasn't expecting to give up the ghost anytime soon, but after leaving her like a fucking candle in the wind for the past nine years when I thought she was protected, I wasn't about to take that chance again.

"You knew a little about her because I needed you to just in case something went south while I was in the army, and because I needed someone other than me to be aware of her and that she was to be taken care of. You and Law are pretty much the only ones who really know anything about her, now you know a little more than you did."

"I think you should know the aunt was a bitch and the man she's shacked up with a piece a shit wanna be rapist…"

"He didn't…" My boy posed up like a rooster; that was just the response I was looking for. "No he didn't or I wouldn't be standing here talking to you right now. But he did enough that I wrung his dick off as in I disconnected the shit from his scrotum.

I'm pretty sure there ain't a doctor this side of heaven can fix his shit. He would've probably been better off if I'd have cut him, then they would've been able to sew it back together, this way he's totally fucked."

"Damn boss, remind me never to get on your bad side." He cupped himself like an ass. "Don't get on my bad side." I said that shit with a straight face because he knew I meant it.

After the betrayal of her aunt I wasn't in the mood to deal with anyone else's bullshit, and there's nothing worse than someone close to you fucking with you like that. I did acknowledge that part of that stemmed from my insane jealousy of anything male being around her.

"So the aunt? Wasn't what you thought? That sucks. Are we paying her a visit or nah?" He would understand, he knew a little of what I'd been doing over the years.

He hadn't been with me as long as Law has, but we go back enough and like I said, I'd saved his life once and he took that shit seriously for some fucked up reason and won't leave my shadow from that day to this.

"I ever tell you I'm glad as fuck I saved you from that gang of cutthroats in that alley?" I clapped him on the shoulder before heading over to the bank of windows that looked towards the house. I didn't feel as heavy anymore with that shit out of the way.

We went over some security measures, shit I

needed to put in place because I wasn't going to have eyes on her twenty-four seven as much as I'd want to, so I needed others to pick up the slack. At least until I knew the danger had passed.

I delegated some other shit we had coming up because I wasn't about to leave her for a while after I took her virginity. Every girl needs a honeymoon period or some shit, or so I'd heard.

As to an actual wedding that was something she was gonna have to put together on her own. I knew fuck all about that shit and the sheep weren't given to such things, not that I would ask them, I'm not that fucking clueless.

"That run we were supposed to make, I'm gonna need you and the boys to take point on that, shouldn't be too much trouble, I'm sure you can handle it just fine without me."

"The cartel?" Or so they like to call themselves. What they were are a bunch of lowlifes who'd watched fucking Scarface once too often and thought they were fucking gangsters.

They were a motley crew of fuck-ups made up mostly of ex-criminals who thought they got a bad rap, not because they were innocent but because they'd been caught.

This band of misfits had made the monumental

cluster fuck decision to run meth in my backyard, no fucking way. I did the grid ratio on my little town and there were more fucking kids per square mile than livestock, and in this neck of the woods that's saying a lot.

Okay that's a bit of an exaggeration, but there were a fuckload of kids. No way were they peddling that shit here. Not to the kids, and not to the parents.

"Don't insult the Italians I don't think those fucks would appreciate it. Anyway as I was saying, pick a crew and go do as we planned. Don't leave a brick standing. These fucking meth labs crop up like weeds so make sure you destroy the root and get their asses out of our town, let them go fuck up somebody else's shit.

Try not to kill anyone, it's not that big a job and the fucks are just stupid not inherently evil okay." He grinned the bloodthirsty fuck he is and saluted me. "As you say boss. Ahem, about the sheep, uh, you do know that some of them thought or at least were hoping..."

"I give a fuck what they were hoping, all I care about is what was said and I never said one fuck. Keep an eye and an ear out, any of them get out of line where she's concerned I wanna know." Yeah, I wanna handle that shit personally so they know the decision, whatever it may be, is final.

With everything squared away to my satisfaction, I let him go and headed back to my office to kill some time until she woke up from her nap.

CREED

I spent the morning with half of my mind on the club and the rest of it in that bed with her. The fucking calendar was mocking me now every time I looked at it; the time was almost here.

I'd called her my wife to the men because that's exactly what she is. I just had to make that shit legit now but I wasn't too worried about that. As far as I'm concerned, the moment I breech her for the first time is as good as me slipping my ring on her finger.

I fucked around with some invoices and shit but it was all Greek to me and I'm not bilingual so that means I got fuck all done for the next hour. All I could think about was her, just across the way, waiting.

I couldn't hold a damn thought so I ended up going back to the house just to be near her. She was still asleep when I looked in on her, all innocent looking under a mountain of covers.

I tried to imagine that fucking pervert standing and looking down on all that beauty and defiling it, and wished I could fuck his shit up all over again. I checked my watch on the back of that thought.

There weren't any sirens heading towards my place and I figured if he was gonna make that play he would've already, so I guess it was wait and see what, if anything he was gonna do next. I left her and went into the kitchen to check the cupboards.

I hardly ever spent much time here before, but now with her in the house I was gonna have to stay on top of this fuckery like food and whatever the fuck else people stocked up on these days.

I'll wait until she was up to get started on that shit because I didn't have a fucking clue. I puttered around impatiently until I heard movement in the bedroom and her voice calling out to me.

"You up? Let's go get some food in you." I yelled from where I stood not trusting myself to go to her. She came out to the kitchen in an old pair of jeans and a shirt that was way too tight across her chest.

"Change of plans, we need to go shopping." No

fucking way she was walking around like that. She blushed and looked down at herself and I didn't have to be a mind reader to know what she was thinking.

"Hey look at me. Whatever is lacking, it's not on you or because of anything you did. I'm to blame mostly, but never you okay." She nodded her head yes and I took her hand and kissed it before leading her out to my truck, she wasn't use to riding yet and I didn't want to overdo it.

I could hardly find my fucking keys; that's how long it had been since I'd been in my ride. She wasn't here twenty-four hours yet and already she was changing up my shit.

I had to lift her tiny little ass into the passenger seat, which got me to thinking about getting her her own car. I knew she had a license because she'd taken the classes at school, but Dee had convinced me that she didn't need a ride as yet since the town was so small and my girl hardly ever went anywhere.

I'm not even gonna think about the real reasoning behind that shit this morning. I'm working on a fresh start. Thinking about that bitch would set me back a couple steps. All good thoughts Creed.

I buckled her in, kissed her cheek, which made her blush sweetly at me, and walked around to my side with a brand new boner. There was no use hiding that shit because I was sure it was going to be an all day thing, or at least until I bedded her and got the shit out of my system.

She gave a start of surprise when I took her hand in mine as we drove, but I didn't make a big deal out of it, just gave her a little squeeze and kept my eyes on the road. I didn't miss the little smile on her face though.

Fuck, I hope she doesn't look at my lap, or if she does she doesn't run screaming. That's another thing I have to think about, how the fuck am I gonna get inside her? She's tiny as fuck and even women twice her size, have a hard time taking me. Good thing I'd stocked up on the lube.

AFTER I'D BOUGHT her a whole new wardrobe, appropriate for her new life, I took her out to eat. She was now the proud owner of enough jeans and tanks to outfit half the state.

She had about ten new pairs of shoes for every occasion and I still didn't feel like we were done yet. Like any other female on the planet she'd enjoyed herself even though I'd had to talk her into it in the beginning.

I found myself flirting with her and touching her more than usual throughout the afternoon. She didn't seem to mind, in fact she kept getting closer as if seeking my touch. She had no idea that I was training her to do just that.

I wanted her to crave my attention in every way, to always seek me out no matter where we were. I was obsessed I realized, totally taken by the idea of her needing me for everything, at every turn.

At the table before the server came, we sat staring into each other's eyes as I played with her fingers, rubbing my thumb over her palm. I felt like an ass but I'd promised to give her soft for the first until she got used to me. Shit was like to kill me.

She was worth it though, but if she kept biting her lip and blushing that shit was gonna get her fucked in a heartbeat. Not just fucked either, hard and long, the only way I knew how.

The local fucks were all in my shit but nobody asked me any hard questions. No they just stared like what the fuck. I had to give a few of the good ole boys a good glare to get them to act right.

Her tits were the problem. I'd let her choose her own shit because she'd seemed so excited at the prospect that I figured her aunt never let her shop for herself. I see now that I maybe should've done that shit myself.

It wasn't that she was half naked, but the top she had on was hugging her tits a little too well. My dick was enjoying the show so I was pretty sure others were as well, ergo the glares.

I threw my Cut over her shoulders when we were done and headed out into the warm sunshine. I needed to get with Jason and deal with the demise of her aunt, but I didn't want to do that shit in front of her, and since it was her first day in her new hometown I didn't want to leave her cooped up inside.

It was a nice day out, no clouds and a nice light breeze to go with the sunshine. I wish I knew what the fuck to do with it. What the hell did people do on days like today? It's pretty obvious I've never been much for dating; it hit me then that it had been a long fucking while since I'd actually been on one of those.

I think subconsciously I'd known that she was going to be the one. And though I'd had a tangle or two over the years, I'd always kept it light, no entanglements. Now I had to wrack my brain for something to do

She seemed happy enough as we walked across

the lot with her hand in mine, but the fact that she had already missed out on so much already made me want to give her more.

She had this half smile on her face that made me feel good as fuck, because it meant she was happy, to be here, with me. And when she lifted her head to the sun and ran her hand over the soft leather of my cut before dipping her nose into it for a smell of her man, my dick noticed that shit.

We reached the truck and my fuck it meter hit empty. It was her ass in her new jeans that did that shit. I cornered her against the passenger side door. When she looked up at me with those big blue eyes full of questions and fuck me, lust, I didn't hold back. I lowered my head slowly, testing her. There was no fear, no hesitation in her eyes, only need.

I took her face in my hands and lifted her lips to mine, sucking her tongue into my mouth. The feel of her, her taste, went right through me. It was just as good as I knew it would be and I folded her body in closer to mine.

She was sweet and soft in my arms, her little tongue tasting like heaven in my mouth before I pushed it out with mine and fed it to her. "Like this baby." I took her chin and showed her how to suck my tongue before taking hers again.

149

I hope like the fuck the growl in my throat didn't scare her, but I couldn't hold back that shit. Two fucking years and more of pent up hunger was unleashed there in that parking lot. I barely held on by the skin of my teeth.

Her soft tits pressed into my chest and my dick gave her the one eyed salute. I damn near ate her face off I kissed her so hard, but the real beauty of it was that she didn't shy away, didn't seem afraid as she kissed me back. "Sweet." I nibbled her lips before plunging back in for more. If we'd been alone I would've been in her already that's how hot she made me.

I moaned into her mouth and rocked my cock against her middle before pulling away. I held her head against my chest as I waited for our hearts to calm. "I've been waiting for fucking ever to do that babygirl; welcome home."

I didn't give her time for a rebuttal, just opened the door, lifted her into the seat and buckled her in. I whistled my way around to the driver's side, and when I got in she was the one who reached for my hand this time. Fuck yeah.

She was back to being shy and cute and I wanted to eat her the fuck up. When I was running the streets looking for my next meal as a boy, this was never even a dream, I dared not look so high back then.

If I'd known that she was what was waiting for me at the end of all the hell I'd endured in life, I would've run hell bent for leather through it all and not missed a beat. My reward my prize. I lifted her hand and kissed her fingers, letting the beauty if it all wash through me.

"What would you like to do today babygirl?" I had a fuckload of shit to get to as usual, but again, she comes first. Her blush was so sweet I couldn't help leaning over for another taste of her lips.

"Tell me." She made me grin, no small feat that; I'm not one for joviality. Any of the others see that shit they're like to think I'm having a seizure or some shit.

"This." So fucking shy.

"This what?" I nuzzled her ear and neck. I knew I wasn't gonna last the whole three days without touching her, and now with our first kiss out of the way, I knew I was going to mess around with her tonight.

I wasn't going to bust her cherry a promise was a promise after all, even if it was one made to myself. But if I had to be around her much longer without at least tasting her pussy I was gonna shoot myself.

She still hadn't told me what 'this' was, but I had a pretty good idea, I wanted her to tell me though. "What it is it that you want babygirl?" I couldn't keep my hands off of her she was just so fucking soft to my touch. It made my heart swell with pride and longing when she didn't shy away from my touch, but instead seemed to want it.

"Can we go home?" I guess that was as brave as she was gonna get today. She didn't have to ask me twice. I put the truck in gear and sped back to the house. How I missed slamming into the other poor souls on the road was anybody's guess.

And by the time we reached home my cock was a leaky mess and that was just from holding hands. She's gonna give my ass a heart attack if she kept up this sweet shit.

We were both running by the time I took the key from the ignition. I saw some of the crew milling around outside the clubhouse a few yards away and remembered my promise to introduce her to them, but later for that shit.

I bypassed her room and took her into mine with the ocean of bed that I had there waiting. It was a California king, but after the night we'd spent with her wrapped in my arms, I was sure we weren't ever gonna need that much room, well not for sleeping anyway. I could see us fucking all over the surface though.

I don't know what happened, what got into her, but no sooner had we cleared the room to the door, than she was on me. Here I was thinking I was gonna have to be the one to talk her into the shit.

Maybe that would have been easier. Knowing that she might want me as much as I wanted her was going to make waiting twice as fucking hard. "Wait baby."

She was in a rush and her fingers refused to work, so I had to take over getting my shirt off. Her sharp inhalation and the dreamy look on her face as she ran her hands across my chest reminded me that she had never really seen me shirtless before. Somehow she'd missed my tats last night in the hotel room. Could be because I'd put my shirt on over the towel.

I let her play with the dragon on my chest. "You like it?" She nodded her head and went back to playing, and when she lowered her head and licked my flesh my cock jumped.

That was all it took to set me off. I tore at her new shirt to get at her tits. She'd bought some kind of frilly bra in pink, it was sad that the shit had a very short life.

She only grinned at me when I tore that too and dropped the pieces on the floor before lifting her tiny ass up and laying her back on the bed. "Sorry baby I'll get you more."

I looked down at her willing myself to go easy. I didn't want to taint the moment with the memory of what had happened to her, but I needed to make sure she was with me.

"I know this is all new to you, but I don't want you to be afraid. I will never hurt you, ever." I waited until I saw the clarity in her eyes before giving her a quick kiss on her lips for reassurance and to test the waters before nibbling my way along her cheek to her throat.

I licked the spot just beneath her ear in the softness of her neck before pulling it between my teeth, and sucking hard, marking her, claiming mine.

Her body trembled and she bucked beneath me, rubbing her jean-covered cunt into my straining cock. I pressed down hard in the junction of her thighs, making sure to hit her clit as she mewled into my mouth.

She liked to kiss if the way she sucked on my tongue was any indication, but I wanted those tits in my mouth. I hefted them in my hand using my thumb and forefinger to play with her nipple while pulling her ass harder into me with the other hand.

She started the fucking motion, begging without words to be fucked hard. I let her ride my cock like that until it became too much for me but not before she threw her head back and came. "Fuck me that's beautiful." Damn, when I get my dick in her she's gonna go off like a firecracker.

My eyes almost crossed at the sensation of her pussy twitching against my cock through the barrier of cloth. I could only imagine skin to skin contact, fucking dynamite.

"I'm gonna try not to fuck you, but I want to pleasure you with my mouth and fingers." I had to remind myself that I was talking to an innocent when her eyes grew wide as saucers. In them I saw the expected fear, but she nodded.

I hope to fuck I would've had the strength to leave her if she'd needed me to, but I wasn't too sure I could've. Thank fuck her fear was just the usual, of the unknown. Good thing she didn't get a look at my meat or she'd really be scared then.

I undid my jeans but left them on as I laid down beside her, drawing her body close to mine. I came up short, I didn't know where to start. What the fuck? I felt green and unsure for all of two seconds before I reminded myself that she was mine and there was no way I was ever gonna hurt her. "I'm going to touch you now babygirl."

I wanted to go slow, to take my time and enjoy the feel of her under my hands, but she seemed to have the same idea. Her little hand seemed drawn to the ink on my chest and she trailed it with her fingers and eyes.

I let her have her fun, before moving my hand to her breast. It was full and heavy in my palm as I lifted it to my hungry mouth. Her body was already trembling when I lowered my head for another taste of her.

Her hand got trapped between us as I rolled over onto her, taking her nipple completely into my mouth and fitting myself between her thighs. Her pussy was hot. I could feel her sweet heat through my jeans as she ground herself against me in heat.

She was so fucking small under me, I was almost afraid I might crush her. Her hands in my hair held me against her plump flesh as I nibbled and sucked. My cock was thumping away in my jeans, but I knew better than to release him, not yet.

My head was light, something that I'd never experienced before in my life, as I tasted her flesh on my tongue and held myself back from mauling her. I enjoyed the pearling of her nipple on my tongue, the feel of her nails digging into my scalp.

Soon that wasn't enough, I needed more. Even as I held myself in check I wanted to ravish. It was only the reminder of just who it was that I held in my arms that kept me back.

I took a deep breath as I lifted my mouth away from her. Looking down at her sprawled before me I didn't see my innocent little girl but a woman. A woman who wanted to fuck! I closed my eyes against the temptation.

Two more days Creed, you can give her that. I swallowed around the golf ball in my throat and opened my eyes on hers. She was so ready my little innocent, her eyes bright her breath wild and erratic and her body in constant motion.

"I'm going to touch you between your legs now." I lowered her jeans, following the movement with my tongue, licking the warm skin of her tummy as it was exposed. She was already moving beneath my lips and I hadn't even started yet.

When I had her jeans all the way down I dragged them off her legs, hungry for the sight and taste of her. I'll keep my shit covered for now but there was no way I was going another second without having her on my tongue.

I kissed her pussy lips through the sheer silk of her underwear. She spread her legs open making room for me. I tore the silk from her body and sniffed her cunt with my nose pressed against her. Don't fuck Creed; you may not fuck. I had to repeat that shit to myself a couple times when her scent rushed through me.

Her hands captured my head holding me in place as her legs widened even farther and she begged me in short disjointed sentences to help her. I took her up on her invitation and spread her farther with my shoulders. Lifting her ass in my hands, I brought her up to my mouth and tasted her for the first time. "Ohhh." So responsive to my touch!

I licked into her pussy and tasted her juices. She was salty sweet and I prepared to feast. I growled low and deep as her taste burst forth on my tongue. Her natural sensuality had her moving against my mouth in wanton heat as I tongue fucked her until she came. "I love the way you cum for me babygirl."

I licked up her spilled juices from her pussy lips and the crease of her thighs. Young pussy has a taste all its own. Like nothing I've ever experienced in my life.

I added a finger to the mix, my heart beating faster as I went in search of an answer that had been plaguing me. Something I hadn't let myself think about. Thank fuck, the barrier was there, I wasn't gonna have to hunt some college kid down and maim his ass, and better yet she wasn't due a severe punishment.

I know it was a fucked up double standard, and that it was even more fucked because I'd never told her that she was off limits to other men. I just took it for granted that somehow she'd know. The shit doesn't make sense but who the fuck cares?

I could rest easy now knowing that she was untouched; perfect, mine. I licked and sucked on her flesh to my heart's content while she made the sweetest sounds, encouraging me to do more.

The thoughts in my head were way ahead of me. I wanted to fuck in the worse damn way and not being accustomed to denying myself anything, it was a battle of wills as I ate her pussy 'til my mouth hurt.

I reached down between the mattress and my dick and squeezed it off to stop the flow and give myself some relief. Her pussy was spilling into my mouth like a busted pipe and I was happy as fuck at her responsiveness to my touch. "Creed?" Her voice was thick with her need and it was all I could do not to answer her call.

I felt like I was gonna explode from wanting in

her so bad, my heart pounded under the strain of holding back. I knew she would do this to me, that she would be the one woman on the earth to bring this shit out of me. I'm not gonna make it, fuck.

"Fuck, I wanna fuck you." I had to grit my teeth and hold myself still. I counted to ten and told myself to just get her off and get the fuck out of the house. I opened her with my fingers, trying to distance myself, but there was no way. Her pussy was calling me to fuck. I eased two fingers inside her tight hole and sucked her clit into my mouth.

She went up in flames, her back arched off the bed and her pussy clamped tight against my mouth and fingers. Her sharp nails dug into my shoulders and back as she rode my tongue. I sucked her dry and then rolled off the bed like the shit was on fire.

"I'll be back." I sounded pissed I know, but what the fuck did she expect? You need to calm the fuck down Creed, she didn't tell you to put your mouth on her you fuck.

I ran my hand over my head as I left the room like the hounds of hell were after me. Shit, you can't just leave her there like that, not after her first time with a man; but it was either that, or fuck. That damn promise was like an albatross around my neck

I dunked my head under the sink in the bathroom and took some deep breaths. When had I ever felt like this? Not ever. I had to talk myself down and glare myself into fucking submission in the mirror. Who the fuck's idea was it to wait any damn way? Yours asshole! Eighteen was the legal age why the fuck did I do this shit to myself?

When I felt like I was in control again I went back to her. She looked scared as fuck when I went back into the room and I felt like a fucking animal. She didn't look like she'd moved an inch since I jumped off the bed, and her body was stiff as a board while she looked close to tears.

Just like that my protective gene kicked in and I wasn't in danger of fucking her too soon any longer. We'll see how long that shit lasts.

"No baby don't do that, you didn't do anything wrong." I ended up back on the bed with her anyway, taking her into my arms to console her. "Why did you leave then, wasn't I any good?" She was clutching at me like she thought I was gonna run away.

"Yes you are babygirl, too good. That's why I left, I don't want to take you like this, I want it to be special. I have…it doesn't matter now, just know you are perfect." I kissed her precious little face until I reached her lips again and sunk in. She didn't seem to mind her taste in my mouth as I fed it to her. That shit just made my dick even more unruly as she climbed onto my chest in her bid to get closer.

I held the back of her head and eased her away before she hurt herself when she became agitated. Poor baby, her pussy was awake and she didn't know what to do with herself. I couldn't resist taking one last nip of her swollen lips though, or grinding my cock up into her.

When we were both a little calmer I made her look into my eyes because I needed her full attention for what was coming next.

"Do you understand what's going on, do you know why I brought you home?" She shook her head no and made herself more comfortable on my chest, her fingers once more tracing my ink. My cock was still straining against the bit and the sight of her plump tits pressed into my hard chest was all that was needed to get him going again.

"Fuck it, I'll tell you later." I rolled us over and pushed her back on the bed, this time lying flat on top of her. I fitted all thirteen and a half inches of my cock against her pussy. Fuck me this is torture. Her tits were like some kind of fucking magnet for my mouth and I dove right in again, moving from one to the other as I bit sucked and licked.

My cockhead was peeping out the top of my jeans and I used that to titillate her clit as I mauled her tits. I dry fucked her as I sucked on her mounds, leaving my mark all over her in my feverish need. She keened and moved beneath me as her legs shook and her pussy creamed.

I wasn't about to nut on her stomach, not for a long time anyway, but... "Don't be afraid, I'm going to put the head of my cock inside you, I won't breech you I promise." I wasn't sure if I could do this shit, if I had that much control, but I was sure I was going to fucking die if I didn't at least feel her.

Reaching down between us, I released my cock, piercings and all. She reacted to the feel of the cold metal against her heated pussy. My shit was fully decorated from tip to base, so I knew that in a minute her pussy was going to be feeling like heaven.

I rubbed the underside of my cock up and down her clit, letting the fat leaking head slip into her pussy hole on each upward thrust. Her bush was soft against my rod, cushioning it in warm strands of silk.

I was close as fuck from just this and I had to stop myself from fucking into her. Instead, when I felt her body tremble with a massive orgasm and her hands clutched at me desperately, I put my cockhead just inside the rim of her pussy.

I started shooting as soon as the pussy snapped around my meat. She was a tight fucking fit. "Hold still baby don't move, fuuuuuuuu..." I cut myself off just in time.

Far from heeding me, she moved even harder against me, sending my dick deeper inside her. I butted against the barrier deep inside her cunt and a second volley left me.

I had to pull out fast, but stopped short of hotfooting it out of there again. If just that little taste was anything to go by I was going to need at least a week alone with her when I finally took her.

I looked at my watch, one and a half days. While I was trying to catch my breath, she got cold feet or her shyness kicked in and she tried rolling away. "No way." I reached out and pulled her back into my arms.

I took stock of everything then. The way I felt whole for the first time in my life. The warmth that filled my chest at just the feel of her in my arms. I squeezed her gently and lifted her mouth to accept my kiss.

I ran my hands up and down her naked back soothingly. "I love you babygirl." I whispered the words against her lips. Her body stiffened next to mine before she melted into my chest, and my eyes popped the fuck open when I realized what it was I had said.

Shit, I hadn't meant to blurt it out like that, but now that the deed was done I felt even more of a weight lifted. I held her closer as her little body vibrated next to mine.

This conversation was long in the making. There were things I needed to do to make up for the past before I could embark on our future, but this I could give her now.

I didn't want her thinking for one second that she was just another fuck to me, so I needed to set shit straight before we went any farther. I'd planned to do the shit before I had my head between her legs but shit happens.

She didn't run screaming from the bed so I figured she wasn't spooked, and the way she clung to me while I had my cockhead in her told me she wasn't disgusted.

"Creed?" Damn, will she always have that soft innocent voice? I hope to fuck she does, that life with me never robs her of that shit. "Yeah babygirl?" She was back to running her hand over my ink and down my stomach, stopping short of touching my cock that was lying against my stomach half hard and just waiting for an excuse.

I took her hand in mine and raised it to my mouth to save us both. "What is it love?" Her eyes were still dreamy and her skin still flushed when I looked down at her. "I love you too." She said the words fast together before hiding her face in my chest. I felt like fist pumping the air but my ass was way too cool for that shit. Instead I turned her onto her back again and studied her face.

"If I didn't just off load inside you I would eat your pussy again, but I'm not sure I'd like the taste of my jizz." She went red as a cherry making me laugh. By the time I was done with my little innocent she was going to be uttering some of the nastiest shit to ever leave a mouth. I love a nice dirty fuck complete with commentary.

"Now let me look at you." I hadn't really had time before, since I'd fallen on her like a starving carnivore as soon as her clothes were off. Now I reared back and looked my fill at her slender form with the centerfold tits. I took my time and perused my bounty, thankful as fuck that I was the only one lucky enough to claim her as mine.

"I like your bush, don't ever shave it. I'll shape it up sometimes but I like the look." I reached between her thighs and slipped two big fingers in her sopping wet pussy. My seed and her juices started leaking out of her into my palm as I finger fucked her sweet cunt. I wanted to hear her moans again.

I went after her tits again until her nipple pebbled on my tongue and her pussy clenched around my fingers. "Cum for me baby, that's it." She rode my hand in search of her next cum as I made love to her tits with my mouth. "Creed...?"

Her voice shook and her body trembled. "Does any of this scare you baby?" She shook her head and moved against my hand in the last throes of her orgasm. I took her mouth in a soft gentle kiss as I eased my fingers in and out of her softly. Her breathing went back to normal and her body was pliant as she looked up at me in wonder.

"Are you ready to learn how to please me with your mouth?" She tensed up in my arms, such an innocent. "There's nothing to be afraid of. Did you like when I used my mouth on you?" She hid her face in my chest making me laugh again. I don't think I've ever known anything this fucking pure in my life. "So fucking sweet, don't ever change babygirl."

"I love eating your pussy, in fact I love everything about your body." My eyes went to her huge tits as I finger fucked her harder. "Sometimes, I'll wet my fingers in you and play with your pussy and clit for an hour, just to make you feel good. Most of the time though I'm gonna be inside you, in fact for the first year or so I'm gonna be in you so much you might start to think that's all you mean to me, don't."

I used my jizz to lubricate my finger before easing it into her ass. "Easy it's just another way for me to share my love with you." Her ass was tight as fuck. It was going to take a lot of work to open her up there.

I fucked her pussy with my thumb while teasing her asshole with the first knuckle of another finger. I wanted her nice and primed before I let her get her first eyeful of the monster.

With her tit in my mouth and each hole stuffed I brought her off three times. My cock had been hanging out the top of my pants since the dry fuck, just waiting his turn. I brought her little hand down and wrapped if around my meat, it didn't reach all the way around but it was good enough.

She jumped in surprise when she felt the steel that decorated my meat. I had a ladder going the full length of the underside of my cock shaft plus an Apadravya and a Prince Albert in my cockhead. For someone as green as she was I'm sure she wasn't ready for a close up of my shit.

"Stroke me, move your hand up and down." I didn't want to take my fingers out of her pussy long enough to show her so I just instructed her. She played with the studs that lined my cock and the ring at the very tip while my boy put on a good show and leaked like fuck into her hand.

"Can I see?" She moved before I could answer and her eyes were soon widening in fright. I didn't even try to bullshit her. "He's a beast I know, and he will hurt you." I pushed my fingers deeper until I reached her hymen. "But he's a part of me and trust me I'll make it all good. Give me your mouth sweetheart."

I kissed her to take her mind off the beastly one, but I was sure that would only work for so long. I could feel her hesitation mixed with curiosity as I played in her pussy while she ran her hand up and down my drooling cock.

Time to move this shit to the next phase. Her hand felt good as fuck but I knew something else that would feel even better, and since I couldn't fuck her pussy for another day and a half, I wanted the warm wet cavern of her mouth. Fuck!

"You see how he's leaking and jumping in your hand? He wants your mouth." I don't even know how I got those words out. Having her service me with her soft hand was more pleasurable than any intercourse I'd ever had with anyone else.

I had no doubt that it was because of who she was, the fact that she was my heart. I kissed her again, long and hard as sudden emotion overcame me. She was really here with me, my woman now and soon, completely owned by me.

"I don't know how." She fretted as she said the words, like that was a bad thing. "You better not fucking know how. That's my job; to teach you everything you need to know about pleasing me. Now give me your mouth."

I wrapped her hair around my arm and took her mouth a little rougher this time. Her statement had spooked me so much I'd forgotten my rule about swearing in front of her.

She rubbed herself against me in heat so I pulled her over on top of me with my cock hitting her just where she needed me. I whispered soft words of encouragement to her when my boy poked her from her pussy slit to her navel and she got nervous. "I won't try to fit all of him inside you at once, not the first couple of times anyway, but eventually you'll learn to take him. Feel this. Don't you like that?"

I took my cock in hand and rubbed the swollen head against her pussy, up and down to the crack of her ass. It wasn't long before she was mewling into my mouth and making fuck me noises of her own. I pressed her down hard on my cock shaft and let her fuck herself on my hardness until her juices flowed again.

Now that she was loose, I turned her around so that her head was over my cock and her pussy was spread in front of my face. I opened her pink cunt and licked as her mouth went around my cockhead slowly. I wasn't going to tell her what to do, just let her feel her way around.

I knew there was no way she was gonna fit my whole length not to mention my four inch girth into her mouth, so I wasn't even gonna try. I figured it would only take about six inches 'til I hit the back of her throat.

Her teeth scraped against my cock rings and I gritted mine and tensed up waiting for the pain to set in when she bit into my shit, but she caught on real quick and soon all I felt was the sweet softness of her tongue and the smooth insides of her cheeks.

I could concentrate on feasting on her snatch now that I wasn't in any danger and went back to studying her pink gash. I kissed it like I would her mouth before letting my tongue go on the hunt. She didn't need any instructions on how to fuck my tongue. Her body took over that little task all on its own.

While I was tongue fucking her, I pushed my finger into her asshole again, going a little deeper this time. She really got off on that shit if the way she humped my face harder was any indication. So I upped the ante and forced the whole fat digit inside. She jumped and swallowed more of my dick, which made her cough and that shit was on.

The sensation of her throat closing and releasing around my meat, mixed with the excitement of finally having her here with her pussy on my tongue was more than my poor dick could take. I fucked up into her mouth making sure not to go too deep as she gagged and tried her best to hang on.

She did some shit with her tongue and licked around the piercings in the tip of my cock and that's all she wrote. I came a fuckload in her throat and held her head in place to take my load. I think I went blind there for a second as I offloaded the heaviest load of my life so far. "Fuck babygirl, fuck."

Her breathing was all over the fucking place when I flipped her back around to sit on my face so I could continue to tongue fuck her. She held onto the bed head as I held her spectacular ass in my hands as she rode my face.

She was wilder now, less inhibited as she enjoyed her man eating her out. When she filled my mouth with her pussy juice in one massive orgasm I had to hold her so she didn't shake herself off the fucking bed.

"You good baby?" She couldn't even answer me as her body slumped forward onto the headboard. I pulled her down into my arms as her body went through mini aftershocks. I soothed her with whispered words of love and the soft touch of my hands even as my own heart knocked against my chest. "That was amazing baby."

I held her on top of me until we were both back to normal then smacked her ass to get her moving. "Lesson one. You did good."

CREED

I couldn't very well fuck all day so at some point I had to go back to the clubhouse. The men had already been warned so they knew the deal, and I was sure they had passed that shit on to the women.

There weren't that many wives or girlfriends around this time of day, people had jobs and shit, which reminded me, I had to get her school situation squared away.

There would most likely be a few sheep hanging around looking to get fucked though, but like I said, she's gonna have to get used to the way things are around here. I held her hand the whole way over because she needed that shit.

I was very aware that my baby was green as fuck,

and had missed out on the teenage dating scene. And her entrée into sex was me for fuck sake. She didn't seem any worse for wear though, unless you count the high color in her cheeks. She was my innocent little babygirl, new to all things sexual thank fuck.

That was mostly because of me in a roundabout way. Even before I'd decided to stake my claim, subconsciously I had been cutting her from the herd. I used the protective guardian line back then though, but it was enough to keep her focused on school and not boys.

"You can sit in here with me." I didn't want her walking around out there on her own, not yet anyway. She'd had enough of an education for the day what with me shoving my dick down her neck and releasing. I didn't want her getting culture shock and looking for the closest exit.

"Come here." I didn't even want her the few feet away from me in the chair across from my desk; instead I sat her on my lap. It wasn't long before my tongue was halfway down her throat again and my hands were busy, one on her tit and one up under the skirt I'd insisted she put on for just this reason.

You'd think I hadn't just cum twice the way my cock sprung to life. "Damn baby you're so sweet." She tried hiding her face in my neck like a little kitten. "I wanna touch you again." Her eyes flew to the door in question. "Not to worry, no one will come in here."

I finger fucked her slowly as she tried not to make any noise to alert the people milling around outside. The scent of the soap she'd used to clean up after our little interlude wafted up to my nose, but as sweet as it was, it couldn't beat that underlying aroma of cunt. And hers had its very own bouquet.

"I wanna fuck you so hard it's killing me to wait." She gets shy and cute when I talk to her like that, and now was no different. "Give me your tongue babygirl let me taste you."

She might be shy but she was a hot little number. All it takes is my fingers on her clit and she's open. I was sure she'd have no problem letting me fuck her how, when and where I want. "I'm happy as shit you saved me your cherry." I pulled her head down and kissed her hard while my fingers worked her pussy over.

"You want me to eat your pussy again?" I'm addicted, so the fuck what? It's my pussy isn't it? I can stay in the shit all day if I want to. I didn't think it was the newness either, the novelty effect. It was all her and what she did to me. She nodded shyly and I helped her up onto the desk.

"If you don't want anyone to know my head's buried between your thighs I suggest stuffing these in there." I passed her her panties, which were pretty to look at but served no real purpose.

I'll be getting rid of those shits soon. When I wasn't around she would be wearing industrial strength fucking titanium drawers. I don't need the bells and whistles personally; she can go bare as long as I'm home.

She sucked on her panties while I went to town on her pussy. Her bush tickled my nose and my chin while I feasted on the nectar she produced. I wouldn't tell her that her pussy was the best I'd ever tasted, no point in reminding her that I'd been around, but her shit was on fucking point. Sweet and fresh.

I had to make it quick, no doubt someone had seen me come in and around here that meant an open invitation to come fuck with me with bullshit. I ate her out like she was dessert while she rode my tongue and cooed at me from behind the silk stuffed in her mouth.

I think I brought her off about three or four times with my mouth and she just laid there begging for more with her pleading eyes. Looks like I had a hot one on my hands. Who would've thought the shy little thing who blushed at the slightest provocation would come alive like that, damn?

I sucked up her juices as she kept cumming in my mouth. If she keeps this shit up I'm gonna be the one needing to keep up with her. She looked like she could go all day and all night. We'll see how that plays out when she rides the monster, he ain't no tongue that's for sure and her tight little pussy might go into hiding after the first taste.

"Creed, please…" Her fingers in my hair told me she was getting antsy. I finished eating her out to a massive orgasm, before pulling back to give my mouth a rest. She dropped down from the desk into my lap and without words tried to fight my cock inside her.

"No babygirl, not like this." She was frustrated poor thing, her pussy was hot and in her innocence she was doing the only thing that made sense. She wanted to ride my cock.

I held her off with soothing kisses and soft caresses while telling my dick to stand the fuck down. He didn't give a fuck about me or my half ass promises, he wanted to fuck yesterday.

She made these noises like a kitten in heat or some shit and that fuck went right to my dick. The more I tried to hold her off the more restless she became, rubbing her soft flesh against the harsh denim of my jeans.

"Look at me, baby, look at me I said." Fuck, her eyes were dilated and her breathing was gone. Fuck baby." Damn I've been cussing in front of her all day. It was her damn pussy's fault. How the fuck was I supposed to control myself with that shit in the mix?

It was nice to know that I could break down her inhibitions so easily though, but I'd be fucked if I was gonna take her on my desk for her first time. "Okay here." Instead I pulled my cock out and let her slide her pussy slit up and down against the cock rings that lined my shaft.

That seemed to satisfy her need for now and it wasn't long before I was catching her screams in my mouth. I held her while her body shook with pleasure and she tried to suck my tongue out my head.

"Go sit over there and let me get some work done babygirl." I was huffing like I'd run the Boston marathon or some fuck. I think I underestimated this virgin shit; shit was a fucking con.

Of course she was back to blushing and being shy, but I had no doubt that if I whipped the monster out she'd be on him before I could blink. Fuck if I didn't like that shit.

Now she's sitting on the chair across from me because it was the only way I was gonna get shit done, and complaining that she was bored because she couldn't get at my dick.

"You have the cutest little pout, now behave yourself while I take care of this. If you're really good I'll let you have my mouth again later." I smirked at my little freak in the making as she blushed all pretty and shit.

"Can I go look around then?" she looked over her shoulder out the door where I could hear movement. Fuck no I didn't want her out there without me where there were other swinging dicks; it was too soon.

Shit, I'm gonna have to get over this whatever the fuck it is and quick. I wasn't always going to be here, there were going to be lots of times in the future when I had to leave her to go handle shit, but not today…

The ringing of the phone with the outline reading Jason decided for me and I let her go explore with the admonishment not to leave the building. As soon as she cleared the door I answered the call. "What you got?"

"It's done, we got the cash and I put the house on the market after hacking into their accounts. Did you know they have a vacation place in the Rockies? Looks like they rent it out to the skiers. I went ahead and took that one too. All in all you look to gain a few hundred grand when all's said and done."

"Great, how soon before they're assed out? I want this shit over like yesterday."

"It won't take that long, we just need a buyer for the house, the rental is a snap, already have buyers lined up and of course none of this comes back to us."

"Good job." Next I called Law to see if there'd been any buzz from Sal and his asshole crew, but he hadn't heard anything on that front, not yet anyway. I went back to work and all but got lost.

I hadn't heard any screaming so I figured her ass was okay and though it was killing me, I left her alone to find her way around, though I must've checked my watch a thousand times. Fuck I'm a mess.

"So, that's how you do it huh." I looked up at the intrusion and threw my pen down on the papers on my desk. My face was already ice cold because I wasn't expecting this meeting, not after the way things had ended the last time I'd been in the same room with her.

"Sonia, to what do I owe this displeasure?" I knew how this shit was gonna play out, like a fucking soap opera, like I had time for bullshit. She came farther into the room and tried to close the door.

"Leave it open, my woman's out there I don't want her getting the wrong idea." If this little impromptu meeting hurt her in anyway I'm gonna drop this bitch out a window on her damn head. I'm not sure who'd told her about babygirl, most likely it was one of the sheep. Fucking females and their shit.

Granted Sonia was a different breed. She was one of those high-class pussies that think her shit's lined with gold, and all men should worship at her feet. The type that likes a little wild under her belt before settling down with some limp dick asshole who'd let her run him.

I'd fucked her once months ago and probably would've gone back for seconds had she not played the role. Apparently she hadn't been banking on the 'beast' when she decided to take that walk and it fucked up her program. In short she became hooked on my shit and wanted a hell of a lot more than was on the table.

She was one of the last tangles I had before I decided to purify myself for my girl so to speak, so that shit was dead in the water. Which I'd told her the last time we spoke. I thought she understood. What she was doing here now was anybody's guess; as long as she didn't fuck up my program we were straight.

"Did you really think it would be that easy? I told you, I'm not like the other women around here, that you use and discard at your whim. I'm taking you to court for breech of promise and deferred affection."

I laughed out loud I couldn't help it. "What the fuck are you on?" Just then I saw Jessie making her way back to the office. "Fuck, you've got to get the fuck outta here." She looked over her shoulder and her true purpose was written all over her face

"Don't even think about it bitch." My warning came too late. She went into a long-winded spiel about everything we'd done to each other that night. What the fuck, had she been taking notes? I kept my eyes on babygirl as she stood off to the side witnessing all this and that's when I heard it.

It was the same hurt sound she'd made that night in the bed. The one I'd thought was because of Sal but... I got up from my seat and moved over to her side so I could whisper in her ear. "What is it baby what hurt you?" She shook her head at me but I wasn't about to relent. The bitch behind me kept talking but I tuned her out.

"Don't shake your head at me babygirl something hurt you what was it?" The look in her eyes made me want to fuck someone's shit up royally. I looked around for the danger but there was none that I could see, so taking her face in my hands I asked her again. "What?"

"You, and her…" There was a world of fucking hurt in her voice; that shit went to my gut.

"There's no me and her sweetheart." Then it hit me, that noise, it was because of me, she hurts when she thinks…what?

"Why do you make that sound babygirl?" I saw the answer in her eyes even though she couldn't say it. "Merciful fuck." I pulled her into my arms ignoring everyone, and everything else. She makes that noise when she thinks she can't have me. I don't know how I knew, I just did.

"I'm all yours, have been for a long fucking time now." I know that even with all we'd shared this day those words must've been a shock to her, but I figured she needed that shit.

"I had a life before we met, but none of that has anything to do with us now. I never once loved any of them and I damn sure never gave anyone what's yours." I whispered the words to her for her ears only as I held her shaking form in my arms.

She didn't exactly relax but she wasn't as stiff anymore. "Look at me." I held her head back so that I could look into her eyes. "I need to deal with this, but there's nothing for you to worry about, ever; not where another female is concerned okay." She nodded her head and gave me her sweet smile before I stole a kiss.

I took her hand in mine before turning back to my unwanted guest. "You done? I got shit to do that does not include me going to jail behind your misguided ass. The door's that way." If looks could kill my ass would be toast. Too bad for her I didn't give a fuck that she had a gash instead of balls. She hurt my baby; I'd fuck her shit up no problem if she didn't get the fuck gone.

She had some choice words to say to me on her way out but my focus was on my woman and what that shit was doing to her. I ignored the empty threats and other bullshit that meant nothing.

Damn where was that venom when we fucked? Women got way too many fucking faces for me. Thinking that shit reminded me of her aunt and only soured my mood farther.

The mood was broken and the way my girl was clinging to me I knew she wasn't really as fine as she made out so I took her out of the clubhouse for a little tour around the property to take her mind off of that fuckery.

It didn't take long for her to relax completely. Maybe because I kept her hand in mine, or my hand on her ass, or an arm around her, the whole time we were walking around.

We talked about school and getting that shit taken care of and she was soon my sweet girl again, no shadows in her eyes and that sweet smile that melts my heart.

The rest of the afternoon went by without incident, thank fuck and I only had to threaten one motherfucker for ogling her. His excuse that it was because she was new might've saved his ass.

By the time the sun was going down and we'd been back in the office for a few hours with her reading, and me pretending to work, while daydreaming about the many different positions I couldn't wait to take her in, she was over this afternoon's little blip altogether.

CREED

*T*hat night there was no question of where she was gonna sleep. Her birthday was in two days and I had a shit load of stuff for her, but there was no party planned. I wasn't ready to share her yet.

I knew there was no way I was gonna have the kind of patience it would take to live through that shit knowing what was awaiting me at the end of the night any damn way.

After I'd fed her and put her to bed we'd slept with my fingers in her pussy while she slept sprawled on her back after I'd eaten her sweet cunt to orgasm.

It was the hardest fucking thing to wake up the

next morning and not fuck right away. My dick woke up looking for the pussy. I rolled out the bed mad as fuck at myself but at least there was only one more day to go.

All the day before her big day I walked around with my dick hard as fuck. I couldn't concentrate on shit all day so I rode out with her on the back of my ride. Big fucking mistake. Her body pressed into mine only took my mind to places better left untouched.

We spent the evening at the local fair grounds of all places. I guess that was as close to a party as she was gonna get since the whole crew thought their ass was invited and tagged along.

I'd finally introduced her all around and she seemed comfortable enough in the company of the big louts so I was able to rest easy on that score. She'd only met the wives and official girlfriends and when she looked at some of the sheep that were milling around I did my best to explain that shit to her without getting too in depth with it. She'll learn soon enough no use in piling it on.

I'm pretty sure that everyone within a ten-mile radius saw the dance between the two of us. We were practically joined at the hip, and if I wasn't touching her, which was a rarity, she was hanging on to some part of me.

I stayed on her ass all night, literally. There was barely two inches of space between us at any given time the whole time we were there. "You having fun babygirl?" Her eyes were bright as she moved from one display to the next.

It was such an innocent reaction for someone her age that it reminded me of the shit that I had left her to. That shit pissed me off all over again and it was only because I didn't want to spoil it for her that I kept a cool face on.

"This is so much fun Creed, and you say they're here all the time?" She was working her way through a jumbo spool of cotton candy. I had to keep an eye on her, make sure she didn't make herself sick with all the junk she'd talked me into getting her.

"Yeah baby you can come here as often as you'd like." I probably just signed myself up for a shitload of fuckery seeing as I hated this happy shit like poison, but for that look on her face I'd do pretty much anything.

I wasn't blind to the fact that in the last couple of days there'd been a kind of pattern forming between us. She's been running circles around my ass since I got her home.

I think I was overcompensating for the shit her bitch of an aunt had put her through by letting her do whatever the fuck she wanted, but I also knew that shit could be dangerous in more ways than one.

"No baby you're not getting on there." Now this fair is about as old as Methuselah's nuts give or take a couple years. I brought her for the sights and sounds but there was never any intent to let her get on the fucks.

Now she was dragging me off to what they call a rollercoaster. I could see from the ground that the tracks were missing a few slats and shit and the fuck sounded like a bucket of bolts that was about to fall the fuck apart. I don't know if it was the sugar, the sun, the atmosphere or what the fuck, but my girl kinda lost her damn mind.

"Fine I'll just go by myself then." That cute pout wasn't so cute any more, especially not when the five nosy fucks that were on me like Wolverine on Sabretooth's ass were all fucking ears. I tried glaring the fucks away but they didn't even bat a lash.

They were bent out of shape because I'd had to share a little of what was going on with them and then leashed them. Not necessarily what had prompted me to get her a few days early, but the fact that Sal's people might be seeking retribution at some point.

They seem to forget that I had served in some of the world's shittiest hellholes for the better part of my life, but then again according to Max, my sharp-shooting skills didn't mean fuck up close and personal.

If I didn't know better I'd think he was calling me a punk but I let that shit slide because my mind was on the pussy. I could deal with his insubordinate ass later. But this shit was a fucking no-no.

"Jessica, come here to me." She'd started to flounce off in the direction of the death trap that if the fucker in charge let her get on I was gonna shoot. My tone didn't alert her but my boys got restless. Their old women were old hands at this shit and were off doing their thing. They'd wanted to take her exploring with them but no.

When she was standing in front of me looking up at me with her stubborn little ass I took my time and tried to remember that she was enjoying her first taste of freedom.

"One, don't ever walk away from me when I'm talking to you, and two, if I say no, then it's no. There's no debating, no arguing, you tow the line. It can mean the difference between life and death, you understand me?"

She didn't look like she understood shit and I wondered why the fuck she had to save this shit for me. "Why can't I go? The others are going." She turned to look at the other women as they lined up. I glared at my boys who were too fucking pussy whipped to deny their women anything.

The fuckers shrugged their shoulders and pretended interest in one of the brain dead games they had here where you had to throw a ring around a bottle to win a prize. The fuck.

"Why don't I win you a bear baby wouldn't you like that?" she shook her head at me looking like twelve with big open eyes and a pout. Fuck this shit. I heard the snickers when I took her hand and went to join the line to get the damn tickets for the fuckery.

"Go on ahead babe I'm right behind you." I waited until she took her happy ass on ahead in the line looking like she'd won the lottery or some fuck. How can I deny her that kind of joy?

"Hey you, asshole, if anything happens to her on here I will skin you alive in front of all these people and feed your ass to that bear you got over there doing fucking tricks." The fucker looked at the contraption that he knew was a fucking danger waiting to happen and back at me with his Adam's' apple working overtime.

"Sir, uh, maybe you shouldn't…"

"Listen you fuck if you didn't want people getting on the shit then it should be closed. Now she wants on there and it appears what she wants she fucking gets. If she gets so much as a fucking splinter it's your ass."

I walked off and left him to ponder that shit and if he valued his life he'd make sure this piece a shit didn't so much as lurch. I raised a finger in the air at the disrespectful laughter that followed me as I climbed on the shit next to her. I'm gonna have to have a serious talk with her about her stubborn streak.

How did it look that my boys could tell their women no and stay on the ground, while I ended up here? I'm gonna make them pay for that shit too.

I forgot all about it when the death machine started up and she grabbed onto me in fear and excitement. I sat there like an ass trying to keep her fear away and making sure she enjoyed it when I didn't want her on the shit in the first place.

Her nails dug into the skin of my arm, she screamed bloody murder as she buried her face in my chest, and the whole time I was plotting the demise of ticket guy and every fuck who had anything to do with this place.

I was only too happy when it stopped and we began to file off. "Can we do it again?" I looked at her in disbelief. Now mind you, I didn't have much of a childhood so I'm pretty sure I missed a lot.

But I was also pretty sure that if something scared you to the point that you almost took the skin off another human being's arm that that would be a clear indication that you shouldn't be doing that shit again.

On top of that, tomorrow was the day I was getting inside her for the first time and I needed her ass whole for that. "No."

I grabbed her arm and pulled her away while she looked back over her shoulder. She sulked for all of five minutes, that's how long it had taken for me to win her one of the ugly ass stuffed animals they had there.

My only joy was in the fact that since I'd gone on the ride with her, the rest of the women saw it as an offense that their men hadn't done the same and were giving them hell. Now it was my turn to laugh as I had my girl under control while their asses were being dragged to hell and back.

~

Dinner that night was at an out of the way Honky-Tonk. The kind of place the locals frequent and the clientele runs to bikers and out-of-towners passing through, who wanted the Western experience.

"You have to have something more than salad and chicken wings baby, how about a steak?" She looked like I asked her to eat the whole cow. I knew she wasn't one of those tree hugger types who only ate grass and shit, but I had yet to see her eat anything substantial.

No doubt it had something to do with her home life. "A burger?" She gave me the look and I knew I was going to be in trouble with this one. I nodded my head yes and she almost levitated out of her seat.

It was going to be hell keeping shit on an even keel. Because of everything she'd been denied, I'm going to want to make up for that shit, but how do I keep from going too far left?

She seemed to have already tested the waters and knew which way the wind blows, because she knows she has me wrapped around her little finger. I'm thinking that may not be such a good thing, because if she pushed me too far she could end up hurt. Ergo the need to keep my eye on shit and keep a tight rein.

It's strange but now that we were down to the last twenty-four hours I wasn't checking my watch as much. I didn't feel that near panic feeling that had been hounding me the last month or so. She was here now and there was no force on earth that could come between us.

"You want dessert baby?" I whispered in her ear just before nuzzling it. She giggled and scrunched up her shoulders and it was so damn cute I couldn't help stealing a kiss.

My PDA was off the fucking charts. Something I'm sure the others were getting a kick out of since they'd never seen me so much as hold a woman's hand in public.

The place was starting to pick up and the noise level had risen a bit. The guys weren't exactly on alert but they weren't looking like the most inviting types either.

That shit usually drew out the crazies, a lot of these grizzly motherfuckers always have to prove who has the bigger balls and since I wasn't about to start shit with her there I wanted out as soon as possible.

"I'm stuffed Creed." She was also dragging ass if

her half closed eyes were any indication. I kissed her head and wrapped my arm around her shoulders. Her hair still had the scent of the sun and the way she just sagged into my chest made my heart kick in my chest.

"I'm taking her out of here she's beat. You clowns keep shit together." They've been known to close down a place or two just for the sake of showing their asses when I wasn't around. And since I knew that I wasn't going to see the light of day for at least the next twenty-four solid, I thought it prudent to hand out that warning.

I gave Max the 'you're in charge look and headed out with my half asleep baby. It was a quick ride back to our place, which was about all she could handle since it seemed the day had taken the wind out of her sails.

Back at the house she could barely keep her eyes open as she walked into my bedroom and threw herself down on the bed. I smiled at the way she just moved to my bed, our bed, like it was the most natural thing in the world.

By the time I took a leak and came back in she was fast asleep. I contemplated undressing her, but then thought better of it. My emotions were so high that I knew if I went anywhere near her now I'd break my word and there were only a few hours left.

I didn't think that I would sleep. I was wound so fucking tight I was all but bouncing off the walls. But somehow as soon as I laid my head on the pillow and pulled her into my arms I was out.

CREED

*J*rolled over some time later and looked at the clock. My dick and my heart thumped, it was after midnight. Fuck yeah! First time I had no issue with being awakened at fuck this shit o'clock.

She was out cold next to me looking cute and fuckable. "Happy birthday babygirl." I nibbled her ear and kissed my way down her cheek to her lips, with my hand between her legs feeling her warm pussy beneath her underwear, until she stirred.

"*Creed?*" Her voice was sleep soft and sexy, her body warm. "Yes baby wake up, I need you." Fuck, need wasn't even close to what I felt. Everything came down to this one moment.

I played in her pussy with my fingers stretching her for the last time that way before I introduced her to my cock. Her tongue in my mouth was soft and slippery as she slowly played hide and seek with mine.

I pressed my cock into the mattress to ease the throbbing pain, wondering if maybe I should've fisted myself first before taking her, so that I could at least be halfway gentle. It was too late for that shit now because her pussy juice was on my hand.

Taking my fingers out of her wet cunt, I lifted them to my mouth and sucked. She was still half asleep and cuddly when I licked the inside of her mouth, sharing her own pussy taste with her.

She came fully awake when I rolled her onto her back and settled between her legs. She was still dressed in the clothes from the night before but I was ass naked with an iron hard cock.

I let my hands do the talking in the darkened room, letting them roam at will as I continued kissing her lips a little gently at first until she started following my tongue with hers and the heat went up a couple notches.

I cupped her tit through her bra and shirt until her nipple tightened and had to grit my teeth not to rush her. No words were spoken between us when I lifted her to remove her top and bra. Just the hungriest fucking kiss I'd ever shared. I think she liked the taste of her cunt because she chased my mouth with hers, begging for my tongue.

I reached over and turned on the light needing to see her when I took her the first time, wanting her to see me. To know who it was that was claiming her now and forever.

I laid her back on the bed and pulled her skirt up over her silk covered pussy. Her scent rose up to my nostrils as I gently rolled her underwear off her ass and down her thighs. "Spread for me baby. I'm going to take you, but I need to know that you're with me every step of the way."

She was shy about it, but she soon had her legs open so that the wet pink gash between her thighs was on full display. "I'm going to eat your pussy first." I enjoyed shocking her with my raw speech, liked the way it made her nipples pebble and her ass twitch against the sheets in heat.

Licking my way down her body, I nibbled on the flesh around her navel while letting my fingers play in the hair covering her cunt. "So soft." I said the words against her flesh making her tremble.

"You ready babygirl?" I looked up at her as she nodded shyly and bit her lip. She looked so innocent and afraid I reached for her lips again. "Don't be afraid I promise to take very good care of you."

Kneeling between her legs, I let my nose run up her thigh to her pussy lips, which I sucked into my mouth. For such a tiny thing she had a fat pussy. I played with the plump lips with my tongue before pulling them open with my thumbs and staring into her pink depths.

My sons and daughters were gonna come from there, and that was only one of the many pleasures she was gonna give me from that sweet tunnel. I licked into her deep, until the tip of my tongue butted against her hymen.

I played with it a little, stretching the elastic skin before easing my finger in her to play. I fucked back and forth with first one then two fingers being sure not to break it, I wanted that shit destroyed at the end of my cock, it was my right. Mine.

I eased my tongue out and another finger in and fucked her on those until she whimpered and fucked herself hard against my palm. "I can't wait to get my rod inside you." She was tight around the three fingers I pushed inside her as I licked her clit.

Slowly drawing my fingers back from her heat, I

stuck my tongue back inside just as I felt her body tremble and quake. I was just in time to catch her nectar as it flowed from her body.

Her natural sensuality soon had her moving against my mouth as I tongue fucked her to satisfaction again and again. My jaw hurt like a son of a bitch after half an hour, but she needed this. There was no way to avoid splitting her, but I wanted to make shit as easy on her as I possibly could when I finally drove my dick inside her.

Getting up from between her thighs I grabbed the lube from the nightstand and poured a hefty amount in my hand before greasing up my pole. I didn't put any inside her, not this first time, but I knew as wet as she was, she was too tight still to take me without any extra pain.

Settling myself between her thighs once again, I stayed on my knees in the bed as I hooked hers over my arms, keeping her pussy open. "Look at me." As soon as her eyes touched mine, I let my dick nose around her pussy's entrance.

I watched as it spread her fat cunt lips around my cockhead with the steel in it on both ends. "Easy, easy." She was already starting to show strain from my entrance and I had barely breached her.

I thumbed her clit to keep her juicing as I

watched my monster spread her. My poor baby, the head of my cock was the smallest part of my rod and that shit was not small at all. "It's gonna hurt baby I'm sorry but I'll make it up to you."

I held the shaft in hand and fucked back and forth inside her with just the tip, opening her up for more. My heart was wound tight as I fought to hold back, when all I wanted was to slam into her over and over again until I emptied my life inside her.

When her pussy juice started to free flow until it was running down to the sheets beneath her ass, I let go of my cock. I hit her hymen after about inch five with eight and a half more to go fuck. Shallow pussy!

She was already hissing and cringing and I hadn't even started. My dick juice was running out her pussy mixed with her own pussy lubricant as I did a little back and forth motion in and out to loosen her up even more.

"I'm sorry baby." This shit wasn't working I was just trying to avoid the inevitable. Hard and fast, that's how I went in. She screamed and lost her breath as I held still in the tightest pussy I've ever had around my cock. "Oh fuck!"

I waited until she sucked in air and breathed again before easing halfway out and sliding back in again. Words escaped me for about two minutes while I took the time to enjoy the beauty of having her under me like this for the first time.

The reality far surpassed my every dream. There was no way I could've ever imagined the soft heat of her pussy and what it would do to that organ in my chest that I had kept out of the reach of others for so long.

I whispered softly to her as I held her close, licking the tears from her face. Releasing her legs I laid my body flat against hers so that she could feel all of me, all of her man as I moved inside her slowly, gently, loving her with my body, mind and soul.

I kissed her eyes shut before nibbling my way down to her lips for a soft lingering kiss. "So fucking sweet, my babygirl, only mine." I told her how proud I was of her for being my big girl and taking my cock that way she was. How much I'd wanted this, wanted her for so long.

Her body moved beneath mine faster and faster as her breath quickened. "I love the way your tight pussy feels around my cock. Nothing has ever felt this good before, nothing." All of this was said in a whisper as I rocked back and forth into her tight cunt.

She reacted to the words and her body tightened and squeezed as she wrapped her arms and legs around me harder. I could feel the runaway beating of her heart as our tongues mated in time with my cock slipping in and out of her.

I reared back and looked down at her. At this little bit of a thing that was drawing so much out of me so effortlessly. It was like all the bad had been wiped away, none of it mattered, not if it led me to this one moment inside her.

"You with me little love?" I held her head in my hands and watched her eyes for the truth. She was straining to take me, her pussy stretched and packed to the max.

I kept up my easy strokes in and out of her continuing to take it easy on her pussy for the next few minutes until she adjusted. Her pussy was still tight as fuck and there was still about eight and a half inches of my dick left to feed her.

I knew it wouldn't be long before my beast popped his leash and showed his ass. In fact I was amazed that he had held on this long, but as soon as she gave me the go ahead by wrapping her legs around me and tilting that pussy up to catch my cock, I went full tilt up inside her.

"Hang on babygirl, it's gonna be a rough ride but I promise to stay with you every step of the way." I'd seen the fear in her eyes and thought it wise to reassure her.

That look in her eyes, love-lust-fear. The combination pulled at my heartstrings, in a way nothing else ever have, or ever will, only her. "I will love you for as long as I draw breath."

Her cry of joy was music to my ears and sucked me in as I wrapped her up in my arms and prepared to claim what was rightfully mine. I used the steel in my cock to stimulate her even more as we begun to fuck. I'd enjoyed those few minutes of lovemaking, it was a nice introduction for my baby, but now I wanted, no needed to fuck and fuck hard.

Lifting her ass in my hands with a firm grip, I plowed into her newly awakened pussy over and over again while holding her eyes with mine. "That's it babygirl, enjoy what your man is doing to you."

She was a fucking natural the way she clung to me, digging her nails in as she cooed at me and fucked herself on my cock as I picked things up a little. I was in pussy heaven, not even in my wildest dreams did I think a pussy could feel like this.

"Fuck me that's some good pussy." I covered her

lips with mine and sucked her tongue into my mouth as I prepared to fuck her the way I've been wanting to for the last couple years. Her pussy revolted when I went too deep on my next stroke, but I had to get all the way inside her, it felt like I would fucking die if I didn't.

Looking down between us as I prepared to pound into her, harder, deeper, I saw her blood ooze out around the trunk of my thick cock and had mixed emotions. The man in me felt pride that she was mine and there was the evidence. The lover hated that he had to hurt her.

When her pussy stopped throbbing around my meat I eased my upper body down onto hers so I could hold her close and comfort her. "It's gonna feel better soon I promise."

Soft kisses to her lips and whispers in her ear soon had her relaxing beneath me again. Meanwhile, my cock was thumping away inside her impatient to fuck again.

"I have to move baby please." She shifted around beneath me. "It's okay Creed." Now she was the one soothing me with soft strokes up and down my back, opening her legs wider around my hips to accept me.

I needed that shit because it was hell holding back. I wanted to fuck and fuck hard, but her tight softness warned me that I couldn't, not to mention the blood she'd left on my dick.

I started out slow, testing her to see just how much she could take. Although I had reached the end of her pussy I still had a few inches left. If I wanted all of me in there I would have to go into her womb, would she be able to handle a womb fuck? Not many can.

I looked down between us as I drew my cock out until only the fat head was left inside, stretching her pussy lips obscenely. Then I watched her face as I surged back in, stopping just outside her cervix.

I did this a few times until she got more relaxed under me and started to move her pussy on my dick. "That's it baby, doesn't that feel good?" I rubbed her clit to get her even more stimulated, making it easier for me to slip and slide in the pussy.

I was barely hanging onto my control for her sake. When her pussy finally eased up a little on my cock I slipped deeper on my next stroke and hit her spot. Her mouth opened wide in a silent scream as her body bucked and sucked at me.

"Yes baby fuck, yes." She was taking me beautifully, her legs opening wider to accept my thrusting hips as I sped up little by little. Her tits bounced on her chests begging to be sucked, and I leaned over and sucked one into my mouth hard, while flexing my cock inside her hot cunt.

When she tugged on my hair to bring my mouth to hers I knew she was finally with me all the way. "This what you want?" I let her suck on my tongue while I concentrated of giving her the fuck of her life.

The bedsprings squeaked with each pound into her and her moans got louder around my tongue. When we both needed to breathe I pulled away and buried my face in her neck sucking the skin between my teeth.

She squeezed around my cock when I bit into her and I took the risk of fucking into her harder, going after her G-spot again and again. Her soft walls scraped along the metal piercings in my cock and had pre-cum streaming out of me.

In the back of my mind I kept telling myself to ease off, go slow, but my cock had a mind of its own. "Too long, I waited…" Couldn't finish the words, too fucking caught up.

I pulled her chest harder into mine as our hips moved faster and faster together. "So good baby." She called out my name in that high-pitched voice tinged with a little bit of fear as her body shook in a massive orgasm.

Her pussy clamped down around my dick and locked my shit down. I shot off hard, volley after volley of thick cum shot straight into her womb. This set her off again and she damn near skinned my back down to the bone as she bucked beneath me.

I pulled back and looked down at her face as she got lost in her pleasure. "Fucking amazing." I let her fuck herself to another orgasm on my cock as my balls drained inside her; I was already looking forward to round two.

I eased out of her pussy and dropped to my side pulling her with me. Her body was going through aftershocks and I had to soothe her as we both caught our breath.

"Come." I lifted her into my arms and took her into the bathroom to clean her up. She stood in the shower while I set the water temp. When it was doable I pulled her in front of me and got busy washing the blood from between her thighs.

I took my time and cleaned out her pussy until I ended up dropping the cloth and fingering her. I moved slower this time, now that I knew what she felt like I wanted to savor the buildup.

"Hmm, spread your legs for me baby." She opened and I used my fingers to fuck her while she leaned against me and let herself feel what I did to her. "This no longer belongs to you, I claim it as mine, what's mine I keep, and I don't ever fucking share; never forget that." I guess that was as good a proposal as any.

"Here!" I gave her the soap and watched her face turn three shades of red as she took my cock in her hands and returned the favor. As soon as my boy was clean I wanted in her again. "Are you too sore to take me again right now?"

She seemed fascinated by my dick as she ran her hand up and down the metal that decorated it. "What are these for?"

"Did they feel good inside you?" I countered her question with one of my own. She blushed and nodded her head as she examined me.

"That's what they're for, to make your pussy feel good." She didn't need to know that I'd done it in the last year or so as a distraction. It was part of my countdown, my cleansing ritual if you will, when I was preparing myself for her.

I'd never fucked anyone else with the steel in my rod she was the first and the last. We were both playing with each other now, her hands on my cock, my fingers stuffed in her cunt. I was soon helping her to her knees in the shower so she could take me into her mouth.

"Suck my cock babygirl." She was a little awkward at first, but that was more from shyness than anything else, but she soon remembered what she'd been taught and went to work, teasing my piercings with her teeth and tongue.

"Pull off." I knew it was because it was her that I was so close so fast, but I didn't want to cum in her mouth. Tonight, all my seed was reserved for her womb. That shit had a purpose.

I wrapped her in my robe after drying her off and sat her in the sitting room so I could change the sheets. "Here drink this." I gave her a shot of whiskey and grinned at her sour face after she downed. I knew she was gonna need that shit before the night was over though.

I folded the sheet with her blood on it, my chest filled with pride as I placed it carefully into the bottom of the trunk at the end of my bed. Don't think I didn't give serious thought to flying that shit from my porch. Let all the motherfuckers within a fifty-mile radius see that shit and know that this one woman was claimed. Lock stock and barrel.

"Come." I held my hand out to her to come to me once the bed was nice and freshly made. I winced a little at the way she walked like her pussy hurt. Shit

213

Creed, if you were any good you'd let her heal before going at her again.

That shit sounded good but I knew there was no way it was gonna happen. I was gonna do my best to go easy on her little pussy for the rest of the night though, but almost three years of pent up lust was waiting to be unleashed. And now that my boy had had a taste he wasn't about to put up with the waiting shit.

I hit the play button on the stereo and filled the air with nice seventies music, before getting the little box I'd taken out of hiding and placed in the night stand. I knew exactly when I wanted to give her that particular gift.

I laid down beside her and just held her naked warmth against me, neither of us saying anything just holding each other and letting the night sink in. When she started playing with my ink, my dick twitched and I brought her fingers to my lips.

"How are you feeling, your pussy still sore?" I tested her with my fingers and thought she wasn't as hot as before, her cunt was still swollen. I eased my way down on the bed until I was between her thighs.

Opening her up with my fingers I studied the damage. Inside her I could see the remnants of her hymen just a torn piece of flesh, but it was her red, swollen inner walls that concerned me.

I licked all around her pussy to try to bring some comfort, before pushing her legs back towards her ears and licking from her tight ass hole to the tip of her clit. I lapped at her flesh until she juiced, then being ever so careful, I sank my tongue all the way inside her.

Her pussy clung onto my tongue as the sweetest fucking thing I'd ever tasted burst forth in my mouth. I gulped that shit down as fast as I could, still some dribbled onto my chin.

I made some inhuman sounds in my throat that I don't think I had ever heard before as her taste overpowered me. I pulled her pussy on and off my stiff tongue as I tongue fucked her to a screaming orgasm.

Only then did I feel safe climbing up her body and slipping my hard cock deep into her belly. I held still as we both adjusted, and reached over to the nightstand for the little box I'd left there.

My heart opened and flowered in my chest as I lifted the three and a half carat diamond solitaire from its cushion. "Give me your hand." She lifted it to me, her eyes wide with wonder.

"This says that all of you is mine." I slipped it on

her finger and only breathed easy again when it fit perfectly. "To the grave baby." I took her mouth as tears rolled down her face.

WE STAYED in bed all that day and I think I fucked my cock raw more than once. Her pussy had grown accustomed to being pounded by round four and by midday that day she was the one on my dick whenever she caught her breath.

We talked about the future, and what we both wanted. I thought it best to get everything squared away from the get, now that she was officially mine.

"So I can't have male friends?" It was the second day and we were in the kitchen making breakfast together. I'd just told her some shit that was a big fucking no-no.

"That would be negative."

I didn't look at her to see how she was taking what I had to say to her, because at the end of the day, it really didn't matter. The shit I was telling her was for her own good. Most of it would most likely save her from future ass whippings.

Like, the fact that she was never allowed to go anywhere without my knowing ever. All friends had to be vetted by me, and the one that she'd lathed onto, no fucking swinging dicks allowed in her vicinity.

"Fine, not like I've really had that many before, but…what if the teacher pairs me up with someone and it's a he?" I'ma have to rethink this school shit.

"Then I guess you'll be failing that fucking class. The only men allowed anywhere near you are the ones under my command and even them you keep your fucking distance from…wait, they're males in your class?"

I don't know why the fuck that shit made her hoot and holler and throw herself off the stool I was dead serious.

After she calmed down and went back to flipping the pancakes I went back to squeezing oranges. She was looking hot as fuck in the shirt I'd taken off a few nights before and I could still smell my scent now mixed with hers on it.

"Hit the switch babe." I moved in behind her and lifted the back of the shirt exposing her fine ass. She caught on fast enough and turned off the fire while I walked her over to the center island and leaned her over.

I ran my piercings along her slit up and down to her ass hole, before slipping into her pussy. There was still that little catch in her breath at my first entry and it was going to be a while before she was able to take me completely without slight discomfort, but she was handling me very well for being new at this.

"Push your ass back and spread your legs I'm going in deep." As soon as she heeded my words I gave my dick free reign to fuck into her pussy. I grabbed two fistfuls of her ass and started pounding the shit out of her pussy for the second time that morning.

The first session had been not long ago in bed as soon as I rolled over. I'd slid my morning hard into her from behind while cuddling her close and rode us both to a nice sweet climax.

Now this was the way I needed to fuck her to get my day started. Nice hard and deep! The kind of fuck that made her look back at me like 'what the fuck' with her mouth hanging open and her pussy grabbing my shit like it would never let go.

What a sight she made. Shirt lifted to above her ass cheeks, legs spread wide as the morning sunlight filtered through the window and her pussy stuffed full of cock. My little cock queen!

I plowed her belly for the half an hour before giving her my jizz. As soon as I'd emptied the last drizzle into her snatch and pulled out she assumed the position; on her knees with my cock in her mouth to clean up.

She took to that shit like a natural every time, never missing a beat since the first time I'd told her that that's what I liked. I held the back of her head as I fed her my cock, easing into her throat and then back out until she gagged on my shit and a river of spit ran down her chin.

Helping her to her fee I snogged her while holding her ass in my hands. "Morning sweetheart." I kissed her nose and set her away from me so we could go back to what we were doing.

My phone rang but I ignored that shit the same way I'd been doing for the last day and a half. I knew if it was an emergency Max or Jason would've been at my door already. Besides, the shop was right next-door. As long as the shit was still standing we were fine.

"Do you have to go now?" She frowned at me. So fucking cute.

"Nope." I kissed her on my way to the breakfast nook with the dishes to set the table, as she stood by the stove. She was a kick ass cook, but when she told me how her aunt had made her do all the cooking since she was about thirteen I wasn't too thrilled about her skills anymore.

We'd got into it a little bit after that because I didn't want her cooking after she'd imparted that bit of news, but she'd convinced me that she liked doing it, and it was one of the things she was looking forward to doing for me. After hearing that how could I resist?

Babygirl

It's almost like a dream, but I know it's real. The rock on my hand is proof of that, not to mention the constant soreness between my thighs. The ache is like the best thing I ever felt, because it reminds me always that he was there. He's always there.

I blushed at the thought as we moved around the huge kitchen together. When he'd told me that he'd built his home with me in mind, along with all the other things that he'd claimed, it was a little hard for me to believe.

His words were so far removed from my reality.

It was hard to accept that while I was pining away with love for him that he was doing the same. I'm still having a hard time accepting, even after all that we've shared in the last day and a half, but boy do I want to.

The only thing I have to overcome now is this new fear of letting him out of my sight. Each time the phone rings or I hear an engine outside I get this sick feeling in my tummy.

When we're lying in bed together every move he makes, is noticed by me, and I cling to him like a love sick puppy which he doesn't seem to mind, but for how long? I think I've grown addicted.

Before, when my love for him was unrequited, I could keep it all in my head where it was perfectly beautiful. Now he had brought it out into the open and it was real and beautiful and perfect in its own way yes, but Creed was all man and some of that reality was bigger than I could've imagined.

I worried constantly now about the oddest things. Things like did he love me as much as I loved him? Would he leave me now that he'd got what he wanted? I knew nothing about relationships and what I was supposed to do, and quite frankly I felt out of my depth.

Add the fact that Creed is so bigger than life and

everything that is beyond perfect in my eyes, and I just knew I wouldn't be able to hold onto him forever. That thought more than any scares me to my soul.

"Hey, you're making that noise again, look at me. Right here babe, and I'm not going anywhere." He took my face in his hand as I leaned over the table to place the platter of pancakes there.

He stared into my eyes almost willing me to see the truth of his words there. "Come here." He pulled me around the little bench seat that was built into the window behind the table, and onto his lap.

With my chin in his hand he studied me for the longest while before saying anything. I was beginning to get antsy by the time he opened his mouth to speak. "I don't like that you're having such a hard time believing me. If I say I love you, that's just what the fuck I mean."

He frowned at me and I almost laughed because he actually thought it was that easy. That all he had to do was say the words and that would make it so. "I want to believe…"

"What the fuck? What did I say? Do you really think I would've fucked you if I wasn't all the way gone? The fuck you take me for? That fucking lasso on your finger is as good as a branding iron and I put it there." He didn't say anything for the next few minutes just studied me like a bug under a microscope.

"Am I to believe then that you don't really love me either? That it's just my dick that make you cry that shit out when I'm in you?" He didn't seem to like that idea very much and the dark scowl on his face was testament to that.

"Of course not, don't be silly, you know I'm in love with you." My face went up in flames and I was about to throw up, but I managed to get those words out.

"I don't know shit baby apparently around here we throw that word around but it has no real meaning." It took me a minute to realize I'd hurt his feelings or his pride, I don't know which one because I suck at this.

Now it was my turn to reassure and I found that it was easier being on this end. "I'm sorry I didn't mean to make you feel that way, it's just hard for me to accept that someone as perfect as you could love someone like me."

That got me a deep tonsil clearing kiss and a gruff don't be an ass and a pat on the butt. "Stay." I'd tried getting off his lap to go to my side but he held me in place. "Open."

I opened my mouth for his offering of pancakes and that easily the mood changed back to one of lightness.

For the rest of the day when we weren't making love we were whispering to each other. He seemed to know that I needed a lot more than words though, and so set about showing me in all the ways he knew how, just what I meant to him.

By the time he rolled away from me in the early morning hours, I was a lot more convinced that this was real, that he was truly mine.

And when he wrapped his body around mine, as if he were protecting me from the unknown, I dropped off into slumber feeling loved and secure.

CREED

Three days of fucking and I still wasn't done but my woman was. If I kept after her like this she'd walk crooked the rest of her natural life. I slipped out from under the sheet and looked back at her in my bed where she belonged.

Her beautiful hair was spread out on the pillows, her cheek, the one that was turned to me, was a little red from my scruff that I had been trying to keep under control without much luck since we'd been locked away together.

I hadn't had time for anything but her. It was like I'd found my favorite drug and was trying my best to OD on the shit in one go, addictive.

I looked down at my cock, which had dried cum and pussy juice from tip to base because when we'd finally rolled away from each other about three hours ago I was too fucking done to give her her usual after fuck bath.

My morning wood bounced in the air as I walked into the bathroom for a nice hot shower. It was the first one I'd be taking solo in three days. I missed her already because I knew I had to join the rest of the world today and leave her here.

With my head bowed under the spray I let the water beat down on me as I took what felt like the first easy breath in days. I think I've been waiting for the other shoe to drop. There's no way anything that fucking perfect could be mine.

I kept searching my heart for any reason why I would deserve her and what she's brought me. Then at the oddest moments I'd have the most fucked up fears, like losing her, or something else going wrong because that's what the fuck happens when shit's this good.

But then I only had to look at her and that feeling in my heart would make me feel ten feet tall and fucking invincible, and I would be back on track again.

Her little doubt fest the day before still bothered me a little, but I was hoping with time she'd get over whatever the fuck that was. I didn't mind her feeling that way about everybody else, but fuck if I'll accept that from her when it comes to me.

I switched off the water and headed back to the room where she was still out. I got dressed as quietly as I could, all the while wondering if I should wake her to say bye or just let her rest.

Last night she'd cried for the first time because she'd been too tired and sore to take me but her pussy was being greedy. I was beyond fucking pleased that she had the same hunger for me as I did her.

I'd eaten her sore pussy until she juiced up before fucking into her. I didn't mean to be a beast, but knowing that I was gonna have to leave her today, there was no way I wasn't gonna have her.

After I was dressed and ready to roll I leaned over her sleeping form on the bed and nuzzled her awake with my lips in my favorite spot on her neck. "Wake up and tell your man bye babygirl."

"Creed?" She cuddled into my pillow, my sweet little kitten before her eyes came open slowly. She sat up and pulled the sheet over her tits as she looked around the room and then back at me.

"Where are you going?" Too cute.

"I have to go to work today baby, I missed a crap load of stuff and I'm sure there's even more waiting for me to tend to." She pouted and looked up at me with sad eyes.

I'm sure that if I was feeling the pain of separation it must be twice as hard for her. Fuck, in all my planning I hadn't given any thought to what she was supposed to be doing while I was doing my thing.

It wasn't like she could sit in the office all day and watch me, and school was out for at least the next two months. "Baby when I get back later we'll decide on what you'll do with your days, but for now just rest up okay."

She didn't look too happy about that shit if the look that came over her face was anything to go by. "Who's going to be there?"

"Come again?" I wasn't sure what she was getting at. She'd met most of the crew, but why the fuck should she care who was going to be over there?

"Is that girl going to come back?" Damn, I didn't once think she would still be thinking about that shit, she hadn't mentioned it at all in the past three days. She looked so fucking unhappy at the thought that it was the first time I realized she might be just as possessive of me as I was of her.

"Would it bother you if she was?" Don't ask me why the fuck I asked her that since I knew for damn sure she wouldn't be bothered. Not after I'd damn near emptied my life inside her snatch in the last three days and had pledged my undying love with every other breath. "YES."

Whoa, okay I guess she would be. "Then she won't be. Come 'ere." I pulled her and the sheet up into my arms. I was thinking just a hug goodbye to get me through the next few hours, but one whiff of her hot pussy scent and my dick came alive.

"You feel that, that's all for you." I took her hand and put it on my cock, which was straining against my jeans. She did the funniest damn thing then. Pulling out of my arms, she leaned over and kissed my cock behind the zipper making him jump.

"Good morning." She was talking to my dick; get the fuck out, not my innocent little babygirl. She grinned up at me as she rubbed me with her soft hand. "He wants to come out and play."

Okay for the past three days I've had her sequestered pretty much in my bedroom practically tied to my bed. In that time I have seen many sides to her as was to be expected. After all, I had opened her eyes to a whole new thing called sex, which she took to like a natural thank fuck.

We've made love, fucked and hit on about all there is to do between a man and his woman, but in all that time and with all that we'd shared, I hadn't seen this playful side of her.

"I gotta go baby." She shook her fucking head at me and attacked my zipper. "Not yet please Creed." Fuck she's got me and she knows it. All it takes is her saying my name in that way of hers and I'm putty in her hands.

"What is it you want bad girl?" I was pulling the Henley back off over my head as she unzipped me and whipped out my freshly washed cock. "One minute." She hopped off the bed and headed for the bathroom leaving me with my dick hanging out of my jeans.

He didn't give a fuck that I had shit to do no more than she did. All he knew was that his mama wanted to play and he was game. I shucked the jeans the rest of the way off and got back into bed waiting for her.

I heard the water hitting the sink and figured she was giving herself a rush bath to get fresh for her man. She's very self-conscious about that shit, me I'd dive into her pussy after a whole day of hardcore fucking and don't bat a lash.

She came back in and some of her shyness had kicked back in. "Don't back down now babygirl, you wanted to play, let's play." Part of her renewed shyness could be because I was laying back on the bed stroking my cock in wait for her return.

Her eyes followed my hand and fuck if they didn't glaze over and her mouth moved as if it were already wrapped around my meat. I like the way she walked over to me as if drawn to the hunk of flesh between my thighs. I loved it even more when she climbed between those thighs and lowered her head to my cock.

I hissed when she teased my cock rings with her tongue before licking the pre-cum that had gathered on my cockhead. "Umm. Yum." What the fuck had gotten into her anyway? I wasn't about to complain though. Let her have her fun. I hope her pussy wasn't too sore for what I was about to lay on her.

I watched as she made love to my dick, licking and sucking her way up and down my length, teasing my balls with her quick tongue, before heading back to the tip for more juice.

She kept her eyes on mine when I grabbed the back of her head. "Stop fucking with me babygirl and suck this cock." And boy did she suck my shit. She'd been getting her practice in in the last few days and my baby could handle her shit.

When she got too fucking good at taking me into her throat, which I had been teaching her to do the last few days as well, I grabbed fistfuls of her hair and helped her on and off my dick with that amazing mouth of hers.

"Pull off baby, first load of the day, you know the rules. How do you want it?" She gave my cock a goodbye kiss before turning around with her ass in the air. Yep, queen of the deep fuck.

I lined up behind her and played around in her pussy with my fat cockhead, letting it spread her then pulling back before sliding it up and down her pussy slit to her asshole. I let my piercings do the job of titillating her, which made her ass twitch and her pussy leak.

She looked over her shoulder and growled at me like a bitch in heat, fuck yeah I like that shit. "You want this?" I slammed into her pussy hard. Although her pussy was still new and still as tight as the first time, she was a little more comfortable taking me at any pace. Still I was always worried about hurting my woman.

When she grabbed the sheets, arched her back and spread her legs, I knew she was ready to fuck. She wasn't looking for lovemaking this A.M. She wanted me in her belly moving shit around. That's what this position usually meant for us since she was such a tiny little thing and my thirteen and a half inch dick was damn near half her size. I gave her what she wanted as usual; I aim to please her always.

Grabbing a fistful of her hair in one hand I greased up two fingers of the other in her pussy juice and pushed them into her ass. "Let's fuck." I growled in her ear and flexed my dick in her womb as she keened deep in her throat.

Since she'd pretty much showed me what she wanted I didn't take it easy on her pussy, just went in full boar, driving my dick into her as hard and as deep as I could without hurting her. it never failed to amaze me the look of my pierced cock stretching her tight little pussy, and the way she took me.

She still cried for pain even though there were still a few inches left to feed her. But I had learned her cries in the last few days. This was one of those 'it hurt so good' cries so I knew to work her up to the 'my pussy's gonna hurt all day and I'm gonna have to sit on your face' fucks.

I ran my fingers down the deep arch in her back to the top of her ass and smacked her tight flesh, watching it bounce back into place. I slid first one, then two fingers back into her ass and felt her pussy twitch in appreciation.

"I love this ass." I sawed my fingers back and forth in her newly awakened ass and felt her pussy tighten around my cock even more. She was giving my cock quite the workout with her magic pussy that had been made just for me, and soon I needed to get balls deep. Nothing else would do, and I knew just how to get there.

"I want you on your back, I wanna see you when I come deep in your belly." I pulled out carefully and turned her onto her back, lifted her legs over my shoulders and slid my cock back up in her.

"Ooooohhhh…" Her eyes rolled back in her head and her pussy juiced. I took her ass in my hands and leaned into her so I could bite into her tit flesh while I fucked her deep.

Her heels pounded my back as I tried to fuck her through the mattress with long deep strokes. As always I got that urge to consume and it wasn't long before I was leaving bite marks all over her chest and neck.

I sucked the flesh under her left nipple into my mouth and held until I was sure I'd marked her. I was satisfied to see the purple black color appear before I moved to its twin and gave it the same treatment.

"Creed…"She grabbed her stomach just around her navel and I knew she was feeling the pressure of my dick on her organs. "I'm close baby, fuck. Take my cock." I pounded into her as she screamed and her back arched deep.

"That's it, I'm cumming baby cum with me." Too fucking soon, but her pussy always did this shit to me. I reached for her clit and pressed down as I went into her cervix for a nice end time womb fuck.

Oh yeah, she went nuts and rode my cock hard as she came hard enough to lift me off the bed. I shot off inside her like a volcano erupting, giving her a heavy dose of early morning cream.

We were both fucked up for the next five minutes as I laid on top of her breathing like it was my last. I had no doubt I was too heavy for her much slighter frame, but she didn't complain.

Instead she wrapped her arms and legs around me and did that cooing thing she does when she's been well and truly fucked, which has been every time I've taken her.

I pulled out, smacked her ass and dragged her off to the shower where she got her pussy eaten out before I escaped her greedy ass and went to get some shit done across the way.

THE PLACE WAS STILL STANDING SO I guess the fucks

hadn't been up to too much shit in my absence. There was a shitload of messages on both phones, which I'd have to sift through soon but first things first.

"Max anything I need to know about?"

"Nope, we took care of the Cartel situation just like you said, no muss no fuss. It might take the fire department a few to figure out that the shit was arson. But then again they might not look too hard seeing as how everyone wanted that shit gone. Unless the asshole owner goes after the insurance."

"Fuck him he knew what they were doing and he let them, that's the price he pays. Anything else?"

"Yeah, Jason's been trying to reach you, won't tell me what the fuck but something's up."

Shit, I'd all but forgotten about that shit. "I'll get back to him soon, what about this place anything happening around here I should know about?"

"Nah not really, just that Deidre's back."

"De who?"

"You know, Skins, came back last night, wasn't sure what you wanted to do about that so figured I'd wait on your say so."

"What the fuck? Why is she back here now?" As if I didn't know. "Where's her sister?" I'd overlooked this shit; it hadn't even registered on my radar of shit to watch out for.

"They were both here last night 'til late tying one on you know, the usual." Fuck, Deidre is a complicated issue. She was the old woman of one of my boys that had got killed by a rival asshole in a bar fight a few years ago.

After his death we were all pretty fucked up and one night one thing led to another and she and I ended up rolling around on her bed trying to outrun our own demons.

In the morning I felt like shit for fucking my boy's piece even though he was gone, but Deidre was in love or some shit. It wasn't easy getting her to accept that that shit was a one off and that it was never going to be repeated.

She did everything in her power to change my mind and then when she realized that shit wasn't gonna work shit got ugly. She'd played the pregnancy card with me then and pissed me the fuck off because I never took a woman without covering my shit up.

When I'd called her on her shit she'd hightailed it out of here. That had been over two years ago and I hadn't heard or seen her since. Her sister was hooked up with another member and was still here, so I can only surmise that words were spoken about my new living arrangements and that's why she was back here.

"Keep an eye on her and let me know as soon as she shows her face. Jessie's home today but she might wander outside or some fuck at some point I don't want her bothered."

"You want me to put someone on the house?"

"No Max, I'm six feet away I can keep an eye on my woman thank you, you just keep the rest of these fucks in line while I take care of the inventory and shit that I've been neglecting." The jackass grinned and headed out back to the garage.

I had a full operation here, bike shop, garage and the clubhouse where some of the men slept rough. There were rooms where some perverted shit went on that I wasn't even gonna think about and then there was the main room with the bar.

My office was more towards the back near the meeting room. I could see my house from there and had eyes and ears in the place already, something no one knew about but me. Like I said, I don't trust one fuck.

"Yeah Jason what's up?" I called him first as soon as I reached my desk. "Hey boss, I took care of that little thing everything's squared away nice and clear.

Only hiccup is when the new owners go to take possession, you think of how you want to handle that side of things?"

"Not really I've been busy but I'll come up with something." I hung up the phone and went into the account he'd told me the money was waiting in. It only took me a few minutes to transfer it to the account I'd opened for her nine years ago.

With that settled I took care of some of the shit on my desk and made a few calls to suppliers. I had a moment of regret over the whole Deidre situation in the middle of all the shit I was doing.

Even though things had ended badly, I couldn't place all the blame at her door. She'd been a friend once and we'd both been in a pretty dark place after what happened to Ian. I looked out towards my place where my heart was and let that shit go, I can't go back and change shit.

By the time I came up for air it was noon and my guts was groaning at me, reminding me that I'd missed breakfast and mealtime was staring me in the face. I knew just what I wanted for lunch. My dick did too because he sprung right the fuck up.

I closed down the shit that I'd been working on and started to head out when the phone on my hip rang. I grinned when I saw the name in the screen. Nosy fuck was probably calling to tease my ass about being whipped. "Law my man what's...?"

"We've got trouble." His words wiped the smile off my face and started my feet moving faster towards the door.

"Tell me." I looked out the window to where she was just coming out my side door with something in her hand and a happy smile on her face. I knew the only reason he'd be calling me like this is if it was about her.

"You need to get here brother. By the way do you need the priest or whatever the fuck? I think my boys are holding him hostage here or some fuck because he's always under foot these days." I thought of the ring I'd put on her hand while fucking her the second time.

"Yes, we'll be there in a few." If it was really bad he would've told me some of it, but it was bad enough for him to call me in. It was a given that the shit had to do with her fucked up relatives.

I was on the way out to meet her when I heard her voice raised in anger. That shit coming on the back of the call had my pressure rising and I wasn't in the mood. Maybe that's why I didn't stop to ask what the fuck was going on when I came upon the situation outside the clubhouse door, but just reacted.

"What the fuck are you on?" I grabbed Deidre by the scruff of her neck and flung her aside. Babygirl was busy picking up the plate she'd been bringing to me for lunch. When she looked at me with tears in her eyes I wanted to kill.

"Come here baby." She was my only thought, making her feel better and removing those tears from her eyes. I didn't even look at Deidre.

I don't know what the fuck gets into females, but that jealousy shit seems to give them extra strength while at the same time draining every fucking brain cell out their heads.

As she moved towards me, Deidre, a woman I hadn't seen or spoken to in over two years rushed her. By now most everyone was outside watching this shit unfold in disbelief.

I moved to get in between them again but a whirlwind flew past me, and all I saw were arms and legs flying. I stood in shock for a hot minute before moving. "Get this bitch outta he... Baby quit it." What the fuck?

I never saw her like this before, she was pissed the fuck off and breathing fire as I dragged her away while Max got the idiot woman up off the floor.

"Inside." I pointed babygirl to the door behind me trying to get her out of the line of fire just in case it wasn't over. She gave me a look that said she'd kick my ass too and I figured she was at about the end of her rope; I don't blame her.

"Baby please go inside so I can deal with this. I do not want you in the middle of this shit, so unless you want me hauled out of here in cuffs do what the fuck I say."

She gave the now loudly complaining Deidre one last withering look before doing as I said. As mad as I was at this shit, I knew I was partly to blame.

I should never have slept with her, not when she was so vulnerable. It didn't matter that we were both drunk as fuck that night, I shoulda known better. For that reason I couldn't do what I would normally do in a situation like this where she'd put her hands on my woman, which is break her fucking neck.

I turned to look at Deidre then and was faced with yet another fire breathing dragon. I do not need this fuckery at this particular moment in my existence.

"You gave her a ring?" Those were the first words she threw at me. I really didn't have time for this shit, but I couldn't see me treating her like one of the sheep, not after the relationship I'd had with her old man.

On the other hand, my woman had just walked away from me looking like I'd gutted her or some fuck and that shit was not cool.

"Everybody get back to what you were doing. Max I'm gonna need you, Cam and Rog in the next five we got shit to do." I waited until they left and the only ones there were she, her sister and I. "You can leave too."

Pam looked like she wanted to argue but the way I felt right then if she gave me any shit I would've thrown her ass off my place never to return again.

She must've seen the look on my face because she had the sense to walk the fuck away. "You wanna tell me what the fuck you're doing here now, why you'd bring this shit to my door? The only reason I'm not planting a foot in your ass for fucking with her is because of him and the friendship we had, but that was your last get out of jail free card."

"How can you say that? You promised him remember, you said you'd take care of me after he was gone." She was breathing hard and close to tears with fire shooting out of her eyes. After two years of no contact I'm thinking this shit was not normal.

"And you took that to mean what? That I was

going to make you my woman, what the fuck ever gave you that idea?" The whole fucking mess was pissing me the fuck off.

"But that night, in bed, we were so good together." She looked genuinely hurt and I felt like shit. How had I misread that whole situation so badly? "I thought we were offering each other comfort, that's all it meant to me I'm sorry, I didn't mean to mislead you." Hadn't I said this shit before? Why would she think things had changed now?

"It's not fair, Ian was a good man, he was all I had and then you…" She started to shake and it was then that I got a good look at her. She had wasted away to almost nothing in the time she'd been gone. That shit hurt me to my core, that I might've had a hand in doing that to her, fuck.

"What the fuck did you do to yourself? Come here." I didn't think anything of it when I wrapped my arms around her to offer comfort. Before we'd confused shit by jumping into bed together, we'd been pals. A hug between us was as easy as passing a beer.

I'd spent many a night on her couch laughing and unwinding with her and her old man back in the day when shit was just getting started. I guess you can say we'd grown together in this new life, each learning our way as best we could and shoring each other up.

"I'm sorry I hurt you, that was never my intent, but you have to let it go and move on. It's not me that you want it's him. You think you can recapture that by being with me but you can't. And Deidre, I love her, even when I was with you I knew it was going to be her, I've known for a long time now, I'm sorry."

She cried into my chest, heartbreaking body wracking sobs that tore at me and made me relive the loss of my pal all over again. I turned to take her inside and my eyes met Jessie's and fuck me if she didn't look like I'd betrayed her.

"Wait here Deidre." I whistled for Max to come to me and passed her off when he did. "Take her to her sister. Deidre I have to go I'm sorry."

I had nothing more to give her right then, I had more pressing matters on my hands. Like the young girl I'd just had chained to my bed for the last few days, who was now looking at me like I was the worse kind of scum for betraying her. Fuck me side-ways with a claw hammer.

I didn't spare my old friend a second glance as I turned and went to face the woman that looked like she was going to kick my ass or crawl into a hole and die. "Baby…" She evaded my hand when I reached for her and walked away from me. "Uh-uh babygirl, we don't do that come here to me." I stood my ground and waited for her to obey me.

She folded her arms and kept her back turned. I needed this shit today. "Look at me." Still nothing, when the hell did she get to be this damn stubborn?

"Jessica I said look at me." Maybe I shoulda left that shit alone because the look on her face when she did obey me was just evil. "There're things going on here that you don't understand. I told you before that you don't have anything to worry about where other women are concerned…"

She took her ring off and threw it across the room. I have to say, I've been in some situations before in my life, but nothing and I mean nothing had ever surprised me as much as what she just did. I looked from the ring to her and back a couple times before the pressure in my head came down a little.

"Pick that shit up are you nuts?"

"No, I wanna go home I don't want to stay here." How the fuck can you be crying and breathing fire at the same damn time? I knew that the anger that hopped up inside me just then was misguided, but I'd be fucked if she were ever going to get away with shit like this. Total fucking disrespect, fuck no. I moved over to her and grabbed her this time when she tried to walk away.

Without uttering another word I walked her over to where the diamond was glistening up at me from the corner. I held her by the back of the neck and bent her over. "Pick it up." She got the good fucking sense not to rebel this time and did as I said.

I was suddenly pissed the fuck off at everyone and everything. This isn't how the fuck I saw this day going, not four days after I'd taken her for the first time. We were supposed to be happy as fuck that we were finally together, but instead it seems like everyone was conspiring to fuck with us, and she wasn't making shit any easier with her hard-headed stubborn ass.

I marched her through to my office just in case someone entered the club just then; I needed privacy for this shit. I started stripping her out of her clothes as soon as the door closed.

"Stop it Justice, I don't want you to touch me." She's never called me anything but Creed and I didn't know quite how to take the switch, but the last part of that statement was a big fucking red flag. I pulled her up so I could look into her eyes while I told her some home truths.

"I understand you're mad, but you don't ever

fucking say those words to me again, and take that fucking tone down a notch." I never thought in a million years I would be this close to spanking her ass, not so soon anyway.

"I said there was some shit here that you don't understand. Deidre was the wife of a friend nothing more nothing less. I can't just cast her off like I did Sonia, I made a promise."

None of that shit was getting through I realized that shit when she actually put her hands over her ears and closed her eyes, essentially shutting me out. Fuck this shit, it's like she'd been saving all this fuckery up for me. She sure as fuck never defied anyone else.

I took a deep breath and hoped for patience, I wasn't equipped to deal with his shit. Since she wasn't listening and her body was tense as fuck I tried a new tactic.

After I'd stripped her down to nothing I took her over to the chair behind my desk and pulled her down in my lap. "I'm sorry she attacked you baby, I hope you know I would never let anyone harm you."

How could I explain that I was complicit in this shit? That I had my own guilt to deal with where this situation was concerned? I didn't even know what the fuck was going through her head because she wasn't talking, and this was new territory for us.

"Babygirl…"

"Don't call me that you don't mean it, you chose her…" She started to fucking hyperventilate and scared the fuck outta me. "Baby calm down, I didn't choose her over you, please listen to me." I tried hugging her to me to get her to calm down.

She wasn't having that shit; she stiffened up on me and tried to get off my lap. "Stay where you are." I held her even tighter, my guts in shreds because I'd hurt her and I hadn't meant to. How had I fucked this shit up so royally?

"I hate you." I took the blow but held on, telling myself that she didn't mean it, that it was just the hurt talking. "Jessie please don't do this, give me your ring." I took it out of her tightly closed fist and forced it back on her finger while she cried like her heart was broken in a million little pieces.

"Ian and I served together. When I timed out he followed me here. He was never the strongest guy but he had a good heart and was loyal to a fault. Deidre loved him, when he died she…we both took it hard.

One night not long after his death she and I…you

were too young baby, I wasn't a monk you know that. I can't just throw her out now, she's just a little hurt and confused." I was saying that but I knew if she insisted I would do everything to make her happy.

"How many others?" That certainly did not sound like my little peach.

"Pardon?"

"How many other women have you slept with and are they all HERE?"

Well shit. "Babe…"

"Tell me or I'm leaving." I'm thinking my sweet little innocent was no more. I wonder if it was her introduction to my dick that had made her lose her damn mind. Whatever it was, once again I couldn't let her get too out of hand, that shit could prove dangerous.

"Let's get this straight." I grabbed her face and turned her to look at me. "You'll never leave me, not now not fucking ever, so calm your little ass down before you go too far."

"I won't stay here with her or any of the other women you've slept with and you can't make me. You made a promise to me too remember, but then again this wouldn't be the first time you broke a promise to me." I could see that she wished she could take those words back the moment they left her mouth, but it was too late.

Baby-Girl

I COULD HEAR myself saying these things to him, but could hardly believe they were coming from my mouth. I was so mad and hurt though, that in that moment I really didn't care.

I knew he'd been with women before me and yes I hated all of them. I sure didn't want to share space with any of them. I knew from everything he'd said to me in the past few days that he was insanely jealous at even the thought of another man near me, wasn't it supposed to be the same for me? Wasn't he as much mine as I was his?

I didn't mean to be mean to him though, to throw it in his face that he'd left me with that horrible woman all those years and had no idea what my life was really like. But seeing him hugging that girl who'd attacked me was the last straw. It was the last betrayal I was willing to take.

It was as if every horrible thing that had happened to me in my life had bubbled up to the surface. He was in shock at my words I could tell, that's why it took him a while to answer. I was a bit surprised myself and was wishing them back two seconds after they were said, but my anger still burned bright.

"Explain yourself." Oh he was mad, but after the last three days spent with him, I knew I had nothing to fear, that he'd never hurt me physically.

I was also almost certain because of the things he'd said while we were being intimate with each other that he would never cast me aside. He loved me, and I him, but that didn't mean I had to be a doormat.

With my aunt I was always afraid, never feeling that I had the right to speak up for myself. In the last few days since coming here he'd freed me. He was probably going to regret that by the time this day was over, but I couldn't turn back now.

"I've been in love with you, seems like from the first moment we met. I built a whole dream world around you even when there was no hope of us being together because I was so young and you, you were already a man with a life separate from the unwanted kid you'd taken on."

"I used to live for the days when you'd show up out of nowhere, and because you never gave prior warning, everyday was a day of hope that you would. You were the only bright light in my life."

"When you came, I was your little princess for those few days, but then as soon as you were gone, I went back to being nothing. Aunt Dee was mean to me, so mean, but when I tried to tell you that, you didn't listen. Instead you sided with her, just like today."

The memory of it made me mad all over again and next thing I knew I was pummeling his chest and screaming at him how much I hated him.

He did nothing for the first few minutes it seemed before springing into action. He tried his best to get me to stop, but I couldn't pull it back in. All the anger and disappointment from the past came spewing out and I yelled some pretty horrible things at him. The truth is I was angrier about today than all the things I'd endured at my aunt's hands all those years.

Seeing her in his arms had loosed something in me, something that I had no idea was even there.

"**W**hat the fuck?" she'd lost her damn mind, that's the only thing I could think of when she started hitting me and yelling about all the shit I'd done wrong. I tried wrapping my arms around her to calm her the fuck down, but her anger seemed to have given her added strength.

I wasn't too fucking thrilled about some of the shit she was hurling at me either, seeing as how I'd spent the last three fucking days buried inside her and promising to make shit up to her, shit that I'd had no control over anyway because I'd been off fighting a fucking war and trying to keep her little ungrateful ass safe.

"Fuck this." I lifted her off my lap long enough to unzip and pull my cock from my jeans. When I had my shit where I wanted it I sat her down hard on my cock.

"Umph." I knocked the air out her ass as I fucked up into her hard and deep. She was still on her shit trying to fight her way off my dick. I got to my feet with her impaled on my cock and bent her over the desk.

Grabbing a fistful of her hair I turned her face to the side so I could look down into her face. "You're mad, be fucking mad, but you don't fucking threaten me ever, you understand me?" I fucked into her and had her scratching at the desk as I pummeled her pussy from behind.

I held her head down as I punished her with my cock because now I was mad as fuck too. She was calling out to me whether for mercy for her abused pussy or to apologize I didn't know, and was too fucking far-gone to care.

"Give me your fucking mouth." I pulled her head around since her stubborn was still acting the fuck up. She tried to bite me but a thumb on her clit soon had her singing a different tune. Her fucking tears were killing me though and I had to let go the anger for now.

"I'm sorry baby, I'll make it right I promise." Fucking sap that I am, I would've promised her anything to get her to stop crying. Instead of the hard fuck that she'd earned I held her back against my front lovingly while whispering encouraging words in her ear.

"I love you only you, stop crying." I held my cock still inside her as I kissed her lips softly and played with her tits. "No one will ever mean more to me than you do babygirl, not even fucking close."

I kept telling her the shit that was in my heart until her body loosened up and she started kissing me back. I bit her lip once I had her full attention and eased my cock out of her womb slowly before driving back in.

"Since you threw down the gauntlet I have to reaffirm ownership, brace yourself." It was all the warning she got before I pushed her head down and away from me towards the desk, kicked her legs open wider and grabbed her ass in my hands.

She was bawling for a whole other reason now, because although I was no longer angry at her, she had to learn never to challenge me. "You want to act grown, this is what grown women get, hard fucking cock. Every time you act up or act out, this is what you got waiting for you."

"Creed..."

"Oh so I'm Creed again?" I fucked out the last

hour's frustration in her belly pounding her pussy hard with each thrust. "Tilt your pussy the way I taught you, that's it. You wanna give this up? Where the fuck were you going? I'll find you, anywhere anytime, don't ever threaten me with that shit again."

"I won't I'm sorry please." Her hands and nails were scrambling to take hold of the desktop but each time she got a grip I slammed into her until her ass shook and her pussy leaked.

She was crying out for mercy but her pussy was enjoying the shit out of what I was doing to her, if the amount of juice that ran down my dick was any indication.

She came on my cock three times while I tickled her clit and nibbled her ear and neck, all her sweet spots. With each stroke I searched out her G-spot and I knew the metal in my cock was making her pussy feel extra good. The last time she came, I had to hold her up before she flew off my dick; she was a wild one.

I was close, very close, now I had a decision to make. Do I give her my seed after the way she'd behaved, or do I teach her a lesson? I went with the lesson and pulled out. "Get dressed." She looked over her shoulder at me questioningly.

She had learned me well enough in the last few

days of nonstop fucking, so she knew I roared like a fucking beast when I came, not to mention she had told me more than once that she could actually feel my shit shooting into her.

"You didn't...?"

"No." I pulled my jeans back in place and ignored the pain in my cock. I wouldn't give her the satisfaction of cumming in her back or going to the bathroom to rub that shit out. She was going to learn that no matter what, she never fucking go against me.

I saw the hurt and ignored it as I walked away. If I caved now she'd be running fucking circles around me for the rest of my life; that's not how this shit works. "Go get cleaned up we're leaving in ten minutes."

She lost the color in her face and I knew what she was thinking, but before I could set her straight she was across the room, throwing herself into my arms.

"Please don't send me back, I didn't mean it." She held onto me like I was her lifeline. I wasn't mad enough to let her go on thinking that shit even for a second. "Hey, look at me."

I took her face in my hands and looked into her tear filled eyes. "Never, I will never send you away no matter what you did, no matter how mad I get, you got that? Don't ever think that, now go clean up." I kissed her forehead and set her away from me.

She didn't want to leave, like she thought I was lying to her, but in the end she went into the bathroom and closed the door.

How the fuck did I get myself into this shit? I'm either gonna have to talk her into letting Deidre stay, or go back on a promise, hard fucking thing to do when your word is your bond. But nothing means more than she does so if it came down to it, she wins. I had the next few days at least to try to get her to see reason; we'll see.

While she was cleaning up I went out into the clubhouse and called Max to gather the others for a little briefing before we headed out. I hadn't even had time to think about what the fuck Law had waiting for me before this pile of crap was thrown in my lap.

The guys filed in one by one looking bored as shit but I knew that was a con. "Cam, Rog, you're gonna need to grab an overnight bag we're headed to Law's for a few days. I don't know what exactly he's got going on but I'm pretty sure it has something to do with my girl. Pack your hardware, something pops off I don't want us standing around with our dicks in our hands."

"Max, everything looks good around here, make sure it stays that way before we head out. If this shit is what I think it is I'm gonna need all my energies focused on the situation and I don't want to come back here to any fuck ups."

"I'll take care of it, meet you out front in ten." He headed out leaving me with the other two. I gave them some last minute orders before sending them on their way to say their goodbyes to their women and get what they needed.

I waited until she came out the office and took her home to pack. "Just grab enough shit for a few days, if you run out we'll go shopping." She kept giving me looks under her lashes to gauge my anger meter I guess, but my mind was already onto the next thing.

"Creed?"

"What is it?" I didn't turn around to look at her when I answered.

"I'm sorry."

"No you're not, you're pissed and you have the right, just don't lose your mind again and come at me like you did. If the tables were turned I'd feel the same way but that shit better never ever happen in this life.

With that said what happened between her and I

was a long time ago and didn't mean shit. You're the one with the ring on her finger, the only one I ever even thought of giving one to.

Like I said, I made a promise to a friend a long time ago, now I have to decide if I can live with myself if I go back on that word to please you. So for the next few days I'm going to be a little sore because the whole fucking thing is fucked, don't sweat it." I left the room because I was pissed, not at her, but at the fucking situation.

SHE CLUNG to me all the way to Law's, which took a few hours. I think she cried some back there, I felt the wetness hit my cheek when the wind was just right and my visor was up. I hated like fuck that this shit was happening, that we hadn't even had time to really get to know each other before shit went south.

On the other hand I was proud of her for standing up, that shit was long overdue. And though I think somehow she knew she was in no danger from me, I was happy as fuck that she felt safe enough with me to do her thing.

Now I'm gonna have to find a way to make this shit up to her, to show her what she means to me. I'd never given much thought to the balance in a relationship, I just always knew that shit was gonna be my way end of story.

That shit was all well and good, but the crying and the hurt was not part of the fucking deal, that's where I draw the line. I signaled to the others who were flanking me that it was time for a stop.

We pulled into the next lot up on the right and the guys headed into the little convenience store. "You want something from in there?" I had helped her off the back of my bike and was holding her between my spread thighs as I sat there. She was still not looking at me as she shook her head no, and when I removed the helmet I saw the evidence of her tears.

Pulling her into me I hugged her as close as I could against my heart. "Why are you still crying babygirl? Look at me." I smoothed the hair back from her face and looked at her without speaking for a while.

"We had our first fight, it was a bad one, you lost your damn mind, but I'm still here. I'm sorry you felt even for one second that I chose her over you that would never happen. Now stop the tears I don't like it."

"Kiss me." I waited for her to lift her lips to mine

before taking them in a sweet kiss. "I'll give you my seed tonight okay, stop fussing." Since she lost that fucking haunted look in her eyes I figured that's what the fuck was wrong with her spoilt ass.

"You want chocolate?" She nodded her head yes when not five minutes ago she said she didn't want shit. I shook my head with a grin and took her into the store to stock up on the sugary sweet shit that she had a weakness for.

She seemed much lighter now that we'd had our little talk. I doubt she knew how much of her heart she'd shown me today. I'll have to be careful in the future not to harm her sweet heart. My girl is a softie.

By the time we were on the road again I had come up with an idea for Deidre that would save me from breaking my word and give my woman what she wanted in the bargain. Now as to getting rid of everyone I'd slept with, there were only one or two of them left, but if that's what she wanted so be it. The boys had more than enough pussy to go around.

She was already changing my shit around and she hadn't been there a month. I guess I was gonna have to rethink some shit because she had proven that she had no problem standing up to me and that shit was going to have to be nipped in the bud before she fucked around and pushed me too far.

The one thing I was not prepared to accept from my woman, is disrespect, no matter how fucking mad she gets. That shit will earn her an ass whipping.

She held me a little tighter the rest of the way and there were no more stray tears hitting me as we rode hard for our destination.

With her little ass under control my mind turned to what could possibly be waiting for us at the other end of this shit. Most likely it had to do with the hate brigade, as Law was fond of calling the local chapter of the Nazi wannabes, who were apparently friends of Sal's.

If that fuck wanted to lose his nuts altogether I had no problem helping him out there, and if I took out a few of those assholes along the way so much the better.

The thing is, I don't think any of that would've prompted Law to call for a face to face, something like that he could've told me over the phone or true to character, the pain in the ass would've handled it himself and then told me after the fact. This shit was just making me antsy as fuck on top of everything else.

My mind ran the gamut of possibilities but all roads led to her. If it concerned her and Law wasn't talking but was asking me to come all this way, then it might be bad. But wouldn't he have given me a heads-up?

Not if it's really fucked and he thinks you'd lose your shit and go vigilante. It would be just like him to try to bring me in to diffuse the situation. And all this guessing shit was just making me more agitated. Better to wait and see before I make myself nuts before I get there.

CREED

*L*aw and his crew were practically waiting for us at the gate when we got there later that afternoon. I took in the whole place at a glance and didn't see anything that would give me any idea as to what the fuck was going on

Law, Brand, Clay, Kyle and their cousin looked relaxed and laid back. I relaxed a little then but not much. These men were all hard-asses each in their own right, I wouldn't put it past them to be holding shit close to the vest.

"What's up brother?" We exchanged our usual hugs all around before Law turned to Jessie. I felt my hackles rise and had to remind myself that Law had his own woman and he was standing at least ten feet from mine.

He must've felt my energy in the air because the ass grinned at me before reaching out for her hand. I couldn't hold back the growl that escaped but was quick enough to play that shit off before the others caught on. I'm so fucked.

"And you must be Jessie, pleased to meet you finally." As he said it I realized I'd never introduced them in all the years we'd been friends and they had lived so close. He'd known where she was of course, because I'd told him, but I never wanted anyone around her, not even my most trusted friend. "Fuck!"

"Problem?" Law looked at me after my outburst as I looked at her. I felt like an asshole, it was so clear, what the fuck had I been thinking? "Nah, just something I have to take care of. Come here babygirl."

She came over to my side and I realized she was a little nervous being around all these strange men. I kissed her temple and left my arm around her as I pulled my phone and walked a little ways away. I looked down at her and kept my eyes on hers as I made the call.

"Jason, I need you to do me a solid. Cut Deidre a check for ten grand for me." I hung up and made the second call which was easier than I thought it would be.

I'd been looking at this shit all-wrong. My first allegiance will always be to her and making sure she's happy. This shit wasn't ever going to make her happy and it was shit thinking to believe it ever could. "Deidre, yeah it's me, listen Jason will be there in a few with something for you.

I want you to take that and go back to your parents'. It's enough to get you started somewhere. We'll be gone for a few days, but I'm gonna need you to be gone when we get back."

I heard her silent tears on the other line and felt my heart hurt for the wife of my friend, the girl I'd known for so long. But it was the one on my arm that mattered most.

She hung up the phone without a word and I guess that was the end of our acquaintance. Even though I hadn't seen her in a long time and we'd parted on such bad terms last time and not too hot ones this go round, there was still that connection. I guess we could call that the first casualty of my love for my babygirl.

"Better?" She gave me a half smile and a sweet kiss before we returned to the others. I knew some shit was up when Law broke off his conversation with my crew upon my return and my boys were looking like they were ready to pounce on some shit.

"Creed I thought since your woman knows Illyana we'd let them get reacquainted while we take care of some things." He looked towards his place, the main house on the spread. The one he'd inherited after his parents and his little sister had been slaughtered not too long ago, leaving just him his younger brother and the cousin who had grown up with them.

It was then I saw the women all congregated on the porch watching the goings-on. One of them broke away at Law's signal and headed towards us until the men whistled and the others followed.

I almost laughed at the way the women fell in line because I remember these boys complaining about the shit their women put them through and how hardheaded and opinionated they were. Except for Brandon whose relationship was relatively new.

"This is my wife Dana Sue, Dana this is my buddy Creed and his girl Jessie." The introductions were made and the women took her off with them. It didn't escape my notice that these guys weren't too thrilled about their women being around strange men either, friend or no friend.

The atmosphere changed as soon as the wives were out of sight and I was back to playing the guessing game. "Okay Law, you got me here what gives?" He seemed to be taking an inordinate amount of time studying me for some fucked up reason and that shit was not helping.

"You're not gonna like what I'm about to say to you so let's get that shit out of the way now. I know how you are so I'm asking you to keep your cool and let's come up with a plan, no rash moves brother for fuck sake."

Yeah, if that little tidbit was supposed to settle me down it had the opposite fucking effect. If it were anyone else I would've jacked him up until he started talking, but you can't rush this fucker, he moves at his own pace.

His boys and mine started twitching and that shit just sent my radar into fucking orbit. I looked towards the house she'd disappeared into with my guts in knots.

"Tell me what the fuck's going on Law." I didn't like the way everyone was looking like they expected me to lose my shit; that could only mean one thing. That whatever the fuck he was about to tell me was fucked.

"Do I need to send her to the bunker over this shit?" The bunker was fucking hours away at my place. I'd had it built years ago after my stint in the army. You learn things when dealing with Uncle Sam, the fuck.

I loosened my stance and waited. If Law was on his shit then it was worse than he'd led me to believe on the phone. And since it involved her, oh well, shit might get fucked up no matter what he said about keeping my cool. I'll wait 'til he told me his shit and then we'd see.

"I have to show you something, follow me." I looked back in the direction she'd gone and went after him with our guys following behind. His set-up was pretty much like mine only difference is there were less women around. I guess that was compliments of the wives. I'll have to ask him how that shit was working out for him.

We bypassed the play area and the bar and headed back to the meeting room so I knew shit was about to get serious. As soon as we were seated Law threw what looked like a photo album across the table at me.

I looked around the room at his men who for some fucked up reason were lined up against the wall, and Max who was standing like a sentinel behind my chair.

"What the fuck is this a hit?" I grinned to lighten the mood and the feeling of dread that was beginning to grow in my gut. I flipped open the lid of the book and didn't know what the fuck.

"What's this?" It looked like a photo album filled with girls, young girls. I started to relax a little, thinking that the shit had to do with my cause, which was rescuing young kids from fucked up situations and the twisted adults that were supposed to care for them, and nothing at all to do with my babygirl, until I saw her face looking back at me.

"What the fuck is this?" There was nothing written there, no explanation. Only her age, height, weight, hair and eye color. I looked at Law for answers because I didn't like where my mind was going. For someone who'd dealt with and seen some of the shit I'd seen stateside, there weren't that many reasons for something like this and it wasn't a school yearbook.

My head was buzzing an alarm. The shit was already hot and I still didn't have a fucking clue. But I knew whatever this was it wasn't good. I saw another now familiar face in there, and my gut started to burn.

I pushed my chair back and stood when I got to the back of the fucking book and saw what was written there. "Who the fuck put her in there?" I pointed to it accusingly as I tried to keep ahold of my building rage.

Law motioned to his guys and mine and that's when I figured out what was going on with them. He was trying to cut me off, good luck with that shit.

Law stood too and came around the table. "My guess is the aunt or her guy, we're still trying to figure this shit out." He was watching me like a powder keg about to blow or a snake about to strike, I felt like a little bit of both.

When I thought of what could've happened if I hadn't gotten that call a few nights ago, if I'd left her in their clutches… "What the fuck is this sick shit?" Not her; I broke out in a cold sweat and rage fought with nausea as I thought of the implications in front of me.

"Exactly what you think it is. Ironic isn't it? You've been fighting this shit for years and these dumb fucks thought they could bring it to your door…where are you going?"

"I need eyes on her, need to make sure she's fucking okay and Law, get the priest." She was probably gonna have a fit when I told her she was getting hitched in Law's backyard, after all she'd told me about her dream wedding a million times since I put my ring on her finger. Too fucking bad.

We'll have to do that shit another time, right now it was more important that I tie her to me completely. The need was almost overwhelming as I headed out the room and across the yard to where I'd seen her disappear with the other women not too long ago

There was only one thing on my mind; getting to her, looking at her, feeling her, reassuring myself that she was here safe with me, not in the clutches of some fucked up pervert.

CREED

*S*he was in Law's house with his woman and her friends. I released the tortured breath I'd been holding until I got her in my sights. She was fine, still whole and smiling, no lingering sadness. Oh babygirl. I composed myself before stepping into the room.

I figured the one she was sitting next to was the one she'd known from before. They all piped down when I came inside looking guilty as hell and baby-girl had a red fucking face. Uh-huh, up to no good no doubt.

I figured I owed her friend at least a thank you for what she'd done, and since my heart was beating normal again at the sight of my woman, I figured now was as good a time as any.

"You the one who gave Law the heads-up?" I stood in front of the amazingly beautiful woman who had a hold of my girl's hand. "Yes, I'm Illyana, I can't thank you enough for rescuing her."

"She's mine, thanks for looking out. Come here babygirl. If you ladies will excuse us." I took her just outside the door, not even wondering what all the giggles and whispers behind me were about. "Did you bring a fancy dress with you by any chance?" She looked at me like I'd lost my fucking mind.

"No, I didn't know I was gonna need one. Are we going somewhere special?" She looked a little crest-fallen that she wouldn't have anything to wear so I could imagine how she was going to feel about what I had to say next.

"No, you're getting married today." Her eyes all but popped out of her head and she screamed loud enough to wake the dead before turning to rush back inside in her excitement.

"Jessica." She stopped and turned back to me, her face bright and happy, just the way I always want her to be. "Get back here." I had a big stupid grin on my face so she knew I wasn't mad even though I probably sounded like a grizzly with his paw caught.

"Your man needs some sugar." She ran and jumped into my arms, peppering my face with kisses before I took her mouth in a deep tongue fuck. There, my world was settled again. I can deal with whatever the fuck comes at me now.

"I take it you're happy. We'll see about your fancy wedding another time okay baby; be ready in ten." I watched her rush back in to the room full of women and heard the screams and whatnot before I made it off the porch. I headed back to the yard to meet the guys who had followed behind me. Probably thought I was gonna pull a fast one.

"Right, where's the priest?" For some reason that got Law's right hand men to start grumbling and his brother to breaking into laughter and I remembered Law saying something about holding the priest hostage.

Someone ran off to get him while I cooled my heels and tried not to let my inner feelings show. If one more fuck goes wrong today I'ma shed blood no fucking joke.

I better never tell her that on her wedding day her man was plotting murder in his fucking head instead of looking forward to the exchange of vows.

As far was I was concerned she became my wife when I got her blood on my cock, that's good enough for me. But from her reaction just now, the whole ceremony thing meant more to her.

At least I knew that for her it was about more than all the hoopla. She was willing to get hitched in Law's backyard in jeans. That shit, made me feel lighter, even with all of the shit that was going down.

My mind kept going back to her face looking out at me from behind that yellowed plastic. She looked about sixteen there or what I remembered her looking like at that age.

She still had that babyish innocent young girl thing going on then, was now coming into her own as a woman and some fuck had been drooling over her for his own sick perverted fuck reasons.

I'ma end up burning this fuck to the ground, but first before I lose my shit, I'm gonna make her mine officially. The whole fucking town was full of fuck-wits as far as I can tell; who would miss 'em?

The asshole that had done Law's family, and now her aunt and uncle, not to mention the fucking hate brigade assholes. What was the fucking point in letting it stand? Law's place was on the outskirts; he won't miss the shit. What a way to be thinking on my wedding day.

Max nudged me as we stood around the preacher/priest what the fuck ever, who was looking like what the fuck, and I turned to see her coming to me. "Fuck." The clothed one cleared his throat over my shoulder but it was too late, the word was already out.

She looked fucking amazing. How the fuck long had it been since I walked out of that house? She was wearing a yellow sundress that someone had loaned her; it made her skin glow. And someone had put flowers in her hair and she was holding a bunch in her hands.

I wonder what the fuck they would've accomplished if I'd given them more time. Then again I shouldn't be surprised, they had the best canvas to work with.

I tried to convince myself that it was the sun in my eye that made me tear up but I knew different. Every thought went out of my head. There was nothing there or in my heart, but her, babygirl.

I met her halfway, ignoring her new friends and the guys as I walked towards my life. My hands fucking shook when I lifted them to her perfect face. "You're beautiful babygirl, damn." Her smile was wide and bright without a trace of anything but joy. That smile went a long way to soothing my beast.

I didn't let go of her hand the whole time we stood before the man who officially joined us according to the law. Speaking of which, I didn't even ask Law how he pulled off the license that quickly, but I was sure there was a story behind that shit.

I didn't think it would, but hearing those words 'I now pronounce you man and wife', actually lifted a weight off my chest. She was mine now, nothing and no one could change that.

"I'm gonna love you for the rest of your life, get ready." I whispered the words for her ears only as I held her in my arms for the first time since making it official.

Her girls were soon there buzzing around and one very bold one, I think she was Clay's if the way he rolled his eyes was a hint, came over and took her from me with a very saucy suggestion.

There was even a cake after, nothing major but it was more than I'd been expecting and my woman seemed happy as fuck with her lot.

We tabled the bullshit for later as we watched the women enjoy themselves and even the sheep had joined in and the wives seemed fine with that. I'll have to ask Law about that shit as well, but later.

Babygirl sought me out after half an hour and came over to my side with a new pep in her step that hadn't been there before. After the way the day had started it was good to see her this happy.

"Thank you husband." She grinned up at me

looking young and unafraid and I fought not to think of what the fuck I was gonna have to deal with soon.

"You're welcome wife." I kissed her hair and drew her in close to my side as the festivities went on around us. She was happy at least and carefree, if the way she clung to me meant anything.

I too found that I felt a thousand times better now that she was mine all the way. "You're mine, every beautiful inch of you; be happy babygirl." I planned to see that she always was. I was never going to let her know about this shit either. She'd suffered more than enough at those two's hands.

I let her have her thirty minutes but as the sun was going down I knew I had to go take care of shit. I had no idea who all was involved in the shit Law had thrown on my plate today, but I knew from dealing with similar bullshit for the past few years, that it was usually a network of assholes spread out all over the place. Sometimes even reaching as far as other nations.

"I've got a run to make baby." She pouted but didn't give me any shit. I'd taught her not to question that statement ever, and was glad to see she'd been listening when I was laying down the law in between fucks.

"Don't leave this yard for any reason. From here to Law's place that's it. If you lose your fucking mind and forget those instructions come find me in the clubhouse so I can remind you. Now give me your mouth." I kissed her long and hard before releasing her on shaky legs. "Behave yourself."

I left her with her friends and headed for my ride. I was pretty sure Law was gonna try and stop me, he's Mr. Let's plan shit, which I usually am as well when it comes to this shit, but not this time. I'm gonna line both those fucks up and put a bullet in them. There has to be a pack of wild dogs around here I can feed them to-to keep the law off my ass.

"Hold it, they're not there, I checked after calling you in." That brought me up short. It was like the fucker had been waiting for me to make my move all this time. What was he saying though?

They couldn't be gone yet, Jason had only just told me about the house situation. Did they expect me to come back and finish what I'd started the other night? "Where the fuck are they?"

"My best guess, their friends are hiding them out in the hills. Word is you put a hurting on Sal, and made some pretty heavy threats afterwards. You may not be the only reason they went into hiding though.

If they're the ones responsible for putting her in that lineup, then they're in deep shit themselves."

"Think about it, you took her out of there what four, five days ago? From what little I gathered so far, losing her could mean big trouble for the aunt and uncle and whoever is running this shit. They're gonna be holed up looking for trouble so we wait."

"What hills, where?" I looked beyond the walls he'd built around his place towards the hills running along the horizon in the distance. He could wait I wasn't about to. I needed to talk to those two and find out how far this shit had gone. If money had changed hands then the shit could get ugly.

If some fuck somewhere was already fixated on her as it appeared might be the case from all the fucking notations referring to her, then there was no telling what he would do. I'd seen it all already and not my fucking babygirl. The mere thought that someone was even out there thinking he had any rights to her burned my ass.

My experience, some of these sick fucks actually started believing that they owned the people they paid for whether that person had anything to do with what the fuck was going on or not. If I have to hop on a plane and head to the desert to put a hole in some fuck's head for being stupid, I'd rather know right fucking now.

I was on the move, wasn't sure where the fuck I was going but I'd figure it out since Law wasn't looking like he was about to help. "Chaz hold the gate closed, don't let him through." Law gave his guy that order and almost lost his fucking head for his efforts. "You better rescind that order brother." I turned to glare at him.

"Justice stand the fuck down would ya, I said we wait, they're gonna be expecting this shit."

"No." I didn't even stop walking. Law might know his shit, but I know he'd never seen this side of evil before so he could have no clue as to the lengths these fuckers would go to.

" I will level this whole fucking town to kill that one cockroach Law. Unless you want me to go through your crew first you'd better tell these fucks not to fuck with me or I'll make you look like a choir boy."

"Calm your ass down. Why the fuck am I saddled with hot headed fucks? You can't go after them this hot, let things cool down for a day or two. I've asked around, it seems this shit is running rampant in these parts, fucking breeding programs or some shit. Girls have been going missing going back years.

There's more going on here than we know. We go in now before we know more we're putting a lot of fucking lives at stake."

"Besides, I'm waiting on another call before we move. I think this shit might be tied into something else that runs through a big chunk of the country."

"What the fuck are you talking about Law?"

"You remember Lo and his boys, got out and settled somewhere in Georgia?"

"I heard something about that so what does that have to do with this?"

What the fuck do the SEALs have to do with this shit? As far as I know those guys never ran Ops on domestic soil. But then again they were part of an elite squad so who knows what the fuck.

"Seems it might be connected. One of their birds flew down here, or they think they've traced him down here somewhere, after he worked over Ty's woman or some shit. It was their digging on an Op that discovered the album."

"They know I'm from down this way, and when they saw the references to this place they asked me to look into it until they can get here."

I saw him flex because I don't think those boys had any idea just who was in that little ledger when they sent it to him. I knew those boys, had gone on

Ops with them more than once, stand up guys but crazy as fuck.

Still, I couldn't wait around for them to get here to deal with this shit, and I'm a hundred percent sure that if the tables were turned they would feel the same.

"Wasn't your wife on that list, how the fuck can you think of waiting around?"

"She wasn't mine then or the fucks would already be six feet deep." He folded his fists and I just quirked my brow at him. Who's hotheaded now?

"As it stands I'm gonna make them bleed for even thinking about putting her in there, but we're gonna do this right. The fact that she's in there has given me a string I can tug, but I gotta give it some thought. But back to those fuckers in the hills and the rest of your boy Sal's pals.

The fucking sheriff is in their pockets and he already has a hard on for me, which I don't give a fuck about, but if he fucks with you I'm gonna lose my shit and I've got shit to do.

Not to mention a wife that was looking kinda green this morning when I rolled out of bed, which tells me she might be breeding or some fuck. Like my life isn't fucked six ways from Sunday already. I need this shit."

I found my first laugh in a long time. "Hey congrats brother, may the little fucker be just like you." I could take a minute to be happy for my boy. After the fucked up year he'd had with his family being slaughtered while he was off fighting a war, he deserved some happy.

"Fuck you asshole, then again that might not be so bad. Heaven forbid any of them should come out like Dana Sue, fuck me." He actually looked horrified at the thought and I couldn't believe I could find anything to laugh about at a time like this.

"A handful is she?"

"You laugh now but I'm telling you, that sweet little thing you got over there is gonna be a whole new person any day now. I don't know if it's the ring on the finger, or taking them to our beds, but they change overnight on your ass and life as you know it is at a fucking end. Look at this shit."

We watched as the women walked from one of the set up tables to the other laughing and hooting at who the fuck knows what. I saw my little one in the middle of the pack holding her own, and my heart did its crazy dance.

"I think we're already there brother and I think it has to do with them feeling confident after they've caught their man." I thought of the shit she'd been through this morning and the words she'd said to me in anger.

Now knowing that the ones I'd entrusted her to had put her in danger, had my temperature rising again, and just that easy my mood switched back to dark.

"You said this fuck messed with Ty's girl? And he's still breathing? Those boys get soft stateside or what?" Didn't sound like the Ty I knew. I wonder how they got him to stand the fuck down?

"Nope, I'm pretty sure his ass is still as hotheaded as yours, but we have to play this shit right. We don't know who all is involved as yet and how far it reaches. From what little those boys shared with me, there're some heavy hitters involved. I'll wait until they get here and see, but I smell a shit storm.

And let's not forget there're about two hundred girls in there that we have to account for before this shit is all said and done."

What he was saying made sense, but it went against the grain to let this shit slide for even a second more. She was safe now that's true. No one was gonna get anywhere near her that's for sure, but I needed this shit dealt with yesterday for my own peace of mind.

How had I not known this shit was going on?

How had I left her in danger so long? I didn't like feeling like a fucking tool. Somebody's ass was gonna burn.

"Fine, if we're gonna find out who those kids are we're gonna have to put them through the special identifier. I didn't bring mine with me obviously…"

"We've got one here brother the fuck you think I am a slacker?" He clapped me on the shoulder as we headed back to the clubhouse. The women were still gathered around gabbing and laughing and who the fuck knows what, but there was no danger, and Law had men on patrol, good enough.

"Rog, eyes on mine." He stayed back to protect her. Not that I didn't trust Law, far from it, but I don't take chances where she's concerned. I wasn't expecting anything to happen here, but I hadn't expected to find her in a flesh catalog either so what the fuck, who knows?

It was with a heavy heart that I went back to that room and picked up that damn book. There were a million thoughts going through my mind. This shit looked like the sixteen year old Jessie, so that would make it five years ago.

Most pedophiles didn't like women that old, they were more into younger innocents. So what was the real deal here? Had Law said something about breeding programs?

"Law what was that about breeding programs?" He turned from setting up the machine. "That's what Clay and Brand said it looked like. Apparently they dealt with something like this a while back as part of a sting, and the set up was pretty much the same.

If the girls were younger it would've been a pedophile ring, but because of the fact that the girls are a little older and it has obviously been some time since those pictures were taken, they've surmised that they were chosen for the magazine for rich men to choose from."

"And when you said Dana Sue being in there gave you an idea, a string to tug on, what did you mean?" He took a minute to compose himself before answering.

"I meant I think I have an idea of how this shit works. Her father all but sold her to someone, who sent her to some fancy school to train her to be the perfect wife or some fuck. So I'm wondering if the others were chosen the same way and already have a fucking buyer."

I took a moment to let that shit sink in. "I gotta say, if you want me to leave your little town standing that was not the right thing to say to me at this fucking juncture."

"Take it easy, it's just a theory we don't know that that's how it's done for sure. Until we know one way or the other I'm not going to be comfortable going in.

You think I don't want to go up there and have my boys smoke these fuckers out and pick them off one by one as they scatter like roaches? But that's not gonna get me any answers.

I know the fucker who 'bought' my woman already bled out, but I don't know about the others. So we chill until we know and then we move and take out the whole fucking program once and for all."

"I'm giving this shit until tomorrow and then I'm going to find answers my way. All I need is two minutes with one of those fucks and they'll talk."

I turned back to the fuckery on the screen and left him to his mumbling about hardheaded fucks. If he thought I was bad, I wonder which planet he was on when we were dealing with the SEALs in the past. And just what the fuck he thought they were coming here to do.

We'd both ran special Ops with those boys when we were in. They're the fucking elite's elite of Special

Forces. The motherfuckers you call in when you want to snatch a fly off of dog shit at high noon in the middle of Abbottabad.

I knew if they were involved then the shit must be really bad, and my baby was caught in the middle of it. Was this on me too? Fuck!

"Just be cool for me brother. I know how hard that shit is, seeing your woman in some shit like that. But like I said, we've got all those young girls in there that might be in danger. Ours is safe for now and they'll stay that way. Let's try to give them that."

Fucking right they'll stay that way. I scrolled through the pictures with a bad taste in my mouth. It wasn't the first time I'd done this, but it was the first time it had ever hit this close to home.

CREED

I didn't know any of the other faces staring back at me thank fuck, but they were still someone's kid, so he had me there. There was no way of telling if they'd already been snatched, or if they were still home tucked up warm in bed, with no idea that their lives were in danger.

The book was obviously a few years old because of the wear on the plastic, and the fact that I knew babygirl's picture was at least five years old. Whether that was a good thing or not remained to be seen.

It was painstaking work, running each one through the system, because some of them weren't in there, unless they'd committed a crime or some shit. So there was no real way of knowing since there were just numbers in the book with their stats listed.

Lately though, or in the last ten years or so, some states had been making it a law that you had to have your kids taken to a local precinct to get printed and photographed. With technology being what it is, there's a lot you can do with that shit.

Still I wasn't holding out much hope, especially if most of these kids were from these parts. We're not exactly known for following the pack.

Sometimes living here can feel like you're separated from the rest of the country, our way of life is so different here. Is that why some son of a bitch had chosen to use it as his playing field?

"Oh fuck!" I looked up at Law's exclamation. "What is it?" His face was almost white, what the fuck?

"This shit just got a fuck of a lot more complicated." How the fuck was that even possible? I stood to move over to his side.

"How so?" He pointed at the screen where a young blonde kid in her early teens stared back at me. Her face didn't really ring any bells even though there was something vaguely familiar about her. "Do we know her?" I squinted for a better look but nothing doing.

"No, but we know her father, he made our bikes."

"Oh fuck."

"Are we calling him in?" I was trying to calculate in my head if we had enough manpower to keep this fucker in check. He wasn't army, navy or none of that shit, but what he was is fuck mean when it came to his woman, so I could only imagine how he felt about his little girl.

"Have to, he's one of us." That would be the brotherhood of motherfuckers who got shit done. "We might have to tap that tree of yours before it's all said and done since this is your thing Creed."

"You're cool with Blade right?" He asked me about another ex soldier turn cop turn restaurateur who we both knew, that was also into doing the ride-along with abused kids the same as my crew and I were.

"Yeah we were supposed to have a meet at Jake's with some other crews who're down with what we do but I couldn't make it, had a job come up last minute."

"Jake, shit, forgot about him. We might need to tug on that string since he's law enforcement. I better make those fucking calls. My little town is about to be overrun with crazy fucks." Yeah cause he was sane.

Shit, in all this fuckery I hadn't even asked about his parents and I knew he was still raw from that shit. I heard his voice drone on as he made his calls and I watched the screen as more and more information poured out.

"Lo wants to talk to you since you know more about this shit than I do." He passed me the phone and took over watching the monitor. "Yo."

"Creed, how's it hanging brother, heard you got hitched congrats."

"Yeah thanks, word is you're not too far behind."

"Nope, but we got some shit going on down here that may be tied in to what you boys uncovered in your neck of the woods and it's putting our shit on hold."

"Explain that to me, Law didn't go into detail."

"Long and short, that book we sent him was taken from the personal library of one asshole who resided in our little town up to about a couple weeks ago. He grabbed Ty's woman…"

"How the fuck did y'all let that happen?"

"She wasn't his yet, well not all the way. Anyway he pulled a runner soon after and we did a little B and E, that's where we found the book. I saw the reference to the place in the back and we happened to trace him there afterwards. And since Law's down

297

there and it's gonna take us a few to get down that way, we figured we'd give him a head start.

We had no idea though what the shit was about, we just knew it wasn't good. Now he tells me your woman is in there."

"Did he tell you who else is in there?"

"No who?"

"His wife and the daughter of the guy who built our rides."

"Shit; Law doesn't have a bead on our guy but we're heading out tomorrow should be there around midday. Stand down 'til we get there soldier, let's run this shit like an Op."

Law and his snitching ass probably ratted me out for wanting to go in hot. I realized it had been a couple hours since I'd had eyes on her and that it was now full dark outside and it was her wedding night.

I hung up the phone and stood to stretch. I missed my babygirl. I wish shit would stop getting in the way of my fucking joy. "I gotta go see to my woman, not much we can do tonight since you've got me on a fucking leash, so we can just leave this running for now and see what we see in the morning."

"Sounds good." He handed me a set of keys.

"What's this?"

"Keys to the cabin, it's your wedding night you need your privacy. Your guys can bed down here there's plenty of room and I think some of the sheep already got them on lock."

"Am I supposed to know where this cabin is?"

"Yeah it's the same one we used to escape to when shit got to be too much." Damn, I'd forgotten all about that place.

"Fine I'll take your truck because if I remember correctly that'll be a ways out otherwise."

"Key's on there truck's out front waiting."

"Had it all planned out did you?"

"Just had my own wedding night not too long ago, I'm an old hand at this shit."

I went to collect my woman who was drooping by the time I reached her. "Grab your stuff baby let's go." She rested against my chest as I kissed her hair before going to get our shit and heading out after the long ass goodbyes. I had to browbeat fucking Max into staying put since he gets antsy whenever I'm out of his sight in unknown territory.

"Max the place is still on Law's land, I use to go there when I'd come back here with him on leave chill." He grumbled some but in the end one of the skirts sidetracked him and I was able to slip away without my watchman.

"You tired baby?" I squeezed her hand as we drove along over the terrain. It wasn't that late yet, it just gets dark here sooner than most places because of the locale, but she'd had a long day nonetheless.

"Not anymore." She sure didn't seem tired anymore when I glanced her way. Her eyes were bright with excitement all of a sudden. I wondered what the hell that was about but put it down to wedding day bullshit.

We reached the place less than an hour later on account of I drove like I had somewhere to go, and I helped her down out the truck. It looked much the same as it ever did, but Law had done some sprucing up it seemed like because it was no longer the rough number I remembered.

I could tell someone had been there recently too, since it still had a shine to it, or knowing him he'd had it done that very day. Always thinking ahead my pal.

"I think I'm supposed to do this." She laughed like a loon when I picked her up and took her over the threshold. That laugh went right to my gut and I was reminded for a split second of just why we were here. That shit sobered my ass up right quick.

"Are you happy baby?" She stopped laughing when she sensed the seriousness in my tone. "Yes, more than I can say." Her kiss was a lot less innocent than I was accustomed to from her, and I tasted wine on her tongue.

I walked in the direction of the bedroom or where I remembered it to be while carrying her in my arms with our mouths fused together. In the room I laid her back on the bed and leaned over her.

"I missed you all day baby." I'm such a damn sap, but when she reached her arms up and around my neck, pulling me into her, I all but forgot the shit that was going on around me.

"I need to get cleaned up baby." She let me know in no uncertain terms that she would take me as I am by wrapping her legs around my ass and pulling me all the way down between her thighs.

Her kiss was hungry and carnal. And fuck if my dick didn't start leaking in ten seconds flat. I dry fucked her through her clothes with our tongues battling each other while pawing at her tits. The fucking dress was in my way.

"This is a nice dress baby, but unless you want it destroyed we'd better get it off you." She sat up making me straddle her while she pulled it off over her head.

As soon as her tits bounced into sight I was on them. She forced her hands down between us and fought with my zipper, making these noises that I'd never heard from her before. I stopped and watched her, mesmerized by her actions, it was almost as if she craved my cock.

I helped her push my jeans off over my extended cock and off my legs. She got frustrated with my boots and I caught her lip between my teeth to calm her ass down.

"Settle I'm not going anywhere." That didn't have much of an affect and she all but wrestled me to the bed and climbed over me. What the fuck is this? I almost laughed at her desperation but reined that shit in just in case it hurt her feelings.

She rubbed her pussy over my cock and pressed her tits into my chest. "Babe you're in heat." I could smell her pussy's scent rising up to my nose and feel the liquid heat from between her thighs bathing my cock.

I wanted to drive into her, but I wanted to have some more fun with this new wild one. She nipped and licked her way down my chest making keening sounds that went straight to my cock.

"On my cock, now." I pushed her head down when she looked at me in a daze, but she soon remembered her old friend and what it was she was supposed to do.

She kissed my cock slit and hummed. I was watching her to see what she would do next, where this new fever would lead her. She played with my cock rings, licking around each barbell at the ends, kissing the hot flesh in between.

"Now run your tongue across the head of my cock, good girl. That's it, drink my pre-cum baby-girl; taste good?" She nodded her head and dove for more. It still amazes me what a natural she is. The way she laps up my juices and search for more with her tongue.

"Fuck yourself with your fingers while you eat my cock." She pushed her hand between her thighs without hesitation and fed three fingers to her obviously hungry pussy. I wasn't expecting her to pull those fingers out and feed them to me though. I like that shit.

"Ummm, sweet pussy." She did some new shit on my cock and worked her way all the way down until I was hitting her neck, and her nose was pressed against my groin, but she couldn't hold it for too long.

Hop on up here, I'm not trying to cum in your

mouth tonight anyway." Oh no, I had better uses for my seed and it was all going into her womb.

The way her eyes closed to half slits told me she was getting close and we hadn't even started yet. I helped her straddle my head and hold on to the bed head before pulling her split peach down onto my tongue.

She didn't need any direction after that, just started riding my face and tugging on one of her nipples. I squeezed her ass cheeks like I was trying to get juice from a lemon. Her pussy juice ran down my face to the pillow and still I ate her out, looking for more.

She flung her head from side to side as I tongue fucked her deep, hitting the sides of her pussy and making her sing.

I pulled her down my chest until her pussy was rubbing against the underside of my cock, which was lying flat against my stomach. Reaching around behind her, I opened her sweet tight cunt with two fingers and used my cockhead to tease the entrance to her pussy.

She started moving, trying to impale herself on my dick, and when I pushed a finger in her tight little virgin ass she really lost her shit then. I guess Law knew what the fuck he was talking about because she was loud tonight, louder than any other time. I'm sure the whole fucking valley would've heard her if we'd stayed.

When her body shook hard I pulled her down on my cock and went deep. She bucked and went off again, slamming herself down on my cock as she keened and mewled. I left my finger in her ass, sending it deeper while she tried her best to break off my fuck stick.

"Ride that cock baby, fuck." I watched my cock slide up inside her hard and fast. I let go of her hip and grabbed her tit and she went from slamming to grinding her pussy onto my meat.

"Tits, now." She leaned over and I sucked her tit into my mouth hard. She never stopped cumming and her eyes stayed rolled back in her head as I ass fucked her with my finger, while munching on her tits and slamming my cock into her.

I was nowhere near ready to cum yet as she wound down. She was breathing like a racehorse and her body was shaking with mini aftershocks. When she started kissing and licking all over my body I figured she wasn't done with me yet.

Turning us over, I lifted her legs high up on my back so I could pile drive into her upturned snatch. I knew I was hitting her deep, reaching into those places that made her pussy hurt good and she let me know I'd found her spot by digging her nails into me and taking the flesh from my back.

"Right there baby oh fuck." The ring to her cervix snapped around my cock and held me captive while I went in search of her womb. As soon as my boy got in there he started shooting off like a fucking rocket.

I must've nutted a half gallon of my seed inside her that time and the shit didn't seem to want to end. I knew I was too heavy and that I wasn't ready to leave her body yet so I flipped us over again and held her on top of me while we both calmed down.

"Creed I wanna try something." Her voice was hoarse but still had that little girl innocence to it. "Talk to me sweetheart, what is it?" I wonder where all women learn to do this shit? She had grown into the habit of waiting until I was balls deep in her sweet little snatch to ask me for shit.

"Never mind, you'll get mad." I stopped fucking up into her and pulled her head back so I could look into her eyes. "Babe, the only kind of man who gets mad at his woman for telling him what she wants or don't want in bed is an asshole. I'm not that man, talk to me." She leaned over and whispered some shit in my ear.

"Well now, hop off." I smacked her ass hard and

she slid off my dick with a pout as I climbed off the bed. "See, now you're mad."

"Nope, I'm going to grab the lube from my overnight case. If you want me in your ass we're gonna need a tubful of that shit." I didn't even stop to think how my sweet innocent little girl knew about ass fucking. She'd spent the day with Law's woman and her crew, and who knows what the fuck else they'd taught her?

"On your hands and knees." I instructed her as I came back into the room. She was still hot from our fuck so all that was needed was a little warm up. I eased an extra finger in her ass this time instead of just one to test the tightness and was barely able to get past the first knuckle.

"Relax baby." I ran my other hand gently down her back before moving it around to her pussy and her swollen clit. I teased her clit while working my fingers in and out of her ass, before slipping my fingers from her clit to her slit.

"Move your ass back and forth on my finger baby, that's it." When I was able to get both fingers in her ass I pulled out and grabbed the lube. Since she was already there and her pussy was winking at me through her thighs, I gave her my tongue.

She pushed her ass back against my face and her

thighs shook, before I licked from her pussy to her tight asshole and back. She was ready as fuck.

Opening her ass I squeezed a healthy helping of the greasy lubricant into her ass before spreading even more over my cock length. "Play with your pussy for me baby." I needed to keep her primed because I knew this shit was gonna hurt.

She touched herself as I stroked my cock back to its full length, spreading the lube in the process. When my cock was leaking pre-cum until there was a string of it hanging, I eased in behind her and lined up.

I had a moment's doubt when I saw my monster up against her tightly puckered asshole, but she'd asked for this. There was really no easy way to do this, no matter what she was going to feel this shit.

I let just the head of my cock slip into her tight ring until it snapped around the soft rubbery tip. The lube made it easy to slip even farther in her, bet my piercings were going to be trouble.

I eased back and then forward, only feeding her a couple inches at a time. I was beginning to think that was all she'd be able to take because she was already making ass hurt noises, but then she relaxed all the way and I was able to slip even deeper in her ass.

"Fuck baby your ass is tight as fuck." She lowered

her head and raised her ass as if telling me to get on with it. Holding onto her hips, I started a slow in and out fuck into her ass while she kept her fingers stuffed in her cunt.

"How's that babygirl?"

"Uh huh." She nodded her head and looked over her shoulder at me with lust filled eyes. I think I'll give her wine more often, if my ass could keep up with her shit.

It was her first time and as tight as her ass was and as much as I wanted to fuck the shit out of her I knew if I stayed in her too long this first time she'd be fucked.

I reached for her tits and fondled her nipples while riding her ass. With her fingers buried in her cunt she was over stimulated and was soon there again. Not that she'd ever really stopped cumming.

When my dick grew and started throbbing in her ass I pulled out and pushed her to her back. It was that kinda night. I stroked my cock over her until I sprayed her tits, face and pussy hair with my jizz.

LAW

~

"Babe, I'm going to have a lot of company in the next few days, I need you to make sure the place is ready. Give the guesthouse a once over and make sure the beds and shit are all set." The fuck I know about having guests?

She wasn't paying me much mind she was too busy running her tongue up my thigh for her morning dose, greedy fuck. Since she seemed to be in a teasing mood I decided to help her out.

I grabbed the sides of her head and moved her over from my thigh to my cock. "That what you after?" She licked my shit and smiled around my cockhead, my little wanton.

"Suck me to hard so I can give you what you want before this place is crawling with people needing shit." She did a damn fine job of sucking me into her throat and almost had me shooting off in her neck before I caught myself.

When my dick was hard as fuck I pulled her up over me. Usually our first round of the day was a little less rushed, but as it stood I didn't have time to eat the pussy, maybe later.

So I just sat her on my cock and pulled her down so I could reach her tits with my mouth. She rode my cock as I nibbled her flesh, her pussy still tight as fuck.

All the shit that was going, that I was keeping from her, had me straining at the bit. Being reminded that not too long ago someone had all but bought her and seeing her in that fucking book made me want to commit murder.

Royce was dead, but there was still the question of who the fuck was behind that shit. Because of the thoughts in my head I found myself throwing her to her back and slamming into her over and over again while she threw her legs in the air and fucked back at me.

"Fuck Dana Sue, am I hurting you?" I don't know why the fuck I was asking it's not like I was gonna stop. Her pussy pretty much owns my ass and if she ever figures that shit out my life would be even more of a pain than it already is.

As it stood I tried my best to break my dick off in her before emptying my nuts deep in her womb. When she flew off the bed in the middle of our after sex cuddle kiss and headed for the bathroom for the second morning in a row, I was pretty sure that I'd bred her.

I followed her in and held her hair while she was sick as a dog. "Babe, you're pregnant." Why the fuck that should make her give me the evil eye was anybody's guess. It's not like I was the only one fucking, she was there too and if I remember correctly about fifty percent of the time, she's the one begging me for cock.

"Just leave me here to die, you can go." I rolled my eyes at her theatrics before heading into the kitchen to get her a can of Ginger ale. After getting her cleaned up she sucked it down and eyed my dick again. Shit, she was in one of those moods.

By the time I made it out the door once her pussy released me from its hold, there was a cavalcade coming through my gates. It had been a while since I'd seen these boys, but it was always a good thing when I did.

They jumped down out the campers looking around like they were in enemy territory, once a SEAL... I walked over to meet them just as the women were being helped down.

I shoulda known with all the shit Lo had told me was going on in their backyard that they would bring the girls with, that was the reason for the RVs. There was even a baby in the mix.

"Ty you had a kid?" I wonder how he relaxed long enough to get the deed done; fucker was always serious. "She's Zak's we share." The little angel smiled at me before turning to him and jabbering away.

I got distracted for a minute by the interaction because damn if he wasn't answering her back like he understood the lingo. Lo and Connor came over and clapped me on the shoulder bringing me back to the here and now.

I saw Zak, Dev, Cord and Quinn either brow-beating or lecturing the women I wasn't sure which, but it didn't look like they were having much luck.

"How's it hanging brother, where's the wild one?" They looked around for Creed but he and his woman weren't back yet. "Should be here soon, he got married last night so him and his bride headed up to the cabin a few miles in. Say, you boys need the priest? He should still be around here somewhere."

"Don't think so, no offense but our women would mutiny if we deny them the shindig they've been planning for fucking ever. Bad enough we've had to put it off because of this bullshit, but me for one will not be telling Gabriella that she can't have what the fuck she wants."

"Bitch made one and two at it again." Ty had passed the baby off to her mom and joined us. Come to think of it, he seemed more relaxed than I'd ever seen him, a lot less rough around the edges too.

The seven of them were soon surrounding me but no one brought up the reason for them being here as yet, I guess they were waiting for the women to get settled.

They had a kid with them that they just introduced as Davie and I figured he was in training for some fuck and left it at that. His sister was among the women too apparently and I wondered fleetingly since when the SEALs became babysitters.

Dana Sue had got herself together and was putting her fancy East Coast schooling bullshit to good use, playing hostess. Of course she was drooling over the baby, which reminded me of what she'd done immediately after I fucked her just now. Her ass better not be sick like that every morning or I'd lose my shit for sure.

We heard the rumbling of an engine minutes before Creed came barreling around the corner. His stride was a little more relaxed when he walked around to help his new bride down from the truck, and he didn't seem to mind PDA, since he damn near ate her face off with a kiss. Then again knowing him, he could be marking his for all to see.

He watched her walk over to the other women to be introduced before joining us. "Hi boys long time no see." I'm thinking he had a good fucking night because he was no longer looking like he was ready to chew nails. We were in a fucked up place if I was the one monitoring everyone else's mood. I hope my town survived this little get together when the dust settled.

"Are we all here? I need to get a bead on this Stockton fucker if he's around here before he flies the coop again." Now that was the Ty I knew and loved.

"We still haven't seen him yet but if you tracked him here and that book ties in then there are only so many places around here he could be hiding out.

We'll get to the bottom of it. Just one more player, he should be here…"

Just then Chaz opened up the gate and a whole fucking crew of bikers came riding in. The leader dismounted off his custom made top of the line ride with his wife's name emblazoned on the side and headed for us. One smooth motherfucker this one, and the shades just tipped that shit over the edge.

"Fuck Lyon, what did you do, bring the whole gang?" We slapped hands before sharing a man hug while his guys dismounted.

"Well from your hemming and hawing bullshit I gathered this little meet wasn't about bikes so I came prepared." He stopped short when he saw the others lined off in the middle of the yard.

"What the fuck is this Law a soldier boy's convention?" He looked around at the others before returning his gaze back to me. "The government know you soldier boy fucks are planning a coup?"

"Funny! No, this isn't about that…" Shit, how the fuck do you tell an irrational man that one of his was in danger? I know this fucker and though he didn't serve he would've made one hell of a mercenary. Then again that may not be true because he didn't take direction well.

"Is it your family, the deal with your folks and

your kid sister? I told you we'd come down and take care of it, but you said…"

"Nah, it's not that either my bird ran to ground and the other one's six deep." Shit Law stop being a bitch and tell the man already. Yeah, but I was trying to imagine being in his shoes and how I would react to this shit.

I looked across the yard to where Dana Sue and her meddling ass posse were taking Creed's woman and the teams' girls off somewhere. Good, at least they would be safe in case something went haywire with this fucking guy.

"Why don't I show you instead? And Colt, stay cool." I saw his whole demeanor change with that warning. It was the first hint I'd given him that this might involve him, fuck. "Give me a minute."

I walked back over to the boys and pulled Lo aside. "I need a solid brother, there's going to be a lot of heat in that room in about five minutes. I know Colt, and I'm thinking of everyone involved he might be our loose canon."

"How so?" He looked over to where the big guy was being introduced around and it hit me that he was the oldest one here though you couldn't tell from his appearance, fucker never changes. Must be that young wife and the battalion of kids he had.

"You and I, we were trained, there's a point that we can be pulled back from. Lyon doesn't have that and I'm thinking when he sees his little girl's face on that screen all hell's gonna break loose.

I'm barely holding Creed back but that leash is about to pop, and your boy Ty isn't far behind. At least with him he knows what he's looking for, those two don't, we have more questions there than answers."

"And you?" I knew he was gonna get around to asking sooner or later. My grin was what you might call menacing. "I'm holding my shit down for now, but you best believe the shit's gonna get ugly. I need to take care of my boys first though, Dana Sue is safe, let's make sure these other women are."

"Still looking out for everyone huh soldier." We walked back to where the others were exchanging small talk even though the atmosphere was rife with tension. "It's what I do."

"Follow me." We headed for the clubhouse and filed into the back room where the shit from last night was still hooked up. The SEALs lined one wall; only Lo took a seat, along with Lyon, Creed and me. While my men, Creed's and Lyon's held up the other three walls.

"Okay Lyon, the rest of us have had time to look

at this shit in the last day or so. I'm gonna show you what we've got and then we're gonna decide what to do next. As it stands we have more questions than answers..."

"Bro, you're starting to make me nervous, I don't like being nervous, just tell me what the fuck..." I passed the album off to him and waited.

I saw his brow furrow as he paged through and felt my muscles tense when he came to the page I knew his kid was on. "Caitie Bear? What the fuck is this? Who the fuck are these kids?"

"That's what we're trying to figure out."

"Start fucking talking." He looked around the table at all of us, his face set in stone. "Lo?" I turned to the man who'd sent me the book.

"Right. The book you're holding in your hand was confiscated from the home of a man we suspect is guilty of human trafficking among other things..."

The fucker flew out his seat and headed for the door. Everyone in the room got to their feet because that's what the fuck you do when confronted with a dangerous animal on the loose.

"Where the fuck is he?"

"We don't know, that's what we're trying to find out, but I'm afraid this shit is bigger than we thought and it stretches far and wide."

"I need five." He pulled his phone and walked out of the room, with his boy Jared on his heels. "We wait." I told the others as we took our seats. Hopefully whatever call he was making would give him time to cool the fuck down so he didn't destroy my place with his shit. Fuck!

LYON

"Kat." I tried to calm my voice so I didn't spook her, my girl spooks easily especially when it comes to me, and the kids. "Baby, I need you to go get the kids from school."

My heart all but raced out of my chest because I wasn't fucking there. I needed to be there to make sure my little girl was safe, but since I couldn't be this was the next best thing.

"What why, they still have a few hours left." I bit back the anger that was no fault of hers. Now was not the time to lose my shit, and she was not the one, never her.

"Kat, angel, I love you, now do as I say. I need you to go get the kids from school." She'd know that me repeating the statement in that calm tone meant not to fucking question me and just do as I say.

"Okay um Colt, is everything okay?" I heard the strain in her voice and bit down hard. I'd promised her that she'd never know another day of worry and I mean to keep that fucking promise if I have to kill off half the fucks in the known world.

"It will be, call me the minute you and the kids are in the house." I heard her talking to the baby as she got him dressed to go outside. I couldn't help thinking of how she'd looked when I'd left her only a few short hours ago.

The way she always looked every morning in my bed. Well fucked and happy, giving her man shit about something or other. I remembered my kids at the breakfast table noisy and happy, and super imposed over that image was the one I'd just seen of my innocent little girl in that fucking book.

I hung up and called my father in law. "Drake I have a situation here can't get into it now but I just sent Kat to pick the kids up from school. I need you to meet her there with a few of your deputies and escort them home. I need you to call dad and Emory and tell them to get to the house. My family is not to be left alone until I get back there."

"Colt what the hell is going on?"

"I just saw my fucking daughter in some child trafficker's book that's what the fuck is going on."

"You what, okay hold on, let's think this thing through, first where are you?"

"Like I said, can't get into it now, I have to deal with this shit." I knew why he was asking but he was shitting in the wind. That fucker was as good as dead, the fuck.

"Yeah I know but Colt, don't do anything stupid, think about Katarina and the kids. Let the law handle it…"

I'm pretty sure he wasn't talking about Law, but what he didn't know won't hurt him. "Law's already on it." I hung up before he could ask me anything more and headed back inside to wait for the call from my wife.

The shit didn't seem real, I felt like I was outside of my body looking in. The men were in the room brainstorming, while my own guys were giving me looks like what the fuck are we waiting for? I nodded to let them know I understood and we were on the same fucking page.

There was nothing I could do until I knew more, but I know these soldier boy fuck types, they're into that law and order bullshit. I don't have time for that fuckery, not when it comes to mine.

So I sat and I listened and pieced shit together. I didn't give a fuck who did what to whom, I was just waiting for the name of the motherfucker who put the book together. At least they knew one of the players from what I had garnered, I'll start there.

"What's this fuck's name again, the one who had the book?" I directed my question to the Logan guy since he's the one who sent the book.

"Who Stockton, Carlson, why?" I pulled my phone again. It was answered on the second ring. "Lyon isn't our meet tomorrow?"

"Yeah Travis but something came up, I need your dad's resources. Do you know anything about child trafficking in our neck of the woods?"

"There's always some fuck going on, people are too fucking idle. I haven't heard anything but I'll ask the old man. If it's happening around here he'd know; what's going on?"

"Someone put the bead on your Goddaughter." Saying those words burnt a hole in my gut. "What the fuck you say?"

"Yeah, I'm looking at it now."

"You home?"

"Nah, I'm at Law's." I noticed that the room was quiet; they were all listening in on my conversation.

"I'll be there in three let me get dad on it. You got

a name associated or nah?" I gave him the only name we had before hanging up. I felt a little better knowing that shit was being done.

I looked at the SEAL, Tyler I think they'd called him. "I know you think he's yours because he worked over your woman, but if he's the fuck responsible for putting my little girl in that fuck we're gonna tussle."

He moved against the wall and didn't say anything for the longest while, just stared at me. "We'll share, there's more than enough of the fuck to go around." Good enough. I wasn't looking forward to butting heads with anyone in the room out of respect for Law and the fact that they seemed cool, but I will if I have to.

Like I said, that law and order shit is for the birds. I'm not talking over shit with this mother-fucker. I get eyes on him he's as good as dead.

"Creed you said you think your woman's aunt and her man might be responsible for your girl being in there, where are they?" Please give me someone to hunt; this sitting around shit will drive my ass nuts.

"Fuckers pulled a runner but Law thinks they might be in the hills around here being protected by the local hate brigade." He sneered that shit and I could see that he wasn't too far off from what I was feeling.

"Those fucks involved in this shit? Why am I not surprised?" I answered my phone just as a call came in for Law on his phone. "Kat you got them, you home? Good stay there until I get back, do not let my kids out of your sight. My dad and yours and some of the guys are gonna be over soon."

"They're here already; Colton what is going on?" Her voice started to tremble making my gut hurt. "Nothing for you to worry about angel, I'll fill you in when I get back."

Like fuck, she'd lose her fucking mind if she ever found out that her kid was in that shit. After the shit she'd suffered herself years ago, there was no way I was gonna do that to her, she'd be haunted the rest of her life.

I hung up in time to see two new players enter the room. One of them I knew because we'd done charity runs together in the past, but the other though he looked familiar wasn't known to me.

"Blade you got a dog in this fight too?" He reached out a hand to shake but his ass wasn't smiling. I knew he had a kid of his own with his first wife and a few with the second, plus he was always doing rescue missions and shit like that, so this would be right up his alley.

Though my guys and I were into charity drives and Good Samaritan shit, it had been some time since we'd dealt with anything this serious, so it had been some time since we'd ridden together. But we still reached out once in a while. "Law said your kid was involved, of course I'm here."

The introductions were made around the room while each man sized the other up. Fucking high school pissing contest, I give a fuck. The soldier boy fucks seemed relaxed enough until you looked close enough and realized they were strung tight and ready to spring at the slightest provocation.

I had to give it to them; it must take a fuckload of training to pull that shit off. You wouldn't tell by looking at them that they were a crew of murdering bastards, but I know the signs only too well.

"Everyone this is Jake Summers, he heads a special division on the force a few towns over, one of the best." Law made the introductions and I remembered where I'd seen his name and face before. It was in the papers a while ago when he'd busted up some ring, but that was about drugs though I think.

Place was starting to crawl with law and order

types. As long as no one gets in my way when the time comes they could deploy the fucking National Guard for all I give a fuck.

We had another round of catching everyone up, as I sat there biding my time. It's fucked, but I wasn't interested in anything but the whereabouts of the fuckers who were responsible for this fuckery. Call me selfish, then again if I off these motherfuckers, game over, end of story.

They were throwing around ideas and I got to see up close and personal how the military did shit. I can't say it was all that different to how I ran my guys, except for the by the book fuckery. If people would stop catering to the assholes of the world it would leave more fucking breathing space for decent human beings. That ought to take care of climate change, the fuck.

CREED

*E*veryone was here, and I think it was safe to say the room was full of barely leashed anger. I was outwardly calm, not giving shit away as Jake did his thing on the phone with his office.

I wasn't worried about Jake reining shit in when shit popped off. He's law enforcement yeah, but he's not fuck stupid. We rode together before, so let's just say I know how he rolls.

It was like running an Op; each man had his thing to do to bring it all together. Colt and I were tasked with trying to identify the girls in the pictures and passing the names off to Jake who was feeding them to someone in his office who was inputting them into a database of some kind.

The shit was tedious at best, but we needed it

done. Blade, because of his work with kids who'd been abused had a few strings he could pull and was busy making calls, and me I was just waiting for dark so I could head up into the hills.

"Creed, you really planning to sit around here with your thumb up your ass while these fucks molt in the hills?" Lyon didn't even pick his head up or miss a step when he asked me that question under his breath so the rest of the room couldn't hear. "Nope."

We exchanged a look and went back to what we were doing with a new understanding. I need action. Even when I worked with the SEAL team in the past, I only came in on the tail end. I was usually the one in the trees or the clefts waiting to pick a mother-fucker off. Yes that shit took patience, but there was none of that tedious planning shit. Just aim and shoot, it's what the fuck I do.

At about noon we took a break and I went and found babygirl. I took her out of Law's place and headed for the guesthouse next door. "This is going to be hard and fast." I pushed her back against the wall and tore her panties down her thighs, before unleashing my dick.

I played up and down her slit with my swollen cockhead until she juiced and then slid home. I fucked out the last few hours' frustration in her pussy, banging her poor body into the wall until she was begging me for mercy. I pulled her down to the floor and drove into her over and over again until she tightened around me and screamed and I came a shitload inside her.

Only then did the dark haze lift from my eyes and I was able to think clearly again. "I love you." I held her tighter, closer as I left my cock breathing inside her. "I want to have a baby with you." Shit; what the fuck was up with me, and blurting shit out when I didn't mean to?

"You mean it?"

"Of course I do." I pulled back to look down into her face. "I want to have lots and lots of babies with you." I kissed her again as my cock hardened inside her and went for round two.

By the time I offloaded inside her the second time I was feeling human again. "What freaky shit are you and your girls planning for my ass later?" She blushed and ran her fingers over my chest. "Ginger was talking about this new position…"

Her voice trailed off and she got red as a chili pepper. "We'll try it later." I pulled out and helped her to her feet before heading to the bathroom to clean us both up. I gave her pussy a little tongue action from behind while she leaned over the sink, before heading back out to meet the boys.

"Okay, so this is what we've got so far. The shit seems to have started in Georgia, here." I pointed to the map at the area where the SEALs place was located. Everyone had come back from break ready for action.

"You said you found a tunnel running from the water to his house or vice versa. Now we have to figure out how he gets them to his house from the rest of the country."

I was feeling ten times lighter after my little break and because of the fact that when we got back to the room Jake had done his thing and uncovered more info for us to work with. If this shit kept up, we could be making a move in the next few hours, tomorrow the latest.

"We've identified most of the girls, but sadly, most of them are already missing. I have someone working on some kind of pattern to see how they're choosing them and when they started." Jake gave his report of what else he'd done so far.

"There's no real connection between any of the

girls on this list, but I'm thinking there is and we're just overlooking it somehow, there has to be a connection. I hate to say it, but the fact that two of us in this room, make that three, have been affected by this in some way, might be key."

That shit had been plaguing me all the way back here. Jessie didn't know Dana Sue before yesterday, or Lyon's kid. So how did all three end up in the same book?

"So let's look at it. Ty how are you and I connected? We ran Ops together in the desert."

"The problem with that is I didn't know Victoria-Lyn back then." Ty pitched in.

"Doesn't matter, let's go back. This is the starting point, your new hometown, where your old CO used to live."

"Do we know when the shit started?" Lyon moved around on his chair and I knew he was getting antsy, can't say that I blamed him. My woman was across the way and so was Ty's. His kid, though he'd put eyes on her, wasn't close enough for him to protect himself. That shit would make anybody nervous.

"According to the old timers a little over a year before we got there. We now know that the CO was onto whatever it was they had going on, so it could've been up to six months before that." Logan rocked back in his chair as I tried to clear my mind. The answer was there but I was just not hitting on it.

I walked over to the board we'd had set up and looked over it all again. There was the name of the town, the CO, Stockton, Dee and Sal, but what was the connection and where the fuck did Colt come in?

"Okay thinking out loud again. Ty, you and I are connected through the Ops we ran together, under your CO, which mostly involved…" I looked at the SEALs in the room.

"Something you wanna tell us?" Everyone got quiet as my blood started a slow boil. So far all they'd told us was that they thought the local barracks was involved somehow but they hadn't expounded too much on that. Now Lo sat forward in his chair before looking around at all the players.

"All non military personnel have to leave."

"Fuck that, try me." Lyon didn't even break a sweat when he stared down the big tough SEAL; guy has balls. Logan studied him long enough to come up with his decision while Law, Blade and I gave the go ahead for our men to file out.

"Your kid's involved you get a pass."

"Uh-huh." I'd forgotten what a hard ass Lyon

tended to be. He nodded to his boy Jared who did not look too pleased as he gathered the rest of their crew and headed out.

Now it was just Law, the SEALs, Blade, Jake, Lyon and I left in the room. "What I'm about to share doesn't leave this room, your word on that." Each man nodded his agreement before Lo got to his feet and approached the board.

"We have reason to believe that this man is involved, if not actually running the whole thing." He added the Desert Fox and I felt another piece of the puzzle slide into place. Still there was something missing.

"Who the fuck is that?" And there you have it. Lyon had no dealings with him, unless he was building bikes for terrorists.

"He's a very bad man who we hunted for three years and were under the impression until here lately had been annihilated. His name was found in some files in the same raid in which we found the infamous picture book."

"Now this guy Stockton." He drew a line from the Fox to Stockton. "Is just a bit player, he works for the Porter family...."

"The fuck did you say?" Lyon was out of his seat moving towards the board as if he'd seen a ghost.

"You know them?" Lo watched him out the side of his eye. I would too, that fucker looked like he was about to blow.

"If it's the same, their son tried to rape my woman before she was my woman years ago. He and his pals actually succeeded in raping her friend who went on to kill herself. Their son got off while the others did time in jail. They never made it out."

He looked around the room like, 'make of that what you will soldier boys I don't give a fuck.' What he didn't know is that every man in the room including the law enforcer would do the same as he was implying to protect their own.

"If these fucks are fucking with my kid you're never gonna have the chance to solve your deal here. They're fucked."

"I feel you brother, but that's not the way to go. We safeguard your family, but we have to find these other girls, and look it, we have another piece of the puzzle." Lo turned back to the board.

"Okay so with this new information, we know that The Fox is the common denominator. So far he's gone after all of our women in one-way or another, with the exception of you Lyon, he went after your kid. Maybe as a favor to this family, since you had nothing to do with him personally."

Yeah, that's the piece that was missing. "How the fuck did they get into bed with this guy? They're not in Georgia either..."

"The oldest son was in army intelligence, we only just found that out through a source that we are not at liberty to name."

After that we tried to piece the shit together with what we had, but it was obvious we were still missing huge chunks of information. For one, how did The Fox know anything about Jessie, unless he was having me followed? And how had he gotten to Dee and Sal?

I understood them doing it for the money, that part was self -explanatory, but who had made the approach, how and when?

Lyon was prowling the room like his namesake and this shit was not gonna end well for anyone if we stood in his way. I'm thinking we need to get to the bottom of this shit and soon before this boy pops his leash. Then nobody would know shit and the rest of those kids would be fucked.

There was a knock on the door and some smooth biker type stood there looking like he owned the place. "I'm looking for Lyon."

"Travis you made it." Lyon moved across the room to greet the newcomer before introducing him to everyone except Law who already knew him.

He looked around the room with a smirk on his face that I didn't understand until I caught his last name. "Fuck! Lyon you play in the big leagues don't you brother?" Everyone knew Travis' old man if not personally, then by reputation. The man just might make The Fox look like an innocent.

Jake was eyeing the kid who wasn't paying anyone any mind. He was there for one reason and one reason only, to share information.

He passed off an envelope to Lyon who snatched it open before scanning the contents and then passing them around.

"He's here." I looked up at the Travis guy who was leaning against the wall at ease.

"Yep. But he's a small fish in a big pond. My dad's doing some more digging, but since my boy Colt needed this shit yesterday and it involves my Goddaughter I figured I'd bring what I have for now."

"He's a small time crook who somehow made it onto one of those military contractor deals a few years back. There's no record of exactly what he did there, but he came back with new connections and a whole new group of friends."

The SEALs shared a look and a grin. "Damn son you just answered one of our questions for us. We couldn't figure out how he went from small time crook to the big leagues. Funny though, we didn't find any record of him being a contractor and our connects would've known that." Lo didn't look too pleased about that.

We went back to the board and put all the new pieces together until shit was starting to make sense. At least I had a name and now a face.

I went down the line until we came to Stockton and why he might be hiding out here, which was another piece of the puzzle that was missing. I was still trying to figure out how he came across her and how they made the connection to me.

Jake took over from there since his people had been feeding him intelligence the whole time we were in there.

"Your boy Stockton came home, he was born here. Folks moved up east when he was too young to know. Guess who's his great uncle? The- Grand-whatever-the-fuck himself.

It looks like they've been using this area and some of the surrounding towns as their hunting ground; lots of missing teenage girls in the last few years.

You guys were the exception to the rule it seems like. The other girls in this file and their families have no known association with this Desert guy or the family you mentioned.

What it looks like is this ring has been in existence for a while. We'll have to dig farther to figure out who started it, but somewhere along the way someone started using it against at least a few of you in this room.

From what Logan has said, it appears the Fox guy is calling the shots and this family is his puppet on a string stateside. He used this to go after your women I'm guessing because you fucked with him for three years.

And in turn, the family used this opportunity to get back at you Lyon for whatever happened to the son that I just found out has been missing for as long as you've been married give or take a few weeks."

I have to give it to him Lyon is one cool fuck. He didn't even bat a lash even though I was pretty sure a top ranking law enforcement officer had just accused him of murder.

"I only have one question, when do we ride?" Lyon stopped his prowling shit long enough to ask.

"Boys, I can't officially be a party to any conversation that deals with vigilantism." I guess Jake felt the need to put that shit out there but we all got his meaning when he cut the connection to his office.

"Okay what's the plan?" That's what the fuck I'm talking about. Enough of this talking shit it's time for some action. I wasn't as interested in the Stockton guy as I was in Dee and Sal. I figured we'd get to the bottom of the rest of this shit in due time.

I'm pretty sure Lo and his boys were gonna go after the Fox at some point and maybe I'll get in on that, but for now I was more than ready to take care of my problem.

We brainstormed for what felt like hours until the women broke that shit up to feed us. After that it was time for a break anyway since we'd been at it for fucking ever. So we each went our separate ways except Lyon and the Travis guy, those two seemed deep in thought.

When we were finally alone for two minutes I took her for a stroll around the property. It felt like we hadn't had a moment to ourselves since we got here.

The shit was playing heavy on my mind and it was on the tip of my tongue to ask her some things, but I kept pulling myself back. I wasn't about to ask her anything that would tip her off to what the fuck was going on.

Brand, one of Law's boys, had promised to talk to his woman and see if she knew anything, if maybe she saw something that she hadn't realized or some shit while she was living with her grandfather the racist before he rescued her.

"How're you doing baby, you having a nice visit with the girls?" I think it was the first time she'd ever had this much time with friends if the stories she'd told me were accurate.

She perked right the fuck up and went into a spiel about all the shit they had planned for the future. I wonder if Law and his crew knew that their women sat around all day planning out their lives for them?

When she got to blushing and biting into her lip I figured she was remembering some other nasty shit they'd introduced her to, like some of the shit she had me doing the night before. Damn!

They were too many warm bodies moving around to fuck, definitely later, but for now I pulled her into me for a much-needed kiss.

"Yo Creed." I picked my head up to see Lyon, Travis and Tyler heading our way. Oh fuck, this can't be good. I looked around for Logan and the others but everyone seemed to be really taking their break.

"Go back to the others baby, if they're busy head

to the guesthouse and stay there until I come get you." I patted her ass and sent her on her way.

"What are we doing?" there was no point in pretending this wasn't about the four of us going off on our own, I could see it written all over their faces.

"Travis just heard from his old man, the book, that's old school. I'm thinking this Stockton guy kept that shit as a souvenir. They've upped their game, now there's a whole database of potential targets. We'll work our way through that in time. Right now we need to get our hands on this fuck and make him talk. I wanna know who the fuck set them on my kid and who the fuck was her potential buyer."

"Ty? Lo know you doing this?"

"Nope." Shit, he'd already zoned so there was no use in even trying to talk him down, not that I really wanted to.

"So how do we plan to do this?" They let me in on their plan to slip away unnoticed as soon as it was dark enough. Lyon had got hold of a rough map of the hills from somewhere and Ty said he would handle some kind of explosive.

For the rest of the evening we went back to the grindstone only this time with the new info from Travis' old man. Halfway through that shit there was a fucking roar that had each of us going on alert.

Cord, one of the SEALs was being held back my Devon and Quinn, two of his SEAL brothers. "What is it?" Logan their leader got into the fray as the rest of their crew gathered around them.

They were all looking at the screen before Cord broke away and headed for the door at a dead run. On the screen was the girl they'd brought along with them earlier, the one with the brother.

"Damn, she his?" I looked at Ty for an answer. "Yep." Shit, there wasn't gonna be enough of that old boy to go around. Ty and I exchanged a look over the others' heads before going back to work.

There were fucking thousands of girls there. I tried not to let it fuck with me when I saw an updated picture of my wife on the screen, but I wasn't too sure Lyon was fairing so well when he saw his daughter scroll by.

So far we still only had the three players, the Fox, Stockton, and the family that Lyon had tussled with. But if this shit went back as far as it did, the Fox wasn't the one who started it, that shit didn't make any sense.

Dig as we might we weren't finding anything that would tell us who. Which told me that they were well insulated whoever they were. That meant money and power.

The four of us never spoke on what we had planned after we'd left the yard. It was just a given between us that when the time was right we'd make our move.

Cord had gone on a tear ever since he'd seen his woman's face and was making sure the place was secure SEAL style, which meant it might take some doing to get off the property but I had no doubts it could be done.

For the last half of the evening I found her and took her back to the guesthouse with me. I actually sat and watched some mind numbing shit on the tube with her, but she seemed so happy just to sit there that I didn't have the heart to tell her that we wouldn't be doing that shit again ever.

I was trying to show her that we weren't just about fucking, that we could be in the same room alone with each other for more than five minutes without me trying to fuck a new hole in her snatch, but that shit was a major fail.

Her movie hit a snag and before she could blink I had her in my lap with her top pulled up, bra shoved out of the way and her tit in my mouth.

I'd insisted she wear jeans and button ups while we were here with a tank underneath, too many fucking dicks roaming this fucking place for my taste. But I was regretting that shit now, especially when I had to let go of her tit so she could lose the jeans.

I just shoved mine halfway down my thighs and had her straddle my cock. "Come up here let me get your pussy wet." I had her climb over me so that her pussy was in my face.

I teased her clit with my tongue while holding her ass in my hands before digging in her pussy with my stiff tongue. She fucked herself to orgasm on my face and damn near scalped me when she came.

I pulled her down roughly and sat her on my stiff cock pulling her down hard so that she was all the way stuffed. "Ride." She moved her fucking hips like my dick was gonna disappear; hard, fast and wild.

"Wait, wait a minute. What was that new position you were talking about earlier?" She hoped off my dick and laid on her stomach on the couch. She placed one leg on the back of the couch and the other on the floor, opening her pink gash for my dick to explore.

There was only one way to fuck in this position so I straddled her hip and drove my cock in at an angle. "Oh yeah." She winced and did her pussy hurt dance on my cock but my boy was in pussy heaven.

I grabbed handfuls of her ass as I fucked into her,

pulling the globes of her ass up tight, which tightened her pussy even more around my cock.

I found a rhythm and picked up the pace, slamming my cockhead into her cervix and beyond. I was pretty sure we were gonna owe Law a couch after this shit since she was flowing all over the seat cushions.

Wrapping my hand around her neck, I squeezed before bending her neck back to feed her my tongue and suck on hers. She ground her clit into the cushion beneath her as I skewered her until she came.

I jerked and spazzed as I offloaded inside her sweet cunt, damn near bending her in half so I could keep our mouths together. When her mouth went slack I realized I'd fucked her into a faint.

I brought her around long enough to make sure she was okay, before I put her to bed, which is what I was after. I wanted her here safe in bed while I did what I had to do. I had no idea what the fuck was gonna happen in the next few hours.

Had no way of knowing if these fucks were lying in wait or if there was going to be some kind of retaliation. One thing I knew was that I was coming back to her no matter what. "I'll always protect you babygirl." With one last look I headed out into the night.

We were going to meet at a certain spot as soon as the moon reached the top of the mountain. That would mean it was headed this way away from the hills leaving the place in darkness, which is when some of us did our best work.

I got there first but Lyon and his boy weren't far behind, followed soon by Tyler. There wasn't much said as we headed in the direction we'd chosen earlier. I was a little surprised though to find our rides waiting there and one for Ty.

"Do I even ask?" I asked Travis who grinned at my question and jumped on his ride before pulling his helmet down.

"Soldier boy you got the explosives?" Lyon was on his shit again but Ty didn't seem to take offense, though he seemed stuck on one-word answers. "Yep."

I'd heard the story about what had been done to his girl so I couldn't be mad at him for going inward like that. That's the kind a shit that makes a man study murder and other fuckery that the average Joe never has to face. For a soldier, a fucking SEAL at that, I can only imagine what he's been holding in.

TYLER

Finally, I was gonna get my hands on this fuck. It had been weeks since he'd flown the coop and I've been getting more than a little antsy. We'd thrown that book aside in lieu of the files when we'd first got back to the compound after the raid.

Back then we were more interested in looking for evidence that would lead us to who was committing crimes in our little paradise. Never once did any of us think it would turn into this.

The first inkling we had that it may be something is when my brother Dev had leafed through it and found the notations in the back. Being in the service all those years, we'd never really ran into anything like that. I'm guessing that was more along the lines of the F.B.I or some shit, but we had a feeling that the shit was off even though whoever had complied it had tried to be slick.

We'd already suspected that there was a trafficking ring working out of our back yard, and this Stockton fuck was knee deep in the shit, but until then we had no real leads. The book had opened up a whole new avenue.

Now these men had come together and we were finally piecing some of the shit that was missing together. I'm sure that we were only tapping the surface, but for now I would be satisfied with getting my own back from this motherfucker.

A few weeks ago he'd done a number on my woman and left her near death and chained up in a hotel room like a fucking dog. Lucky for him he hadn't gotten around to the ultimate violation, not for lack of trying. But my girl had fought the disgusting pig and damn near lost her life for it. Now it looked like it was time to give him his due.

I'd left my woman back there asleep, well fucked and rested. We were still new so every opportunity alone was an opportunity to fuck, not to mention I was on a mission to breed, so every time I looked at her I was in her.

She had no idea what the fuck we were doing here; none of our women did as far as I can tell. Lo had given them some story about visiting an old friend and giving them time away from home where they've been virtual prisoners for the last few weeks.

They ran with that shit and as far as I could see were having the time of their lives. Victoria-Lyn was all healed up and already giving me shit, joining ranks with her sisters and the baby to make us do fucking cartwheels to please them. Fucking females.

Now as I watched the other three mount up, I took their measure. It was the first time I've ever gone on an Op without my brothers and it felt strange, almost like a betrayal. I almost turned back, almost. But then I remembered her battered and broken and decided I could live with it.

Creed I knew but the other two were unknowns. The younger one I now knew was very deceptive with his smiling shit. My brother Con had done a run as soon as we got back to the RV and learned as much as was known about his family, which wasn't much, which in itself was enough of a red flag.

We'd learned enough to know that he was not to be fucked with, which was good enough for me. The other one, Lyon, reminded me of the CO, the man who had commanded us as SEALs. He had that same

353

'give a fuck' attitude, the one my brothers and I had adopted. I like him; in fact I liked all the men we'd met in the last day.

It was for that reason that I didn't mind too much that it wasn't my brothers going on this run with me, though I'd have preferred it. But any way I could put an end to this shit was fine with me.

I rode out behind them since I didn't know where the fuck we were headed. Lo was gonna skin my ass but that's okay, as long as I put an end to Stockton, I can deal with it.

LYON

I hope these fucks know that I'm not leaving these hills without killing this fucker, and if anyone gets in the way they're pretty much fucked too. I missed my boys at my back but this was fine too, needed to get shit done.

Kat was texting me every five minutes because she knew some fuck was wrong and I was running out of excuses. On top of that it looked like I was going to be spending the night away from her for the first fucking time ever. That shit just earned this fucker an extra bullet.

We rode in as close as we could and hid our bikes at the base of the mountain, which was more of a steep hill than anything else. "We walk it the rest of the way in." I gave the order and moved in ahead of the other three.

Each of us had our own reasons for being here, but even if we didn't have a personal stake, this shit was something that any red blooded American male should take care of. Anything that involved causing harm to women or children should be dealt with swiftly and without an ounce of give a fuck.

We got there and walked into a trap. "You guys are late." What the fuck? Fucking soldier boys are slick as shit. "Law, fancy seeing you here." The head SEAL or the one who looked to be in charge of the others was giving the Tyler guy shit but he didn't seem to mind too much.

"Kill the shit Lyon your woman sold you out."

"Kat? What the fuck?"

"Apparently she's been on with you for the last little while up until roughly an hour or so ago, when you went off grid. It doesn't take a genius to figure that shit out."

"Uh-huh, tell your soldier boy fucks if they're not here to play get the fuck down off the hill I got shit to do and bullets don't know no names." He started some shit about my head being hard but I was already on the move.

Ty met me halfway so I guess he'd squared shit with his keeper, and since they all fell in behind us I guess they figured they might as well join in.

I'ma deal with Kat's interfering ass, she ought to know better, damn snitch. The last thing I told her was that I was going to be off grid for a few, so her calling Law was to try to stop me, although she had no idea what the fuck I was up to.

I guess after you've lived with someone for as long as we've been living together you get to know them pretty well. Oh well, she can badger me to death when I was done taking care of this shit.

The SEAL leader and Law headed into the trees. Their plan was to pick the fuckers off as we smoked them out, murdering fucks.

I watched them all branch off in different directions ducking and shit like we were in the middle of the fucking jungle or some fuck. "What the fuck are you doing soldier boy?" I asked Tyler who was the only one left in the clear with me.

"Ambush, we don't know what we're walking into so it's best we approach with caution."

"How about walking up to the fucking door and shooting the first motherfucker to answer?"

The kid actually dragged me off the path and into the bushes. If this is the shit they did in the army no wonder we were gone for fucking ever in other people's country. "What the fuck am I doing back here?"

"We let the others get into position. I'm gonna blow the door as soon as we get the all clear." Now he was whispering and looking around like we were expecting a fucking invasion. What the fuck is this shit?

"What the fuck? You ever think if you soldier boy fucks had walked up to this Fox fuck and put one between his eyes we won't be here now?" Fucker had the nerve to laugh at me.

"Lyon you're alright." We got real serious real quick once the others got into place and started whistling in code and shit. Me, I was waiting for assholes to appear so I could take care of shit and get home to my woman.

"Be right back, stay here." There was a noise on the wind that sounded kind of like the elements to me, but as soon as Ty heard it he sprung into action.

I watched him disappear right before my fucking eyes and my respect for him went up a notch. Next thing I knew the sky lit up like the fourth of July and it was fucking on.

I knew what my pigeon looked like from the pic they had passed around earlier, but I kept my eyes focused in the direction Ty had gone because I knew for sure he had a hard-on as big as mine for the fuck.

Men were climbing out of trees and shit, people were running everywhere, total chaos but I kept moving forward until I found my boy crouched beside the porch just waiting.

"Here he is."

"Fuck." I barely moved out the way when he leapt through the air and took down the fucker. His fists connected with flesh at a rapid rate and all I could think was, when the fuck did we start making super soldiers in this fuck? Shit, wasn't gonna be none left for me if he kept this shit up.

"Okay young'un, we need to ask him a few questions remember?" Damn I thought I was fucked but this motherfucker was blotso, it was like looking at someone else entirely. His eyes weren't exactly dead but close to it, and the weirdest fucking thing, he wasn't even breathing hard.

I dragged the fat fuck away from him and out of the way since the others were running some kind of a raid and there were people running every which way. I'd forgotten that Creed was looking for his own birds too, so focused was I on my own shit.

"Hey asshole, you know who I am?" His eyes were almost swollen shut from Ty's fists and there was blood dripping from his lip. I waited until he focused in on me some.

"No, who are you?"

"I'm the fucker that's gonna end you if you don't tell me what the fuck the Porters want with my kid." He seemed dazed for a minute before it came back to him, then the fucker did the dumbest thing, he fucking smiled.

"I don't have to tell you shit, you think you can stop this?" The next thing out of him was a scream when I capped him in his knee. I'm sure the law enforcement guy was around here somewhere but I wasn't in the mood to give a fuck.

"The next one's going straight to the heart, start talking. Who the fuck was the buyer?" Instead of looking at me he held his knee and sneered at Tyler.

"This is all your fault, you and your meddling friends, and that old man. But I got you good didn't I? How's the little bitch you were sniffing after, did she tell you how good I was to her?"

Ty kicked him the nuts and lost his shit. I knew these soldier types were psycho, all that suave reserve. My ass. I let him work the asshole over until he was tired. In all that time he never said a word, not even when blood sprayed across his chest from the asshole's broken face. That's some scary shit.

Elsewhere the party was going on and I still didn't know any more than I did when I came up the damn mountain. "Hey, you tell me what I want to know and I'll keep this one away from you." I pulled Ty off his dumb ass again.

He was a fucking mess, but everybody wants to live right. "I talk to you I'm as good as dead. You won't stop them; it's too big, even for you and your daddy's money Lyon. Way I heard it your wife was a hot little fu…" I shot the fuck in the head.

"Whoa, Lyon, what the fuck, we were supposed to take him in."

"That was your deal soldier boy, I don't need him to tell me what I already know anyway." Like fuck I was gonna let that piece a shit live after he said that shit about my wife, he's out his fucking mind.

Looks like I have to head to fucking Arizona again to finish what the fuck I started all those years ago. When will this shit ever end?

First the psycho bitch had come after Kat years ago and now the family was after my kid. Why the fuck don't they just come at me head on?

I pulled my phone when I was a good ways away. "Hey snitch girl what're you doing?" I missed the fuck out of my wife and kids. From the moment they showed me my little girl in that shit I'd known the outcome.

As far as I was concerned this was a simple case of one down a whole fucking family to go. I'll end every last one of the motherfuckers before this shit was over. Fuckers kept regurgitating or some fuck.

"Colt, oh thank heavens, WHERE THE HELL DID YOU GO…?" I took the phone away from my ear when she started her screaming shit; she does that when she's scared. When it sounded like she was winding down I put it back to my ear.

"Babe, I don't think I'm gonna make it home tonight." She went quiet on me and swear to fuck she was crying. "But Colt, we never sleep apart." That fucking voice still has the power to make my ass stupid.

I looked at my watch in the moonlight just as Jared and the boys came up on me. I hadn't even seen them since the shit started. They weren't looking too pleased either, fucking old women. It was just after one. "Fine, I'm coming home to you. How're my kids?"

"The kids are fine, your dad had them all camping out in the basement telling them ghost stories, they're all sleeping down there tonight."

"Fuck Kat you left the pothead in the basement

with the kids? You know that's his new hideout, it's where he goes to get high." It felt good as fuck to talk to her like this. The danger wasn't past, not by a long shot, but I was gonna see to that shit soon and I'd got a good fucking start. She laughed on the other end making me feel lighter still.

"Let me take care of some stuff and I'll be home in a few. Kiss the baby for me and get some sleep, I'll wake you up when I get in." I hung up and waited for the others. This had become about more than just me and mine.

These guys had come all this way and done me a solid, the least I could do is return the favor. As long as no one tried standing in the way when the time comes.

CREED

Shit was chaotic, people were scattering like flies but I knew what my prey looked like. I heard a shot off to the side earlier and figured either Ty or Lyon had broken ranks. We'll have to deal with the cleanup later, or maybe not. These boys were loaded for bear. I'm thinking we were all on the same page here.

Right now my only focus was on Sal and Dee. Lo's team and Law's crew were lining up the hate mongers like war prisoners as I walked through looking, but they were nowhere to be found.

I was starting to freak the fuck out thinking they'd escaped when I heard a whistle a little off to the side. "Over here." It sounded like the Travis guy and he was calling from a little distance away, away from the fray. I jogged my way over there and found gold.

"These two were hiding out in the outhouse." He had them by the necks and I'm guessing Sal was still weak from losing his balls because he looked kinda pale in the moonlight and wasn't putting up much of a fight, unless Travis had worked him a little already.

For some reason now that I was faced with them I was more pissed at her than him. She's the one I'd trusted with her, the one whose betrayal cut deep. Sal's fate was already set after what my girl had told me, but this one, she needed special attention.

"What the fuck is she doing in that book?" No sense in beating around the bush. From the look of surprise on her face and the noise he made, they weren't expecting that, which meant they had no idea we'd gotten hold of the book.

"I don't..." This time I didn't take it easy on her. Grabbing her hair, I pulled her head back roughly, twisting her neck. "Don't fuck with me, how did she end up in there? How did he get to you?"

"He said he'd kill us if we didn't."

"He who?" I know it wasn't Khalil or The Fox as we'd been calling him for years, because that fuck has never touched American soil. And since they've been shacked up here with the Stockton dude for the past few days I was pretty sure they knew his name by now.

"I don't know, we never met…Ouch I'm telling the truth I swear, please don't kill us, we had no choice." Okay maybe I was wrong.

"When did it start I wanna know everything and Dee, if I don't like what you got to say I will put a bullet in you. Now make it quick."

She told of being contacted by phone and then receiving pictures of her doing everyday stuff, classic scare tactic maneuver. Then someone had dropped instructions in the mailbox as to what she was supposed to do.

"When did it start?"

"She was sixteen when we were first contacted."

"And?"

"And nothing, every couple of months we'd get a call, a kind of reminder."

"When was the last one? What was supposed to be the end result? And don't tell me you don't know."

"I didn't I swear, not at first anyway, but then we sorta caught on. It was the way he would talk about her ya know, how she was gonna fetch a good price."

"This guy, what did he sound like?"

"Well the first one, he was American he wasn't as scary as the other one."

"The other one, tell me about him." My guts tied itself in knots because I was pretty sure what she going to say next.

"He only started calling coming onto the end. He had a very thick accent, middle-eastern I think, he was not a nice man." She took a deep breath and looked around for an escape.

"What else, why did he start calling instead of the other one and was there ever any talk of collecting?" That was my only real interest. Was I going to have to look over my shoulder now for some fuck coming to collect?

"It was after you stopped calling or coming by." She said that shit almost accusingly and I almost popped her right then and there. "What the fuck are you talking about?" I still hadn't eased up on her hair so I know her neck had to be hurting like fuck.

"After the prom, you just stopped coming by and you weren't calling as much. They had the phone tapped and someone was watching the house because they knew everything.

After you stopped coming around they seemed to lose interest. The calls tapered off and then stopped altogether for a while."

I had to think fast because shit sounded like it was calming down around us and we'd already been here more than ten minutes already. I put shit together in my head and realized she was talking about when I'd pulled back for baby girl's sake. "So after it seemed like I lost interest in her well being, they lost interest too."

"It looked like it but we didn't know for sure, they'd already given us all that money…" She broke off when she realized what she'd said.

"You took money for her?"

"Dude, female." Travis shook his head at me when I put my gun to her head.

"I give a fuck." He just shrugged his shoulders so I guess it wasn't that big of a deal to him after all.

"We didn't feel like we had a choice." She was talking fast now, her eyes trying to see the hard cold steel at her temple.

"So after they stopped showing an interest Sal decided to pay her nightly visits in her room after she fell asleep?" Bitch didn't have an answer for that.

"My friend here's right, you're a female that's the only reason I'm gonna let you breathe, but you still have to pay." I took half her ear off with my Bowie. I did that shit quick so by the time she felt it, I was already moving onto the next one.

"Get her out of here." I passed her off to Travis and took the cowering Sal from him. I didn't need any eyes for this one, and though his dad was a known gangster, I didn't know him, wasn't about to commit a crime in front of him no how.

"Told you I'd be back." I sneered in the pervert's face.

"If she told you I did anything she's lying, I never..." He got a punch in the gut for his trouble. "Tell me the fucking truth. I know Khalil he'd deal with you more than her since the sick fuck has a deep-rooted hatred of women. Who when and where?"

It seemed to take a minute for him to switch gears once he realized I wasn't asking him about his perverted shit. I didn't need to go over that shit again, but I needed to know about the other.

"Why should I tell you anything after what you did to me?" He actually sulked like a little fucking boy, making me sick to my stomach. "Because if you don't you're dead." At least that gave him hope that he might make it out alive.

Jake came upon us then, and the fucker got brave. Probably thought I wouldn't off him in front of an audience, or maybe he smelt cop on Jake. Whatever the fuck his issue was, he decided to go full fucking fuckwit.

"She caught a good price, who knows what the

desert rat who bought her was gonna do with her? He sure didn't mind paying out the nose. But then you stopped coming around and the calls stopped just like Dee said.

We figured we were gonna have to give all that money back but we'd already spent it. We were gonna make a run for it. But then they stopped calling too and we were in the clear, or so we thought." He was sulking again.

"Is that when you started going into her room?" For some reason he balked at this, he had no problem telling me he'd sold her, but he wouldn't admit to this; maybe because the memory of me ringing off his dick was still fresh in his mind. Then his eyes shifted to Jake's and he forgot again.

"So what if I did, wasn't no harm in it, nothing wrong with looking is there?" My hand twitched and I almost did him then but I needed more. "When was the last time you heard from them?"

"Not long after your little visit. It's like they were watching and waiting. How were we to know they still wanted her? And I was just working my way up to getting a taste." The fucker licked his lips and seemed to have gone off into his own little world after saying that shit.

"Fuck this shit." I grabbed him by the neck and started dragging. He came back to his senses right fucking quick then but it was already too late. Not that it would've made a difference whatever he said. He was dead the second he first walked into her room.

"Hey what're you doing? Hey you stop him." He started screaming bloody murder as I dragged him by his neck and carted him towards the edge of the mountain.

"You sold her you fuck and then you violated her, a scared young girl that I left in your care." I tossed his ass over the side and walked away before the echoes of his scream died.

"I'm not doing a fucking day for him Jake so don't even fucking start." Jake I know, he understands the creed. I can take my chances with him because I know if it were his woman or one of his kids he'd do the fucking same.

He clapped me on the shoulder and we headed back towards the others. Blade gave us both the once over as soon as we came into view and went back to hogtieing the assholes that we'd found hiding out up here, at least the ones that hadn't escaped.

"You done?" Law asked as I came back into the clearing. I nodded and kept moving, my only interest in getting the fuck down off the mountain and back to her. "Torch it." Law again gave the order and the night sky went up in flames.

An old man, supposedly the leader of the hate brigade was making noise about calling the sheriff until Jake whispered something in his ear. That shit seemed to quiet him down and the rest of us headed down the mountain. I'll let Law and his crew, deal with the locals. I'm done.

We all gathered in Law's yard after he'd done some-thing with the prisoners. We'd worked off some steam, but we all knew we had barely scratched the surface. It was a given that we weren't done.

"What now? I have to get home to my woman." Lyon was the first to break the silence.

"Well, we still have a shitload of work to do on our end. Stockton I'm guessing wasn't a font of information?" Lo looked at Ty and Lyon, neither of which was looking too guilty.

"And this shit is in Georgia you say? I guess I could pack up the wife and kids for a little road trip. Just a heads-up, I'm giving you all one week to come up with some kinda plan or I'm heading to the

desert. Law give these boys my number, I gotta go."
He walked away with his boys and the Travis dude
like he hadn't just done whatever the fuck it was that
I was pretty sure he'd done.

"Would he really go after the Porters?" Logan
asked Law and I as we watched Lyon and his crew
head out in the dead of night.

"He's already halfway there brother. If we don't
want him to handle this shit his way we'd better get
the fuck on and quick. We still got those kids to
find." Fuck, the sheer volume of it was starting to
give me a headache.

Cord, who was the only one not to join us on the
raid joined us now. Apparently he had stayed back to
keep watch over the women, especially his who had
been featured. From what little I'd gathered he
hadn't quite made her his yet, but I'm pretty sure it
won't be long now, not the way he's been sniffing
around her since they got here.

"You get anything out of him?" He asked his
brothers in arms, who pretty much shook their
heads no.

"Then we've got work." He turned and headed
back the way he'd came. Talkative motherfucker.

I watched over her as she slept with my heart in turmoil. How had we missed it? How had we not put it together? We'd only just received the results of her parentage the day before, but somehow it appeared the Fox had known all along. How?

She was even more precious to me now because of the blood that ran through her veins. She was a part of the man who had shaped me and whatever I'd felt for her before was multiplied because of that fact.

We'd terminated Stockton, or Ty and his new pal had. I found a smile at the thought of our new partner in crime. For someone who'd never served Lyon sure was a militant fuck. But I won't be the one to tell him that since he tends to take umbrage whenever we mention it.

We had formed a tight bond in the days we'd been there at Law's and that was good. Instead of just us we now had a whole network of brothers joined together to deal with what had become more than our little headache.

We'd found out a lot more in the last few days since coming back home. More than we'd known even with all our connections and the technology we had at our fingertips. Travis' dad the mobster was a font of information and a very funny guy, for someone who'd been running his own crime syndicate for over four decades.

They were all headed this way in a few weeks once they'd taken care of their own shit. It seems they were all interested in putting an end to whatever the fuck was going on here.

We'd put Stockton's place on lock down after running his men out of town. Lo had used his connection to the old man to pull that one off. All we needed now was to spread a net and catch who the fuck ever was involved.

Ty was under the impression that we needed to keep an eye on Lyon so that he didn't go after the Porters on his own. We needed to get more out of them than we were able to glean from Stockton and that guy didn't have the patience for conversation when it came to his family.

Not that I blamed him. I looked at her again from my place in the chair that I'd drawn up next to the bed. Someone was after her, the thought sent rage racing through my veins.

I haven't taken my eyes off of her since we'd come back home, but now her mom was making noises about the long absences and her and her brother being out of the house for days on end.

She was going home tomorrow and I wasn't sure how the fuck I was going to deal with that, but I'd done all I could to ensure her safety there. It won't be long before I claimed her anyway, so one night away from me wasn't going to kill me. I hope.

CREED

"Babe, you gotta let go." Her pussy was doing that thing where it locked me down and I couldn't move. Ever since we'd made it back from Law's and all the fuckery that had gone down there I've been inside her as often as I'd looked at her.

"I can't it feels so good." She had the nerve to move her hips under me while digging her nails into my ass. "I can't fuck you if you lock me off in your pussy babe, and I don't want to hurt you so ease the fuck off."

Hardheaded fuck, I pushed my thumb in her ass and that did the trick. "Now you're gonna get it." I lifted her legs over my arms and opened her up so I could drill into her hard.

"I own this pussy say it." That shit was fucking with me again, hearing that asshole say that she'd been earmarked for someone else. And though she'd never know a word of it, I did. Until I ended the motherfucker that had bought her, who thought he had rights to her, I was going to have that fucking monkey on my back.

"Tell me, who the fuck do you belong to?"

"You, Creed, what's wrong?" I guess my crazy was showing because she was looking at me twisted. "Nothing's wrong, give me your mouth."

I only felt whole again when she gave me her tongue and wrapped her arms around me. My heart grew and beat harder inside my chest with the emotion that welled up inside me. "You're mine, my babygirl."

"No one will ever have you but me, ever." I pulled her hair back so I could look into her face as I fed her my dick with steady strokes that went deep. "We're not leaving this room until I give you my son."

I love the fact that every time I even mentioned fucking my kid into her-her pussy creams on my cock. After she calmed down I pulled out and tapped her clit with my piercings until her eyes were rolling back in her head.

"I want to eat you." I slid down her body and sucked her pussy into my mouth, sinking my tongue deep so I could lap up some of that fresh cream.

She fucked herself wildly on my tongue while pulling on my hair until she filled my mouth again. Pulling my tongue out of her I wiped my face in her thigh.

"I want to pierce your clit." I licked her there before climbing up her body and sliding my cock back inside her as I teased her clit with my thumb, just where I planned to pierce her.

I came in her snatch for the third time that night and stayed buried inside her, stealing kisses from her already swollen lips before the phone rang disturbing us.

"Yo! What's up Law?"

"We're heading out to you should be there in a few. We'll stop long enough to fuel up but then we're on the road to Georgia."

"Fuck's wrong with you, why you sound like that?" I ran my hand over her ass as she came down from her dick high.

"Fucking Lyon, have to keep a leash on his ass,

asshole tried to get by us to head into the fucking desert."

"Kabul?" What the fuck; was Lyon planning on going after Khalil himself?

"No asshole, Arizona, then again wouldn't put it past him to head there next with his crazy ass just be ready." He hung up on my laugh. The next little while promised to be fun.

"Up and at 'em wife of mine, we're taking a little vacation." She rolled around on the bed and smiled at me. She knew she was gonna be seeing her girls again soon. It did my heart good to know that someone who had been starved of such things in the past now had that.

I dropped down on the bed beside her, covering her body again. "One more for the road; fuck I love you babygirl."

THE END

Made in the USA
Middletown, DE
28 December 2021

57242062R00225